*'I'd like to start
emphatically.*

Something in Emma'—
notice. The request, punctuated by the Southern
accent he'd come to recognise, was sincere, and
he felt his resolve against her melting away.
Considering her stubborn streak, it must have cost
her a lot to apologise. And when she looked up at
him with earnest amber eyes, he couldn't make
himself refuse her.

'Sure,' he answered.

Her answering smile sent his heart skipping, and
he took a quick, impulsive step towards her
before catching himself. Unless he was very
careful, he'd find himself doing anything this sexy,
tempting charmer asked.

And he had *no* intention of falling under her
spell…

Dear Reader,

Welcome to Silhouette Special Edition®! Every month we publish six wonderful romances full of life and love!

Leading the line-up this month is our **That's My Baby!** featured book from Christie Ridgway, *Beginning with Baby*. However, we are also lucky enough to have new novels from established talents like Gina Wilkins (*Surprise Partners*) and Marie Ferrarella (*Found: His Perfect Wife*).

Prescription: Marriage continues with *Their Little Princess* from Susan Mallery, who gives us a big, strong, earthy hero who discovers he can't give up his baby girl despite having no idea how he's going to cope! Look out for the last Malone's story next month from the pen of Christine Flynn.

Finally, we also have a first Special Edition from Alaina Starr (*A Cowboy's Code*) and a welcome, really emotional return to the list from Jean Brashear (*Lonesome No More*).

Enjoy them all,

The Editors

A Cowboy's Code
ALAINA STARR

SILHOUETTE
SPECIAL EDITION®

*All the characters in this book have no existence outside the imagination
of the author, and have no relation whatsoever to anyone bearing the
same name or names. They are not even distantly inspired by any
individual known or unknown to the author, and all the incidents are
pure invention.*

*First published in Great Britain 2001
Silhouette Books, Eton House, 18-24 Paradise Road,
Richmond, Surrey TW9 1SR*

© Starr Blair 1999

ISBN 0 373 24272 7

23-0201

*Printed and bound in Spain
by Litografia Rosés S.A., Barcelona*

ALAINA STARR

grew up in the Rockies, with one foot in the mountains and the other in the desert plateaus. Ever since she read her first Zane Grey novel, she's been captivated by both, and she finds them an endless source of inspiration.

She's been a fan of love and happy endings since childhood, and when she read her first romance, she was hooked. She began her writing career in school, where she wrote poetry in a spiral notebook, which, thanks to her mother's foresight, she still owns. She confesses to a lifelong love affair with words—arranging and rearranging them until a story unfolds, but it wasn't until she bought her first computer that she considered writing a novel. Though she never thought of herself as a storyteller, she finds spinning tales about love and romance immensely satisfying.

She lives in Colorado with her husband and two sons.

To Patti—I couldn't have done it without you.

My thanks also to Lorraine Preuss
for sharing her knowledge of horses.

Chapter One

"Can I help you, ma'am?"

The voice jarred Emma Reardon out of her thoughts and onto a tall, lean cowboy who stood eyeing her curiously. Taking a deep breath, she got out of her car. In a few days this job and this ranch would all be behind her.

Smiling the cool, professional smile she'd practiced until it came naturally, she smoothed the wrinkles from the business suit she wore. "I'm looking for Nicolas Barlow," she said, using the cultured Midwestern voice she'd spent years perfecting.

"Is he expecting you?"

"No, but I won't take much of his time." A blatant lie. In fact, she meant to take up a great deal of his time, but she saw no reason to mention that. Nicolas Barlow was known for more than his apparent phenomenal success. He'd refused countless interviews, and she meant to persuade him to let her tell his story.

"He's out in the corrals." The man took in her attire and grimaced. "I'll take you there if you like." Emma nodded encouragingly, and he shrugged, then gestured for her to follow.

From a distance, the Uintah Ranch had looked well-ordered, at least, but here, close up, telling little details made themselves known. The picket fence had recently been repaired, but showed its age nonetheless. Beyond it, unpainted outbuildings stood clustered together in silent testimony that paint cost money and there was never enough to go around. Suddenly she was assailed by smells—horses, cattle and hay—odors she hadn't smelled in years. Old memories threatened to rise up again, and she frantically shoved them aside. This was a ranch yard, one of thousands everywhere. It had nothing to do with the grinding poverty of her childhood. She never had to go back, not even in her mind.

She forced herself to concentrate on the man she'd come to see. Her editor had warned her not to fall for him. Emma had nearly laughed in her face.

Handsome or not, Barlow held no appeal. He was a rancher—not much removed from a farmer—and hard experience had taught her his kind of livelihood lay in the hands of Lady Luck. His current success, phenomenal though it appeared to be, could be no more than a trick of smoke and mirrors, an illusion that could turn around in the space of a heartbeat. He had no security, and for her, security was the name of the game. She'd made her decision years ago.

They approached a pole corral where two men in cowboy hats worked on the leg of a showy Appaloosa stallion. One had apparently just finished wrapping the horse's knee while the other bent to help him. The second man was tall. His worn jeans clung just tightly enough to his bowed legs to suggest molded, powerful muscles. His chambray shirt stretched taut across broad shoulders, and it silhouetted a lean back before disappearing beneath a serviceable leather belt.

Hardened though she was, she had to admit he looked good from behind.

"Watch your step, ma'am," her guide said in deference to the white shoes she wore, and she glanced down, barely in time to avoid stepping in something she'd rather not examine too closely. "Nick, there's someone here to see you."

She glanced up again just as the bow-legged man turned. But concerns about Italian leather deserted her when flawless blue eyes met hers across the corral fence. She stumbled to an awkward halt.

He had dark brows beneath his hat, a square jaw and a slightly crooked nose—pleasing regular features that in combination took her breath away. She stood staring, openmouthed and incapable of closing it.

He straightened slowly, radiating masculinity and self-assurance, and her carefully thought out plans deserted her. To her further discomfort, he looked her up and down in blatantly masculine fashion, and it was all she could do to keep from stepping behind her escort to escape his scrutiny. Then, for reasons she could only guess at, he smiled. Two heart-stopping dimples appeared as if by magic in his cheeks, and something elementally feminine in her responded.

Instead of speaking, he took off his hat, revealing dark wavy hair, creased by the hat, but full and thick just the same. He ran his hands through it once, then replaced the hat and started toward her, his eyes never breaking contact with hers. Recalling herself, she stumbled forward to meet him.

Reaching between the poles, she extended her hand. "Hello," she said shakily, "I'm Emma Reardon."

He took it, his grip firm, his hand strong and callused. Electricity sizzled up her arm.

"Nick Barlow," he said in a deep baritone. Up close, his blue eyes seemed to drill into her. Her mind emptied.

The man in the corral with him cleared his throat, and Emma realized she and Barlow still held hands. With a self-conscious tug, she pulled away. Barlow smiled lazily and turned to his companion. "Ms. Reardon, this is Jack Wyatt."

Wyatt smiled and stepped forward. He too was tall, with an arresting face and gold-flecked brown eyes, but he didn't radiate the same masculine energy as Barlow. Emma muttered a greeting, but she had no idea what.

"And the man behind you is Pete Malowich, my foreman."

Thankful for a reason to escape his glance, she turned back and blindly nodded a greeting.

"Keep Cochise quiet for another couple of days, Nick," Wyatt said. "The cortisone should take the last of the swelling down, but don't let him use the leg more than he has to until it's sound. I'll be back in a couple of days to look at it again." Apparently he was a veterinarian.

Together, the men came through the gate. Still frantic to collect her thoughts, Emma studied the horse stupidly. "Nice horse," she muttered.

"Yes," Barlow answered as he followed Wyatt through and fastened the gate behind him.

"Later," Wyatt said. He tipped his hat at her, then he and Pete moved off together, leaving them alone.

"What can I do for you, Ms. Reardon?"

His nearness made her want to step back—get out of range. She couldn't think with him so close. *What was the matter with her?* She'd met handsome men before. But she'd never met a man who affected her like this one did.

"Please, call me Emma," she said, dismayed to hear the twang of her Southern roots creep into her speech.

"What can I do for you, *Emma?*"

"I've a business proposition for you," she said carefully. Convincing Nicolas Barlow to grant an interview would be an uphill battle.

"A business proposition?"

At least he sounded curious. She forced herself to meet his gaze, which was a mistake. "Yes. A partnership of sorts."

He leaned against the fence and crossed his arms in front of him. Giving her the full force of his attention, he answered, "I see."

Nick Barlow had never considered redheads particularly attractive, but this one made him look twice—three times. Hell, he couldn't get his eyes off her.

Her hair was a deep, rich red, streaked almost strawberry in places, but he'd bet money the color was natural. Several strands had escaped the confines of the clip that held it in place at the back of her neck, and they hung in soft curls around her face. Her eyes were the color of aged bourbon, and beneath a light layer of makeup, she wore a liberal dusting of freckles.

She also looked expensive. From the designer suit she wore to those ridiculous high-heeled sandals that he'd bet cost as much as his work boots, she radiated dollar signs. Standing here in his barnyard, she looked every bit as beautiful, elegant—and out of place—as his ex-wife ever had.

"What sort of *partnership* did you have in mind?" Beautiful as the lady might be, she was hedging, which had the dual effect of arousing his curiosity and setting his instincts on alert.

She looked away and refused to meet his eyes again. "You've been working hard here to make a name for yourself and the Uintah Ranch. I'd like to help you."

"You misunderstand," he said, deciding to play her word game with her. "I've been working hard here, but notoriety has nothing to do with it." He suspected she was here to sell him something he didn't want, and she knew it. But she sure didn't look like any salesman he'd ever seen.

She gave him a smile calculated to disarm. "Perhaps I should rephrase that," she said. "Your work here has captured the attention of the rest of the world."

So she was a reporter. A cool one, he'd give her that. He could almost see the gears spinning as she searched for exactly the right words. "And you're here to dispel the mystery?"

Apparently she hadn't been ready to reveal herself just yet.

"Yes, in a manner of speaking," she said clearing her throat. "I work for *American Business Monitor* magazine." Was he mistaken, or did he detect a hint of the South in her voice? "Have you ever heard of it?"

Of course he'd heard of it. Anyone with any business sense at all read *American Business Monitor*. "Yeah, I have a subscription."

She didn't look like she quite believed him, and his mild curiosity of a moment ago amplified. "Then you know," she said slowly, "that *American Business Monitor* watches the climate of the business world, and when they see something out of the ordinary—"

"Tsk tsk, Ms. Reardon," he said, interrupting her, "you must *not* have done your homework. If you had, you'd know I don't give interviews."

Something flared in her eyes, and when she spoke again, more of the sweet honey drawl appeared in her voice as she struggled to maintain control. "I'm well aware of that, Mr. Barlow."

"Call me Nick." He couldn't help but smile. Apparently her sophisticated guise slipped a little under duress. He liked the way her eyes flashed, and he was beset with an urge to kiss her, just to see what she would do.

She took a deep breath, and when she spoke again, she was in perfect control. There wasn't a trace of the South in her speech. "Is there somewhere we could talk?"

Nick had too much to do to dally with a beautiful redhead, but he was enjoying himself and not quite ready to send her on her way. "Why don't you come to the house?"

She looked relieved and fell in step beside him. The spiked

heels she wore, though they did marvelous things for her legs, were all but useless on the uneven ground, and he slowed his steps to accommodate her. "Didn't you know you were coming to a ranch?"

"Of course."

"Then why didn't you put on some sensible shoes?"

She drew her brows together, and he wondered what kind of story she'd try to feed him. But after a moment's hesitation, she looked up and smiled. "They make me taller."

He couldn't help but chuckle. Did she really think a pair of shoes could make a difference? "Ah, well, I'm afraid they're wasted on me, then. The first thing I noticed about you was how tiny you are."

She flushed, but refrained from replying.

They reached an old car parked in the driveway. What was a reporter for *American Business Monitor* doing driving a fifteen-year-old rusted out sedan? He bit back the question— no doubt she had her reasons.

He took her through the back door to the kitchen, where Maria, his housekeeper, was kneading bread dough. Maria looked up in surprise. He'd hired her when he'd grown tired of his own cooking, and since then she'd taken him under her wing like one of her own sons. A quick knowing look crossed her face and she broke into a broad smile as she quickly shook the flour off her hands. Too late, Nick realized Maria had jumped to the wrong conclusion.

Maria wanted him married. She pushed and prodded like the mother hen she was, insisting Nick spent too much time alone. At first he'd humored her, mumbling agreement when she mentioned this woman or that who'd caught her eye. Then she'd gone further, bringing up the summer social at dinner or discussing the Cattlemen's Days dance at length on the telephone when she knew he could hear. Nick recognized her ploys and usually sidestepped her tactless little hints.

Maria had never met his ex-wife, Lynette. She'd arrived

after the carnage had been swept away, the attorneys appeased and the judgment satisfied. Open wounds had begun to heal, but Nick's scars ran deep. Lynette, the venomous virago who was her lawyer, and the suspicious shrew who'd sat in judgment had all taken their pound of flesh, and he'd vowed never again to let a woman, much less a city woman, near him.

But Maria never gave up. In that moment when he ushered Emma into the kitchen, Nick could see Maria's matchmaking hopes ignite with fresh enthusiasm.

"Emma, this is Maria Orizo, my housekeeper. Maria, Emma Reardon."

"How nice to meet you," Maria said. She turned on him with mock consternation. "Nick," she chided, "you should have told me you expected company. I would have made something special—"

"A glass of iced tea will do, Maria." He led Emma into his office before she had a chance to say more. Bringing Emma into the house hadn't been such a good idea after all.

Emma took the chair he offered, and while she'd looked vastly out of place in the corrals, she looked very much at home in his office. He gave himself a mental kick for allowing himself to get caught up in the allure of red hair and enticingly freckled skin. Her clothing, her speech, every cosmopolitan detail reminded him of Lynette and her attorney and the judge who'd threatened to take his ranch away from him. Nothing good had ever come from his association with city women. Suddenly he wanted this interview to be over and done with quickly.

"Now tell me, Ms. Reardon, what exactly do you want of me?"

His question got her attention, and she gave up her perusal of the room to face him. "I would like to do a story on you and the Uintah ranch."

"Then I'm afraid you've made a long drive for nothing," he said. "I'm not interested."

Instead of being cowed, she brightened, as if she'd been prepared for his refusal. As if she had no intention of backing down until she got what she wanted. Yes, bringing her into the house had been a mistake. In the corrals, he could have dismissed her and gone about his business, but now she had her foot in the door and didn't look as if she'd pull it back unless he slammed it on her.

"Before you make up your mind, hear me out. Will you do that?"

It was a reasonable request. "Okay." He'd listen, but he'd never give in.

"I've been doing a series of articles on successful businessmen," she began. "The movers and shakers of the business world. I examine their successes and look for the reasons they stand above the rest in their field. My editor—and I," she added almost as an afterthought, "don't feel the series would be complete without an agricultural angle."

The hesitation had sounded like more than a Freudian slip to him. He wondered what it meant. "Why me?"

"Look around you," she said. "Your operation is big and getting bigger."

"There are plenty of big ranchers out there who are more than willing to talk to the press. Why don't you interview them?"

"Because by all accounts you've taken this ranch and turned it into a showplace in a remarkably short time. Mention registered Hereford breeding stock to anyone in the business and your name comes up. Plus, unless I'm mistaken, that stallion out there is the key to your future as a horse breeder. You've made a name for yourself."

He had to give her credit. She'd done her homework. But the speech sounded as if it were rehearsed, which he could understand, given she must have known he wouldn't be cooperative. But something about it—a slight hesitation, an odd choice of words—made him think she didn't quite believe it. Just as she tried for some reason to hide the drawl in her speech, he suspected she was working hard to hide something else, an inner conviction, maybe, which was at odds with what she said. Most people probably wouldn't see it, but since he'd made such a monumental mistake in judgment with Lynette, he always made it a point to look deeper. An inner voice warned him to steer clear of her, but curiosity made him bide his time. He gave her an ingratiating grin. "You've been reading up on me."

"I have." She smiled, but it wasn't the friendly smile she'd given him earlier. It felt as rehearsed as her speech, and it reminded him again of Lynette. The pleasure of the moment disappeared. "Then you should also know that I've made it clear that I don't want publicity."

"I do. That's why I wanted to meet with you in person. I'd hoped to change your mind."

He waited, not giving her any encouragement.

"Perhaps if you told me why you avoid the publicity, we could come to a mutually agreeable compromise."

She was too smooth, too practiced. He'd been able to distract her before, but now she was focused. It seemed almost as if she'd been coached. "I value my privacy. I don't care to have my life chronicled for all to see."

"But surely you realize what an opportunity this is."

An inkling of suspicion swept through him. Emma's arguments sounded too familiar—he'd undergone this kind of coercion before. If one approach didn't work, she'd try another and then another in hopes of finding a way to cut through his armor.

"Think of the publicity the Uintah would gain from my article. National recognition would double the demand for your cattle. And the stud fees on that stallion out there would more than triple. You could enlarge your operation."

Lynette was behind this.

She had to be, though for the life of him, he couldn't figure out what she had to gain from it. She'd never understood what this ranch meant to him. Yes, he would reap profits, but at what cost? He'd been born here. He'd grown up here, and when his father died, he'd inherited it from him. He'd fought for it when the divorce court had threatened to take it away. More than an owner, he was a caretaker of the land, and he meant to protect it from overuse or the encroachment of people who would violate that trust. The fewer people who knew about the paradise that was his, the better. Lynette and her kind, Emma apparently included, thought there was a price on everything, but this time, they were wrong.

"Wouldn't you like to be recognized as a leading businessman? Wouldn't you like to be seen as a success? By September, your name and your ranch could be household words."

Ah, yes. He was beginning to understand. In September his divorce settlement was up for final review. If he were portrayed as a successful businessman in a national magazine, the vultures circling in the legal system could come in for the kill again. "No, thank you."

She stood and faced him over his desk. He had to give her credit. She was good. Somehow he didn't think the height of her heels made much difference when she was determined. Perhaps he should tell her so. Then again, maybe not.

"I'll write a good story."

"I don't doubt that. I read your last article."

Disbelief showed plainly on her face. "Is that a fact?"

Listening to her carefully prepared arguments had finally shaken his memory loose. He remembered her name now. Actually, he'd read *all* of her articles. "It was about John Quinlan. He owns a textile mill in Georgia. In the past ten years he's brought it up from a shaky little mill facing bankruptcy to a first-class operation. He buys a lot of wool around here.''

Subdued, she sat down again. ''Then why won't you let me do the interview?''

He wasn't about to tell her about his ex-wife. She undoubtedly knew all about her already, and if Lynette's subterfuge hadn't worked on him, Emma didn't have a chance.

Moreover, a sixth sense told him there was trouble afoot. Two weeks earlier, the wheel of his horse trailer had unexplainably come off, jackknifing his truck and nearly killing Cochise in the process. That wheel hadn't just come off by itself; he'd gone over the whole thing before he'd set out on the highway. If he was right, he didn't need a stranger, beautiful or otherwise, poking her nose into his business right now.

''I'm not one for living in the—'' He was interrupted by Maria bustling in with refreshments.

''I made the tea fresh,'' Maria said, ''with a sprig of mint for such a hot day.'' She smiled at Emma, who turned toward Nick as if to ask what kind of red-blooded man drank tea with a sprig of mint in it.

Hell, Maria never put mint in his tea before. Irritated, he watched as she set the tray gingerly on the desk. She'd even dug up some lacy little thing to decorate the tray. What was there about women that they couldn't take a well-placed hint when he dropped one? He supposed he'd have to talk to her.

Maria shuffled out after his hasty thank-you, and Emma turned back to him. He half expected a wry comment about Maria's obvious tactics. Instead, she surprised him by changing the subject entirely.

''How did you know I was a reporter?''

At least she wasn't badgering him again, though he suspected she hadn't given up. ''I've learned to recognize the type.''

It must have been the wrong thing to say. "What *exactly* is the type?"

Her eyes were lit with the fire of challenge, and he couldn't help himself. In truth, he'd never met a reporter before, because none of the others had had the temerity to simply show up at his door. Trying to rattle her again, he said, "I think it was the car."

"What's wrong with my car?"

He must have touched a sore spot. "I didn't say there was anything wrong with it."

"Just because it's old doesn't mean it isn't reliable."

"I'm sure it is."

She took a long drink of tea. "Besides, I belong to the auto club."

He smiled. Apparently the old car had been weighing on her mind. "Where did you drive from?"

"Denver."

Maybe that was where she lived now, but that wasn't where she'd grown up. He'd heard a hint of a drawl in her speech before, but in defense of her wreck of a car, she'd forgotten herself and slipped into a cadence laced with pure Southern brogue. He liked it. Curiosity made him wonder what else he could learn about her. "Well it's a good thing the car's reliable," he said, "because it can be long way between one place and another around here."

The seemingly innocuous comment had the desired effect. She bristled. "*That's* why I belong to the auto club!"

He decided he liked her better this way. A flaw or two made her seem more human. "Do you carry a telephone with you?" he asked reasonably.

"No."

"I usually do," he said. "It can be a long way between telephones, too."

She relaxed somewhat. "Well, I heard that you were a New Age rancher. Maybe that's what they meant."

He smiled and leaned back in his chair. "What else did you hear about me?"

She started to answer, then stopped and smiled slowly. "Who's interviewing who here?"

He shrugged. "Just making conversation. You said the world has the idea that I'm some sort of cosmic cowboy. I just thought I'd find out what they're saying."

"Don't bother. Rumors are almost always false. That's why I always go to the source."

"True enough. But you must have had some preconceptions. Tell me, what, exactly, did you expect to find here?"

She seemed to think about her answer, as if to decide what she dared reveal. "Well, for one thing, I supposed the entrance to the place would be—" she hesitated "—grander,"

He smiled. "More like the gate into South Fork on *Dallas?*"

She nodded, her color rising.

"Well, that's in Texas," he said. "I'm afraid the Uintah is just another ranch around here."

She didn't reply, but he could see that he had her thinking fast. "I suppose you thought I'd be prancing around in a fancy Western suit, smoking cigars and chasing women like J.R., too."

"Of course not." She punctuated her denial with a shake of her head, making him think he wasn't far off the mark.

"Sorry to disappoint you, but I don't smoke."

She stopped shaking her head, and another slow smile spread across her face. Laughter bubbled up, and the transformation had him transfixed.

"J.R. could learn a thing or two from you," she said. "No wonder everyone said—" She bit off the last of the sentence and color flooded her face.

He waited, too entranced with the artless woman emerging in front of him to break the spell. Though he didn't pay much attention to rumors in general, he began to wonder exactly what she *had* heard.

She wasn't aware of it, but he'd cut through the iron composure she seemed determined to wear about her. He didn't know why she felt the need to hide behind an urbane exterior, but he liked *this* woman much better. A momentary thought of getting to know her tripped through his mind, despite his suspicions about her sudden appearance. The urge to kiss her returned.

"I heard you were very attractive," she said finally, her face flaming. She refused to meet his eyes.

"Ah," he said noncommittally, holding laughter at bay. "It is a problem."

She looked for a moment as if she took him seriously, then, amber eyes sparkling, she laughed out loud.

For the first time since his divorce, a spark of interest ignited. Who was the real woman, here? The Southern charmer or the cultured city girl? He wanted to believe she was an innocent pawn in his ex-wife's latest money-grabbing scheme, but if her motive was only to get a story, what was she hiding?

"What do you say we start over?" she asked. "After all, I've already seen through the aura of dissipation around you."

He raised an eyebrow. Would she still feel that way if he acted on his impulse and kissed her?

"Why not let me interview you, and I'll set the record straight."

His pleasant little daydream disintegrated. She'd put on a very convincing act, lulling him into complacency, and he'd nearly fallen for it. He shook his head, angry with himself for not listening to his instincts. "Sorry, no deal."

She stood abruptly. "I can write the article without you, you know!"

He stood, too, sending his chair flying backwards.

''You've got all the bases covered, haven't you? Ingenuity didn't work, so now you're resorting to threats. What else do you have tucked up your sleeve? You haven't thrown yourself at me, yet. Here, I'll save you the trouble!'' In three short steps he rounded his desk, acting on the urge that had been building since he'd first seen her standing outside the corral. He caught her unaware, and before he had a chance to reconsider, he dragged her in his arms, slid her head into the crook of his elbow, and pressed his lips hard against hers.

Chapter Two

She stiffened at once, lips tight, her fisted hands against his chest. She really was a tiny thing—there was nothing she could do against his brute strength. Shame washed through him, but she felt soft and feminine, too good to release. Her light musky scent brought to mind quiet evenings in front of a blazing fire, and he unconsciously softened the kiss.

Then, just as he knew he had to release her, she made a little noise of acquiescence in the back of her throat. Her lips parted beneath his. Her hands slid slowly up and around his neck, and as her response warmed, the kiss became a delectable sampling of warm, inviting lips. He leaned back against the desk, pulling her with him.

Nick raised his head, leaving Emma floating between two worlds. She opened her eyes dreamily to see his deep blue ones burning into hers, and for just one moment she let herself drift in that mesmerizing gaze. Never had she been so soundly kissed, and never had a simple kiss sent her spinning off into space. All her life she'd scoffed at tales of hearts taking wing, but in a single moment he'd proven her wrong.

Then reality came flooding back. She was wrapped around him, practically sitting on his lap after he'd all but called her a tramp. He'd managed to keep her off balance throughout most of their conversation, something no one had been able to do since she'd graduated from college. And she knew now he'd been toying with her—he'd never had any intention of backing down. He'd capped his performance with the ultimate insult.

A smug little smile tugged at his lips as he watched her. He was ready for round two. His sultry eyes invited her closer, and to her horror, she could feel herself leaning toward him. Well, she'd proven herself a fool once, but that didn't mean she would do it again.

The paralysis that held her still disappeared. She was a professional, and no one could accuse her otherwise and get away with it. Throwing his arms off, she pushed away from him and slapped him soundly. Then, expecting the worst, she backed away. To her surprise he didn't try to follow her. He merely rubbed his cheek once, then watched her with narrowed eyes. If she expected remorse, she was disappointed.

She wanted to tell him what she thought of his insulting kiss. She wanted to slap him again for his insufferable attitude. But most of all, she wanted to show him that she would write the story with or without his cooperation—her integrity intact. Coming here hadn't been her idea, but she would do the job she'd been sent to do.

But words failed her. In their place vulnerable tears threatened. For one beautiful moment, she'd been kissed by a man—a very attractive man. A man whose way of life represented everything she'd worked so long and hard to leave behind. Before she broke down in front of him, she fled. Out the door, down the steps, all the way to her car she ran.

There, safe behind locked doors, she took a deep breath. When her heartbeat slowed, she turned the key.

The engine turned over once, popped, then all she heard was a peculiar puffing sound beneath the noise of the starter. In disbelief, she tried again. Nothing.

Nick sauntered out the back door, stopped for a moment, then smiled and walked lazily over to her car.

"Car trouble, ma'am?"

Emma sat in her hotel room at war with herself. The conflict had begun in those interminable minutes while she waited for the tow truck, and continued through the rest of the day and a long, sleepless night. She'd given the article a good shot. Wasn't that enough?

She was sorely tempted to look up one of the big Midwestern farmers who grew thousands of acres of corn, get her interview and get on with her life. Nicholas Barlow had said no in every way possible, capping his final response with an insult that any self-respecting woman would read loud and clear. So why was she still sitting here?

Because if she left now, she'd be running, and she knew it. She'd never backed down in the face of adversity before, and the idea didn't set well now. True, the article she had in mind wouldn't be as complete without an interview, but she had every right to do the story without him. The urge to give up was purely for personal reasons, selfish ones at that. She'd been so certain she'd be immune to his charm. He was a rancher—only a step removed from a farmer. But the truth was everything, from his blue, blue eyes to his steadfast refusal to be intimidated, had drawn her to him like a bee to honey.

At the same time, he made her uncomfortable. She'd never met anyone who kept her so completely off balance. Years of polish, burying her West Virginia roots, had disappeared under the first piercing glance of those eyes. And to make matters worse, she felt as if he'd seen right through her. She'd been bowled over by him, and he'd obviously felt nothing at all for her. His kiss had proven that.

He'd kissed her for the most insulting of reasons, and she'd responded like a naive schoolgirl. He'd awakened a part of her that had been carefully tucked away for half a lifetime. Now she wanted to run. Because what she wanted more than anything was to kiss him again, to feel that weightless sensation when he wrapped his arms around her, to fly into the stratosphere with him as her guide.

How he must be laughing! Even her car had cooperated to make her look like a fool—sitting inside it with arms crossed, waiting for the tow truck like a sulky child. If she left now, he'd win. She'd always be the city girl he'd scared away with one insulting kiss. Most unsettling of all, a deep, secret part of her wanted to believe that electrifying kiss had been real. She'd been warned that women made fools of themselves over Nicolas Barlow, and she'd blandly brushed the warnings aside. No cowboy could make a fool of Emma Reardon.

How wrong she'd been.

"Ms. Reardon, I have a fax for you," the desk clerk said as she entered the hotel lobby.

Emma detoured to the desk. Stranded in town, she'd requested some information the day before. In her befuddled state of mind, she hadn't even realized it hadn't come. She muttered a word of thanks and turned back to the stairway, perusing as she climbed. Halfway up the stairs, a name leaped off the paper at her. Stopping cold, she reread it, then ran the rest of the way up to her room to use the telephone.

An hour later, armed with new information, she stood in front of her closet with renewed purpose. This time she would make certain Nick Barlow found nothing to criticize about her choice of clothing. She needed something suitably professional, yet conservative. His accusation still stung, and she wanted to make certain he had no reason to repeat it. If nothing else, she'd prove to him how utterly wrong he'd been.

She settled on beige linen slacks and a summery silk top. The outfit was cool for a hot June day, comfortable, yet classy enough to show she meant business. Her flat-heeled shoes could take the most uneven footing in stride, and for once her hair, which was wild on the best of days, lay peacefully in the clip she'd used to hold it in place. No one could accuse her of looking anything but businesslike.

Her car was ready, as the mechanic had promised, and she drove back to the ranch filled with determination. But, unlike her first visit, the ranch yard seemed deserted when she drove up. She looked around uneasily. With the abundance of people the day before, she'd told herself that despite appearances, the ranch was a thriving business. Where was everybody?

For lack of other choices, she decided to try the house. The gate into the yard sagged a little, and it creaked when she pushed it open. The paint was cracked and beginning to peel, and for a moment she recalled the weathered boards hammered into the poles around her mother's garden.

How excited her mother had been when Dad had offered to paint the fence after the harvest. The crop was ready, and for once it promised to provide enough money to get them through the winter. That very afternoon a thunderstorm had blown up, dropping six inches of rain and covering the bottomland in six feet of water. That pitiful fence had never been painted, and after a few years it had slowly sunk into the ground along with the rest of the farm. The last time she'd seen it, the vines had pulled the boards down until there was no sign a fence had ever been there.

"Emma!" Maria's exclamation startled her out of her reverie. "You're back! Is Nick expecting you?"

Emma smiled. "No, he's not expecting me."

"I see you looking at my flowers. They're pretty, aren't they? Almost as pretty as you. Come in, and tell me about yourself."

It hadn't taken Emma long to realize Maria occupied a special place in Nick's heart. No one else would ever get away with the obvious tactics she'd employed yesterday. For a moment she toyed with the idea of asking Maria how to win him over. With Maria on her side, she'd probably have a better chance of breaking down his rock-solid defenses. But if Nick ever found out, he'd have her escorted to his property line.

Maria offered her a glass of tea, but Emma declined. Nervousness welled up inside, and she wondered if she was doing the right thing. "I learned something this morning that Nick should know," she said before she lost her courage. Something in her voice must have tipped Maria off. For a second, she said nothing, and Emma wondered if he'd already given Maria instructions to send her packing.

"You got your car fixed?" Maria asked. Not waiting for a reply, she continued, "You should have let Nick look at it for you." She clucked her tongue. "He scared you away, didn't he? He is full of bluster, but he is a gentle man." Her eyes lit with mischief. "And handsome, too."

For one humiliating second, Emma wondered if Maria could somehow read her mind. Realizing she was at the point of nodding agreement, she returned to the purpose of her visit. "Can you tell me where to find him?"

Maria nodded. "He's in the south pasture. I'll call him and tell him you're here."

"No—just tell me where to find him."

Maria took in Emma's outfit skeptically. "You are dressed like a lady. I don't think you want to go out there like this."

With a sinking feeling, Emma wondered what could possibly be worse than the corrals she'd visited yesterday.

She found out when she parked her car at the edge of a rutted lane. Nick was working in knee-high grass about thirty yards away, shovel in hand. He saw her, but made no move to greet her, and he was too far away for her to see his expression. She allowed herself a moment to study him more closely. Like the day before, he was dressed in jeans and a work shirt. He looked tall and lean, every inch a man, albeit a forbidding man at the moment. It took all her courage to get out of the car.

"All right," she muttered. "If you won't come to me, I'll come to you." Swallowing her hesitation, she walked purposefully toward him. She stopped short when her foot dropped ankle deep into cold, muddy water. Irrigation was unheard of on the farm where she'd grown up, and with the single-minded focus of her thoughts, she'd simply overlooked the significance of the shovel in his hand. The shock must have shown on her face, because he abandoned his stony silence for infuriating, unfettered laughter.

Nick knew he probably shouldn't laugh, but the look on Emma's face as she stepped into the water was too good to ignore. It gave him an outlet for the explosion of emotions that surged through him when he looked up and recognized her ragged car creeping up the rutted lane.

He was surprised, of course. After her angry departure yesterday, he hadn't expected to see her again. He'd spent the better part of the intervening time trying to convince himself he didn't care.

On top of that, he was still irritated with the way she'd refused his help when her car wouldn't start. But what surprised him more was the unwelcome surge of delight at the sight of her. The woman, with her silky clothes and lavishly freckled skin spelled disaster unless he gained control of himself. If he'd learned anything from the past, it had been that city women, regardless of how appealing, had no place on his ranch.

Today, at least, Emma wore pants, but the breeze molded them to her, revealing too much about her feminine curves. He wondered if the freckles strewn across her cheeks extended beyond what his eye could see.

Instead of backtracking to dry ground, she merely stood there, glaring at him with self-righteous anger. "You might have warned me."

"Anyone with any common sense would have figured it out." His comment earned him another glare. "I'm surprised to see you here again."

"Why? I have a job to do."

"And I told you I'm not interested."

He leaned against his shovel, waiting to see what she would say next. He was being uncivil, he knew, but the unwelcome urges she fostered left him feeling anything but complaisant.

His actions apparently left her feeling the same way. She looked as if she were ready to bare her claws, and the dagger points in her eyes reminded him of her expression right after she'd slapped him yesterday. Unfortunately, that thought led him backward to her passionate response to his kiss, and his body surged to life. He shifted his weight again, angry for his lack of control and wondering what he would do when his reaction became readily apparent.

"Look," she said after drawing a deep breath, "I didn't come out here to pick up where we left off yesterday. I learned something this morning that I think you ought to know. Could we at least get on dry land and discuss it like adults?"

The smoothly spoken words, devoid of any Southern flavor, did what holding his breath and mentally cursing himself could not. "Be my guest," he said as his body relaxed.

She turned and retraced her steps. But after the first glimpse of softly curved backside, he swore again and directed his eyes at her feet.

She didn't stop until she reached her car, where she slung her shoe off and unceremoniously bent over to wring the water from her pantleg. Nick watched until the sight of beige linen drawn taut against her perfectly formed derriere brought back baser thoughts, then planted his shovel in disgust at the side of the road. He turned his back on her and walked to the front of the car, leaning against it until she was ready to talk.

When she finally joined him, he couldn't help but think the salmon color of her blouse made her skin glow, and he wondered why he'd never noticed before how beautiful red hair could be.

"You were involved in an accident, recently. Would you mind telling me what happened?"

"The wheel came off my horse trailer," he said, wondering what she was getting at.

The color drained from her face. "Was anyone hurt?"

He shook his head, pleased somehow to know that she cared. "Only Cochise. He's lucky to be alive."

She hesitated, giving him time to study her closely. She radiated freshness and vitality.

"Do you think it was an accident?"

The question caught him wool-gathering, and he cursed himself for allowing himself to be distracted. "What's your point, Emma?"

"Have you ever heard of a man named Andrew Warren?"

Nick frowned. He'd spent a long, unpleasant afternoon with the man less than a month before. "I've met him."

"He has plans to build a mountain resort near here."

News travels fast, he thought. But she didn't know everything. "He wants to build it up there," he said, indicating the foothills in the distance. "He tried to buy my ranch last month."

"And you told him no?"

"The ranch isn't for sale."

"Andrew Warren isn't easily dissuaded."

Nick recalled the pompous, paunchy little man and the flashy ruby ring he'd used to tap a staccato beat on the table while he chewed his cigar. He and the two attorneys who'd accompanied him had walked into the meeting hoping to intimidate Nick. They hadn't counted on Nick's hard experience with high-powered lawyers. "I think he understands my position."

Emma smiled at that. "I'm sure he does. But you should know that in the past Mr. Warren has been brought up on charges of using criminal force to get what he wants. Nothing was ever proved, of course."

Suspicion gelled into conviction as the pieces fell into place. He'd known all along the wheel of his trailer hadn't just fallen off, but until this moment, he hadn't been able to figure out who could have wanted to sabotage it. Maybe Andrew Warren hadn't accepted his refusal after all. "Why are you telling me this?"

Emma looked at him levelly, and he wanted to believe the concern he read in her expression. "I thought you should know."

"Thank you."

"I've run up against Andrew Warren before, and he's a dirty player. If you need information, I have quite a few resources at my disposal."

"And in return?" he asked, already knowing the answer.

"You give me the interview."

He frowned. From his short acquaintance with Andrew Warren, he knew the man would be vindictive. He could take care of himself, but he didn't want Emma to get caught in the middle. "No deal," he said more gruffly than he intended. "I'll take it from here."

Emma's brows drew together before she caught herself and smoothed them again, undoubtedly at great personal cost. "Why are you being so stubborn?"

"Why are you being so persistent?"

"Look, I didn't ask for this job—"

"Just tell them I'm uncooperative and be done with it. What's the big deal?"

"The *deal,*" she said, "is *you.* You're the one who's risen out of obscurity. You're the one who's made Uintah cattle the drawing card at every auction. You're the one who's dominating *Who's Who in American Agriculture.* Whether you want to be or not, you are the news. Even I know you're a successful rancher."

She tripped over the last sentence, laying bare what Nick already suspected. She didn't believe what she'd just said, though she looked as though she would give anything to get the admission back. He supposed she thought farming was beneath her dignity, the corrals and fields a little too earthy for her taste.

"Unfortunately, ranching doesn't take place in the squeaky-clean confines of some sterile boardroom," he said. "If it did, maybe it'd be a little easier for you to swallow."

"What? You don't understand!"

"Save it for someone who cares." She looked so appalled, he almost felt sorry for her. "A word of advice. One of the tenets of good writing is to believe in what you write about. Next time, make sure you've got the heart to see it through."

He left her there, grabbed his shovel and strode back across the field. After a few moments, he heard the slam of her car door and the grating of the engine as it came to life. It gave him no comfort to know he'd seen through her. She wouldn't return again, and he told himself he didn't care.

His failed marriage had taught him a hard lesson, but apparently he still had more to learn. Some people didn't understand his way of life, his ties with the land. To him, the earth, the crops, the animals, and every menial task associated with them were all part of a greater plan. Working close to nature, watching the ebb and flow of seasons helped him to understand the cycles of life; he had no desire for more.

Some people, he knew, had no wish to delve so close to their earthy beginnings. What he didn't understand was why it seemed his legacy to desire the very people who found his way of life so abhorrent. He'd wanted to believe Emma was different, that the unguarded glimpses he'd seen revealed the real woman, but she'd just proven him wrong. Perhaps this time he'd learn. It was better to stand alone than to try to alter what couldn't be changed.

Emma frowned as she drove away from the ranch, lost in an angry rebuttal until she nearly missed her turn. Nick was wrong.

She wasn't a snob. She wasn't afraid to get her hands dirty. God knew, she'd spent enough years doing just that. But that didn't mean she had to want it again. She'd left it behind and she had no intention of going back.

Just because she didn't believe in a way of life didn't mean she looked down on it. In fact, given her experience, she admired anyone willing to put their lives so much in the hands of fate. If she was guilty of anything, it was allowing her personal feelings to show.

Why, oh why did that man make her lose control like that? She'd built a career using a cool head and a sound plan. Now, suddenly, she was back at square one, a raw beginner. She didn't believe in her story, didn't believe there was such a thing as a successful rancher, and Nick had seen right through her. Well, she'd given it a good shot. She was through.

Engrossed in her thoughts, she didn't see the stampeding herd of Appaloosas in front of her until she was nearly on them. Just in time, she jammed on the brakes. The car skidded sideways on the gravel, and the horses split, enveloping her in a cloud of dust as they thundered past. Shaken, she watched them disappear in the rearview mirror. They were Nick's mares. She'd seen them earlier, grazing in his pasture.

Conscience told her to go back and tell Nick they were out, but damaged pride urged her to keep going. She could simply call from the next available phone. They weren't her horses, after all. But the next nearest telephone was practically back in Rio Blanco. Something had those horses spooked, and the way they were running, they would be lucky to be rounded up unharmed. She had to go back.

The dust was beginning to settle when she jammed the car into reverse—none too carefully—and checked down the road for traffic. At the bottom of the hill a jumbled shape caught her eye. It looked like a truck of some sort, just emerging from its own dust cloud. With a sick feeling, she realized she'd just discovered the reason for the stampede.

A logging truck stood jackknifed, its load strewn from fence to fence. The driver stood over an inert form in front of the truck, radiating his ill-concealed wrath. Emma drove down the hill and stopped behind it.

"Are you all right?"

"I'm not hurt." He scowled. "But look at my truck! And look at that mess!" He indicated the logs scattered helter-skelter across the roadway. "It'll take the rest of the day to clean it up."

Emma's glance fell on the still form at his feet. She could just make out the spotted blanket on the animal's broad rump. "What about the horse?"

"Hell, I don't know! Fifteen or twenty of 'em jumped into the road right in front of me. I'm lucky I didn't wipe out the whole bunch."

"I'll go for help," Emma said.

"See if you can get someone to bring a tractor out to clear these logs. There's another truck headed down before long. We don't need two loads all over the road."

Nick was working close to the road when she returned.

She laid her hand heavily on the horn the moment she saw him, and by the time she drew up, he was already headed her way.

"What's wrong?"

"Your mares were out on the road," she said. "A logging truck hit one of them. The rest stampeded."

Nick opened the door and jumped in. "Was anyone hurt?" he asked as she shoved the car into reverse.

"No, but the driver's mad as a whole swarm of hornets. The trailer jackknifed and dumped the load. I left him muttering about lost time and wages. He wants someone to clear the road. I don't think anyone can get through."

"Stop at the house," he instructed.

Nick was out of the car before she could pull it to a halt. He ran through the gate and took the porch steps two at a time. In less than a minute, he reappeared, yelling hurried instructions over his shoulder at Maria, who followed and nodded in understanding. He'd traded his irrigating boots for the Western boots he usually wore, and he carried a high-powered rifle.

Emma tried not to think of the import of the gun when he threw it in the back seat. But instead of getting in again, he slammed the door shut and headed for the barn. "Follow me."

By the time Emma got the car backed around, Nick had disappeared into a small door outside the stable. Pete was with him when he returned a moment later, and she caught the tail end of his instructions.

"...saddle up a couple of horses and meet me on the road. If the herd is headed west, they'll probably veer off into the draw as soon as they reach the end of the fence." He threw a heavy black bag into the back seat with the rifle and got in beside her. "Okay," he said, two grim lines bracketing his mouth. "Let's go."

A sense of urgency propelled Emma to hurry. It was possible the horse was still alive, and time seemed of the essence. She wouldn't let herself think about the alternative.

"Tell me what happened."

She relayed what she knew. By the time they reached the scene, everything was quiet, and there was no sign of the runaway horses. The truck driver paced between the logs and the front of his rig.

Nick stepped over the logs and squatted beside the downed horse. Though she wanted to help, Emma couldn't bring herself to go over there with him. She'd always had a soft spot for animals, horses in particular, and she couldn't bear the thought of seeing one suffer. Unable to watch, she turned away.

For several minutes, she heard nothing but the agitated words of the truck driver and Nick's much calmer replies. When she heard a step behind her, she whirled around to see Nick headed toward her, his expression somber. She moved aside for him to reach into the back seat, praying he would reach for the bag.

Instead he stopped short, reached out to her and brushed aside a tear. Embarrassed, she looked into his eyes.

"I like horses," she sniffed defensively. "Is she all right?"

He nodded grimly. "She'll probably live. She has a knot the size of a baseball on her head and a gash on her shoulder, but I don't think any bones are broken. I don't know about the foal."

A relieved tear slid down her cheek. "I'm glad."

His expression softened, and for a fraction of a second she thought she read kinship in his eyes.

"What can I do?"

He looked toward the driver, who'd resumed pacing. "I'm going to see what I can do for the mare. Maria's called Jack and the sheriff, but until we get these logs cleared, we need someone to flag the road. Could you do that?"

She nodded, and he held the door for her before reaching into the back seat for his things. He stopped her with a hand on her shoulder before she drove away.

"Thanks."

She watched as he went back to the horse, who now stood unsteadily in front of the logging truck. With gentle hands, he soothed her, then fashioned a halter out of a soft rope and slid it carefully over her head. Thankful that the horse was still alive, she drove to the top of the hill, thoughts of their earlier argument forgotten. He'd declared a truce between them, and for the moment at least, they were friends.

Chapter Three

"Who's going to pay for this mess? Look at my truck! Do you have any idea what body work on a truck this size costs?"

"Take it easy, Mr. Parker," the sheriff said. "We'll get everything sorted out in good time."

"What about my load? Who's going to pay for getting these logs loaded up again? In my business, time is money and I don't get paid for cooling my heels at the side of the road."

"It's an unfortunate incident all around. Don't forget, Mr. Barlow almost lost a valuable horse in the bargain."

"I ain't payin' for no horse. The whole herd of 'em was running loose in the road. If he thinks he's gonna stick me with the price of that horse, I'll see him in court! The way I see it, he's responsible for his horses and for any damage...."

Emma walked out of earshot. Between the rantings of the irate truck driver and the earsplitting screech of logs being dragged across the graveled road, her head was throbbing. Jack Wyatt had arrived, and after a cursory examination, called for a trailer to haul the mare back to the ranch. Shortly afterward, the sheriff had pulled in. Nick had stayed around only long enough to answer a few questions, then he and Pete had ridden off in search of the runaway mares. She wished she could escape as well.

It had hardly been two hours since she'd breezed by here herself, filled with purpose and armed with Andrew Warren's name. Nothing had gone right since she'd arrived in this town. If they ever got the road cleared, she couldn't wait to leave.

She wandered toward the fence, wanting to put more distance between herself and the hubbub behind her. The field beyond it was broad and green, with a small creek running through it. It looked more like a mountain meadow than a fenced pasture, and she recalled seeing the mares grazing peacefully there just that morning. What would make them get out?

In the distance, she spied a dusty cloud rising just beyond a rise in the road. As she watched, the horses came into view, dancing and snorting in the sunlight. The Appaloosas were magnificent, spirited animals, and she followed their progress as Nick and Pete turned them down the lane. Nick edged his way in front of the herd and trotted toward the corrals, apparently intent on getting the gate open before the rest of them arrived.

Behind her, the engine of the logging truck roared to life. The road must be open. She was free to go. But instead, she stayed to watch Nick's progress.

He sat tall in the saddle, riding in counterpoint with his horse. Even from a distance, Emma could tell he was very much at home there. Once he leaned forward and patted the neck of the lathered animal, as if to thank him for his efforts on his behalf. This was a side of him she hadn't seen before, the horseman who shared an affinity with his mount. His concern for the injured mare and her foal was personal, more than the threat of monetary loss.

Someone else appeared in the ranch yard, and Nick returned to the herd. The mares had slowed to a walk while Pete held them there, neither pushing them ahead nor allowing them to turn back. They watched Nick's progress, ears pricked and heads held high. One or two stopped for a mouthful of grass, but Emma didn't think they were as calm as their actions indicated. There was too much tension in the way they held their heads, too much agitation in their mincing steps.

Then everything seemed to happen at once. Behind her, the truck driver spilt the air with a blast from his horn. In front of her, the horses leaped forward—all except one, which turned and bolted past Pete in a terrified bid for escape. Nick left Pete to deal with the animals stampeding down the fenced lane while he charged after the runaway mare. His horse, a large gray, stretched into a dead run, gaining on the smaller mare with every stride, while Nick pulled the lariat from his saddle. As the mare rounded the turn into the road, he swung the rope over his head.

Emma watched in fascination as man and horse worked as a single unit. She'd seen professional ropers at a rodeo, but she'd never witnessed a working cowboy in action, and the sight was both frightening and breathtaking. The mare slipped on the gravel as she ran past a mailbox planted at the edge of the road. The momentary slowdown was the edge Nick and his horse needed. They rounded the same corner at breakneck speed, leaning hard into the turn. For one alarming heartbeat, Emma was certain they'd both be killed, but the horse dug deep, never breaking stride. A moment later the rope laced out and settled gracefully over the mare's head.

Instead of pulling his mount to a hard stop, Nick let the rope tighten slowly, gently, bringing the frightened mare to a controlled, heaving halt. When she was calm, he dismounted, obviously talking to her, and ran soothing hands over her neck and shoulders. Regardless of the stresses of the day, he was nothing but gentle with her.

A trick of memory brought to mind Nick's hands sliding up her arms, his lips on hers. She had experienced that gentleness, and tingles shot through her, bursting over her skin. She knew the power of his touch, and for one crazed moment, she envied that mare.

The ranch yard was a dusty melee of frightened horses. Pete and his helper patiently pushed them toward an open gate, and by the time Nick returned with the runaway, all the horses were safely penned in the corral.

Emma turned back to her car, still parked at the top of the hill where she'd flagged traffic until help came. The excitement was over, the horses safely rounded up and the road cleared. She was no longer needed. In fact she'd probably be in the way if she stayed, but something didn't feel right to her. There was no sense of closure. A vague uneasiness churned in her stomach. Something was wrong.

She started her car and drove it down the hill, intent on easing it through the single lane cleared of logs, but the sheriff motioned her to a halt.

"Is there something else you need?" she asked, feeling sicker by the minute.

He shook his head. "Just wanted to thank you for your help, Miz Reardon. This whole mess could have been a helluva lot worse—"

He was interrupted by Nick, who charged up behind them on his big gray, sliding to a halt in a spray of gravel.

"Who the hell blew that horn?" he demanded. "Hasn't there been enough damage done for one day?"

"Sorry, Nick. That truck driver, Parker, was hell-bent on leaving and started up his rig as soon as Hank hooked onto the last log. When Hank stopped for a better hitch, he laid on the horn. Damn near gave us all a heart attack.''

''Well I have half a mind to give him more than that.'' For all the patience he'd displayed with the runaway horses, his temper simmered just under the surface.

''I might as well warn you, the man's talking about a lawsuit. Chances are he's just letting off steam, but you should know, just the same.''

Emma had heard enough. The sick feeling congealed in the pit of her stomach. She knew how this story ended. She'd lived it. Nick might have been one lucky rancher up until now, but his luck had changed. In a very short time, he'd wrecked his truck and his trailer, he'd narrowly missed losing his stallion, possibly his very life. He'd almost lost a valuable mare. Perhaps he *had* lost her foal. Now he faced a lawsuit.

Ranching wasn't any different from farming. It was all a gamble, and the tide had turned against him. Next would come the hard winter, a dry summer, record low beef prices. Soon his banker would hesitate to carry him for another year. It was only a matter of time until he succumbed to the inevitable.

No matter how much time and distance she put behind her, she'd never been able to outstrip the old feelings of helplessness and hopelessness. They'd followed her here, accompanied this time by warning bells too loud to ignore. This time it wasn't her family sinking into ruin. This time it wasn't her home under siege. This time it was a stranger, a man she barely knew, but the feeling was strong, just the same. And just like before, she could do nothing to stop it. No one could. The cycle had begun, and she couldn't afford to care.

She was suffocating and she desperately needed to get away. But Hank had a hitch on another log, and the road was blocked again.

The men didn't notice her rapidly indrawn breaths or her

white knuckles on the steering wheel. "...you get all the mares rounded up?" the sheriff was asking.

Nick nodded. "Jack is checking them over now."

"Any idea how the horses got out?"

Nick shook his head, his jaw clenched.

Emma took a deep breath, willing herself to stay calm. "They were all grazing peacefully when I came by this morning."

"When was that?" Both men spoke at once.

She directed her answer at Nick, thankful for something—anything—to occupy her mind. "It couldn't have been more than a half hour before I saw you out in the field."

His scowl deepened, if that were possible. His eyes were steely blue points, but he checked his anger. "I'll check the fence as soon as I'm through here."

"Something must have spooked them," the sheriff said.

Nick nodded. "It'll be a while before they calm down. I'll keep them in the corral at least until morning."

His voice calmed her. He seemed so strong, so sure of himself, as if he were inviolable, even by fate. Suddenly she wanted to believe he was. The suffocating grip in her chest eased somewhat, and she heard herself ask, "Is there anything else I can do?"

Nick studied her with a curious expression, as if he were trying to categorize her somehow. She supposed her concern didn't jibe with the elitist image he had of her, but she'd never be able to explain it to him. It didn't matter. By tomorrow she'd be gone. From the beginning they'd gotten off on the wrong foot. She tried to tell herself that what he thought was unimportant, but even the most cynical part of her knew otherwise.

Finally, he smiled. "Thanks, Emma, but you've been more than helpful already. I'll take it from here."

For one heart-stopping moment, she couldn't look away. The deep dimples in his cheeks exaggerated his smile, and his mesmerizing eyes brought to mind intimacies far more private than a conversation in front of a sheriff. But it was only a flash, replaced by the weighty problems of the day barely half over. She shook herself, trying to break the spell. Now that the road was cleared, there was no reason for her to stay. With a quick gesture she hoped would hide her confusion, she drove away.

She was running. Emotions she'd buried long ago were threatening to explode her well-ordered world. Nicolas Barlow's way of life represented everything she feared most. Fate was chipping away at his livelihood, his security—and the outcome was inevitable. She didn't want to care, but she couldn't stop herself from watching him in the rearview mirror until he disappeared from view.

The need for speed drove her faster. When she saw the broken fence, she was well past it before the implication burned through her churning thoughts. Jamming her foot on the brake, she brought the car to a halt in a cloud of dust.

Nick rode slowly down the fence line, looking for anything that would explain why an entire herd of horses would get out of the pasture in such a short time. He'd checked this fence himself less than a month ago, and there hadn't been so much as a loose staple in the whole thing.

Lucy was one of his favorite mares. She wouldn't have been easy to replace. Pete had christened her as a filly, claiming her red coat and tendency to get into mischief reminded him of the redheaded comedienne. The nickname suited her better than the more ladylike name on her registration papers, and it had stuck. He smiled. Given her changeable nature, if he had it to do again, he'd name her Emma.

He came to a low spot in the fence. The mares could jump here, if provoked. But there were no tracks, no telltale signs of trampled grass. The pasture ended in a dip just out of sight.

The horses couldn't just teleport over the fence. He must have missed something.

"Come on Grayson," he said, urging his horse forward again. "Let's check that old gate up here, just to make sure." The road cut through an embankment and disappeared around a curve, but he and Grayson followed the fence over the hill, still watching for signs of the horses' passing. At the top he spotted a familiar green car parked at the edge of the road below him. Nearby, burnished red hair glistened in the sun, and its owner sat on a rock, twirling something in her hands.

Nick sent the gelding down the rocky hillside, torn between dread of another confrontation and relief that Emma had not yet walked out of his life. She watched him, her expression troubled as she continued to finger whatever it was she held. It wasn't until he dismounted that he pulled his eyes away from her and saw what she'd discovered. The old wire gate his grandfather had built into the fence for convenience in moving cattle lay open. Not just down, but wide-open.

"I think I know how your horses got out," she said unnecessarily.

His eyes dropped to the ground. Weeds and shrubs lay trampled beneath the prints of fifteen sets of hooves.

She extended her hand. Her palm was stained bright orangey-brown from the rusty, mangled piece of wire she held. He took it from her to examine it more closely. It was old—probably the original piece used to wire the gate shut when his father had built a loading chute to haul the cattle to summer pasture instead of driving them up the road. But the surface corrosion was just that. The wire remained strong. On each end the sun glinted off bright silver tips, flattened slightly and angled to a point. Nick recognized the implication at once, but he wondered how Emma had reached the same conclusion. He looked up at her.

"I've seen wire cutter marks before," she said. "Someone opened this gate on purpose."

She was right, of course. And her expression said she meant to pursue it.

She must have read something of his thoughts in his eyes. "Surely you're not going to argue with me."

He took a deep breath, trying to gain control of the frustration surging through him. Anger for the intentional opening of the gate. Perplexion at what could be gained by turning the horses out. Irritation for the way the day had gone sour. A need for retribution, a half-formed plan to fight back. And most complicated of all—confusion about this woman, who seemed to change every time he saw her.

One moment she was vulnerable, the next unapproachable. One moment she'd implied the drudgery of ranching was beneath her, and the next she'd cried over an injured mare. She wore a veneer of cool sophistication, yet she kissed like a fiery temptress. This morning, she'd been an ambitious career woman, now she stood before him in wrinkled slacks and disheveled hair, ready to take on the devil himself on his behalf. Through it all, she was dedicated to getting a story despite everything he'd done to drive her away, and that was what frightened him most. She'd said herself that Andrew Warren was a dirty player. Warren wouldn't stand for Emma's probing, and Nick didn't want her involved.

"I'll talk to the sheriff when he comes back down the mountain."

"That's *it*? That's all you're going to do?"

"What would you have me do? Search house to house for evidence? This is ranching country, Emma. You'll find a pair of fencing pliers in every truck in this county."

"You know as well as I do who is responsible for this."

"I don't know anything except that someone cut a piece of wire. How do I know *you* didn't plant the wire here? How do I know you didn't cut it yourself?"

The air echoed in the sudden stillness. "Is that what you think?"

"Of course not. But I can't make blanket accusations because Andrew Warren offered to buy my ranch."

"What about your horse trailer?"

"There's no proof, Emma."

"So you're going to stand around and wait until he gets careless? How much longer do you think your luck will hold out? How many horses are you willing to sacrifice?"

Something inside him snapped. "Do you think I don't *care?*"

"I *think* if you don't have proof, you have to look for it. Please, let me help you."

She meant to get involved no matter what he said. "Why? Don't you have another story to write?"

"There's a story here."

He raised an eyebrow. "Local news. Regional at best. Not *American Business Monitor* material."

"You're wrong," she said coldly. "Andrew Warren is a power broker. He's got a golden touch when it comes to development. *American Business Monitor* would be *very* interested."

She was stretching the truth. He could hear it in her voice. "Why are you so intent on getting involved? Have you got some kind of vendetta against him?"

"Of course not! But I've seen what he's capable of. I don't mean to imply the sheriff isn't a good man, but—"

"Apparently you don't think much of me, either."

She glared at him. "Is it worth losing your ranch to find out?"

She'd done it again! First she'd implied ranching wasn't an honorable occupation, now she'd as much as told him he didn't have the wherewithal to fight for his own land. After the bloody legal battle he'd endured, he almost laughed in her face. "Rest assured, Emma, this ranch is *mine*."

She said nothing else, just got in her car and drove away. He watched her go, seething with anger and disturbed by the two sides of the woman, constantly at odds with each other. She was working on an agenda of her own, and he didn't suppose he would ever find out what it was. He wasn't even certain he wanted to.

"I appreciate what you're trying to say, Nick, but what you've shown me here proves nothing." The sheriff wrapped the rusty wire around a fence post. "I'm real sorry about the horse, but I can't arrest a man just because someone opened your gate."

"He did more than open the gate, Sheriff. He drove the horses out onto the road. He left tracks everywhere."

The sheriff studied the footprints in the dusty trail made by the horses. "Yes, I'll give you that. But without more evidence, there's not much I can do. I'll take a picture of the prints for comparison in case anything else happens. But I just don't think there's enough here to warrant a full investigation. My guess is you've got some kids around here bent on raising some havoc. It's probably a one-time thing."

"What about the wheel on my horse trailer?"

The sheriff sighed. "There's no proof that was anything but an accident. I'll admit you've had your share of bad luck lately, but it's coincidence."

Nick didn't agree, but it was obvious he'd get nowhere by arguing. Besides, on the surface, there wasn't much to go on. But the sixth sense bothering him since the accident had come to a head with Emma's suggestion that Andrew Warren might be behind the mysterious happenings surrounding him.

What surprised him was the fact Andrew Warren hadn't made a second demand before he set about sabotaging the Uintah. Apparently the man thought, in his underhanded way, he could avoid suspicion if he didn't seem overly eager to acquire the land. Several seemingly unrelated, but expensive accidents might induce some men to sell out, but Nick didn't include himself on that list. Thanks to Emma, he was fore-warned, and in his mind forewarned was forearmed. If any more "accidents" occurred, he'd be ready.

The telephone was ringing when Emma stormed into her hotel room.

"Hi, Emma." It was her editor. "What's the news on the handsome cowboy?"

"There isn't any," Emma replied, unable to curb the irritation in her voice. She related her efforts at getting Nick to talk, but for reasons she didn't want to examine, she mentioned only the business details. She said nothing about his insulting insinuations, the kiss that still had her reeling, his belief that somehow she looked down on his way of life, or his final refusal even for her help.

But instead of accepting Emma's discouraged words, her editor seemed excited. "You mean you've been on his ranch? Twice?"

"Well, yes. But—"

"Emma, you're already ten steps ahead of anyone else who's tried to talk to him!"

"You don't understand." She tried to explain about the accidents she didn't believe were accidental and her suspicions about Andrew Warren.

"You can't leave now. All this would make an excellent sidebar to your story. If you can get this interview, we'll have an exclusive on the man *and* his battles to maintain control. It'll be award-winning material."

Emma felt herself sinking, mired down in her own half-truths. Unless she admitted her personal reasons for wanting to give up, she'd never be able to talk her boss out of continuing her efforts. But was she willing to expose the fears and anxieties that sent her running? Was she willing to admit she was inexplicably attracted to a man who obviously didn't like her at all?

"I think you're making real progress."

"No!"

"Give it a few more days. Concentrate on talking to friends and neighbors, and find out as much as you can about the Warren angle. Barlow will calm down. This has the makings of a cover story. Good work!"

She hung up before Emma could protest. She'd hesitated too long and now she was in over her head. Like it or not, she had to stay.

For the next two days, she didn't allow herself to think about anything but the story. She let the reporter in her take over, concentrating on getting the information she needed. While Anna, her research assistant, checked a list of contacts on the Warren issue, she found and interviewed the president of the Cattlemen's Association. He gave a glowing account of Nick's activities in that organization and confided that he thought Nick would be the next president. He also directed her to Nick's best friend.

Jack Wyatt, it turned out, was also Nick's cousin. He recognized her at once. "Hello again, Ms. Reardon," he said. "What can I do for you?"

"I'm working on an article about Nick Barlow."

"That's odd," he said almost suspiciously. "Since the divorce, he stays out of the public eye."

"Yes." She was curious about Nick's ex-wife, but prudence dictated that she steer clear of the subject. Obviously Jack had no intention of divulging confidences. "My focus is on the unprecedented success of his ranch. I understand you're related."

He nodded, apparently reassured. "We grew up together. I spent all my summers out there when I was a kid." He related a couple of anecdotes, then surprised Emma with his candor when she began asking questions about Nick's operation.

The conversation drifted from cattle to horses.

"Nick's Appaloosas are good horses," Jack said, "but Cochise is the apple of his eye. He's besotted with him. After the accident, he wouldn't leave until he was sure he'd be okay. He stayed here with me for a week."

Emma recalled the showy stallion she'd seen in Nick's corral. "He's a valuable horse."

"No doubt about that. Bill Stratton offered a hundred grand for him. But I doubt if Nick would sell him for any price."

"Who's Bill Stratton?"

"Another breeder. For several years now, he's had the champion stud. But I've heard a rumor his horse is throwing unpredictable foals. It's too bad. The world of champion Appaloosas is a small one, and there's been a lot of inbreeding."

Emma wrote the man's name down, thinking she'd call him to get his reaction to being usurped by a newcomer.

"How did you talk Nick into granting an interview?"

She stopped writing, feeling like she'd been caught with her hand in the cookie jar. "To be honest, I haven't—yet." At his look of consternation, she added, "Don't worry, you haven't given away any secrets. Anything you gave me is just background information."

He smiled. "Well, if anyone can get him to talk, it'll be you." She had no idea what that meant, but didn't ask him to explain. She just wished she had his confidence.

By the third day, she couldn't avoid facing Nick any longer. She had a folder full of notes. She'd spent hours talking with his business associates. She'd even spent a fruitless afternoon looking for more information on Andrew Warren. Now the article needed his input.

This time when she dressed for the meeting, she drew on her years of rural living. She donned a pair of jeans, a

T-shirt and running shoes. The outfit was far from professional, but any opportunity to impress Nick had long since passed.

Armed with the information she'd gathered and hopefully enough determination to face down her fears, she aimed her old car down the Uintah Road one last time. This time, either she'd get the interview or she'd have no choice but to give up.

For two days, she'd been working on a story about Nicolas Barlow, a rancher who'd risen out of obscurity to make a place for himself in the small world of championship cattle breeding. She'd purposely not allowed herself to think about Nick, the man. But now her mind conjured up a vision of him. His appeal went far deeper than a pair of dimples and blue eyes; his charisma struck down the barriers she'd tried to erect between them. Part of her couldn't wait to see him again.

Catching the direction of her thoughts, she reminded herself he was also the man who'd come close to losing a hundred thousand dollars' worth of horse on the turn of a lug nut. His life-style was dependent on the very things that had destroyed her family. Nick Barlow was an interview. He could be nothing more.

A deer bounded onto the road in front of her, jarring her back to reality. She jammed on the brakes but, curiously, the pedal felt soft. It mushed to the floor. She tried it again, and it held for a moment then lost all resistance.

The road angled down and the car began to move faster. Pumping the brake to no avail, her fear mounted. In front of her the road dropped off a long, winding hill that led to the river valley. Without brakes, there was no way she could make it to the bottom. She was already picking up speed. Unless she thought fast, the crest of that hill might well be the edge of the world.

Chapter Four

Nick turned his pickup truck onto the road, his attention divided between his driving and the countryside, watching for anything out of the ordinary. It had been three days since the incident with the open gate, and he almost wondered if the sheriff was right after all.

As a precaution, he'd moved most of the mares to a protected pasture away from the road. He'd kept Lucy stabled to care for her cuts and bruises, and to monitor her unborn foal. Now the idle pasture lay lush and peaceful in the sunshine, far removed from the chaos of the past few days.

Passing by the newly mended fence where the old gate had been, his thoughts turned for the hundredth time to Emma. Apparently this time he'd succeeded in sending her away.

She'd left, but he was not at peace. Since they'd parted, she'd haunted his every thought. To fight back, he'd listed the times she'd pushed the boundary of his good humor, trying to convince himself he was glad she was gone. But he felt a twinge of melancholy when he recalled the last time he'd seen her, when harsh words had finally driven her away.

Work had always been the magic prescription. Whenever a problem loomed on his horizon, he could apply himself to his chores while he sorted through the quandary. But this time his daily tasks, most of them solitary pursuits, gave him too much time to think. He'd checked the perimeter fences with a vision of silky hair in the back of his mind. He'd changed the irrigation water in the hayfields, recalling the shock on her face when she'd stepped into the ditch. Avoiding thoughts of her hadn't worked, so he'd tried dwelling on her pretensions. Instead he recalled the tears she'd shed over an injured mare.

Kissing her had been a monumental mistake. His body recalled every detail of her petite form straining against him, the way she'd returned that kiss. Everywhere he went, the memory of her saucy, freckled face robbed his peace of mind.

At the bottom of Sweetwater Hill he passed beyond his property line. If anything was afoot today, it wasn't along the road. Shifting his concentration, he set the truck onto the winding grade. Halfway up, he thought he caught a glimpse of a green car above him. It looked like Emma's. He thought he saw her everywhere, he decided sourly. If he meant to get on with his life, he'd better get rid of that mindset. She was gone for good.

But when he rounded the next curve, a car *was* there, stopped at the side of the road. And the driver, a redhead with riotous hair, sat with her head against the steering wheel. The battle to forget her fell in defeat, buried by excitement that would not be contained. Not only was Emma still in town, she was on her way to see him. Except, if appearances could be trusted, her car had broken down again.

"Why don't you just sell that thing?" he asked, only half

in jest, when he pulled up beside her. At this rate, the car would get her into serious trouble.

She didn't respond with the acid reply he expected.

"What happened?"

"I lost my brakes."

The lightness of the moment faded. If the car was in that bad of shape, it was a danger to her and everyone else on the road. "Are you all right?"

"Yes," she said, but her unsteady voice and luminous eyes told a different story.

He shut off the engine of his truck and opened the door.

She got out, too. For once she wasn't dressed as if she were headed for the boardroom, but he had only a moment to admire the way her jeans clung to her figure before her wobbly knees gave way. He caught her just in time.

She was trembling all over, and he wrapped his arms around her. "You're okay now, Emma," he whispered into her hair. In response she held him tight, and he found himself shaking, too.

Telling himself she was frightened and needed reassurance, he rationalized holding her against him. Her hair smelled faintly of green apples, but it felt like spun silk against his cheek. She held on with surprising strength, considering how tiny she was. Without the benefit of elevated heels, her head barely reached his shoulder. But before long, his body recognized her as all woman, more appealing than even the most vivid daydreams from the past three days. Awash with emotions that had nothing to do with comfort, he put her from him.

Emma, who'd been too absorbed in Nick's solid embrace to comprehend what she was doing, felt him push her away, and it hit her like a lightning bolt. He'd made it clear again and again that he wanted nothing to do with her, yet here she was clinging to him. She felt her face flame, made worse by knowing he'd see it, too.

He must have thought she still needed a steady hand, however, because instead of letting go, he propelled her toward his truck and nudged her down onto the running board. When he turned away and reached for something in the cab, she used the reprieve to compose herself as best she could, still burning with the humiliation of having made a fool of herself again over this man.

"Drink this," he said. "It's the best I can offer."

He held out a half-finished can of soda. She took it and tipped it against her lips, trying to ignore the awareness that swept through her, knowing his lips had been there before hers.

"Tell me what happened."

She took a deep breath, made herself raise her eyes from his dusty boots to his face. His blue eyes pierced her shaky defenses, making her feel as if the raw emotions inside were exposed to view. Unable to endure the scrutiny, she dropped her gaze.

"A deer ran out in front of me at the top of the hill. I hit the brake and the pedal just—" she paused, looking for the word "—let go." She looked up again.

He frowned. "Didn't you try to pump it?"

"Yes, but the pedal just went limp."

"Have the brakes been soft lately?"

"Not at all. They worked fine when I left town."

He frowned again. "How did you get stopped?"

"I used the emergency brake."

"I'll take a look at the brakes. But first, I need to move the truck out of the road before someone else comes barreling down here. Can you stand now?"

She stood and moved out of his way. Now that the crisis was over she felt more foolish than ever. Of all people, why had it been Nick to find her here? For ten years her car had been as dependable as night following day. Then, in a week's time, it had left her stranded twice, and both times Nick Barlow had been on hand to witness it. Some perverse twist of fate had her in its sights, presenting her in the worst possible light.

Thankfully, when he returned, he'd decided to lighten the mood, although she wasn't certain she liked his choice of topics.

"So, Emma, what brings you out this way?" He sauntered toward her with a cocksure look that made her want to wipe it off his face. But there could be no mistake where she'd been headed. She might as well get it over with.

"Why, you do, Nick."

His eyebrows raised into the shadow beneath his hat. "Was there something you forgot to mention the last time you called?"

"As it happens, I did learn something that might interest you."

"And what might that be?" He opened her car door and slid in beneath the wheel, his knees bent double as he fumbled for the adjustment lever.

"I spoke with my editor a couple of days ago. She feels encouraged."

He tested the brake with his right foot, pumping it several times. "Now why would that interest me?" He glanced up at her, dimples dancing in his cheeks. She flushed under his regard.

"I doubt that it would. But it meant I couldn't go home. It seems you've never let a reporter get out to your ranch before."

He released the hood latch and got out with a chuckle. "True enough. You slipped in when I wasn't looking."

She followed him around to the front of the car. "So I've spent the past two days gathering background information."

"I see." He peered under the hood, checking first one side and then the other. "And what have you learned?" Spotting what he was looking for, he moved around to the side, reaching for an oily looking cap.

"The Cattlemen's Association plans to make you president," she answered.

He grunted in reply as he unscrewed the cap with a gritty, metal-on-metal noise that set her teeth on edge.

She clutched her hands to her jaw. "What *is* that?"

"The master cylinder."

She had no idea what a master cylinder was, but he spoke with authority, so she didn't question him further. What had she been about to say? Oh, yes. "You devised a cattle-breeding plan in college. You even published a couple of papers about it. Apparently you haven't *always* avoided publicity." No reply. "Anna, my research assistant, is looking for a copy of them now."

"Don't bother," he said as he peered into the hole. "It's all out of date. I have the whole thing on computer now."

"So I understand."

"There's a flashlight in my glove box. Would you mind getting it for me?"

She did as he asked, recalling the times she'd done the same thing for her father. Nick was still bent over the fender when she returned, and she slowed her steps to admire the view. Dad had never looked like that when he'd worked on the old station wagon. She pressed the flashlight into his outflung hand.

Nick shined the light into the hole with a noncommittal "Hmmm," and replaced the lid. He backed out and turned to lean against the car. "Sounds like you found a fountain of information. Who, might I ask, is your source?"

She handed him a wad of tissues. "I talked with several people."

"One of them wouldn't have been Jack Wyatt, by any chance?"

She smiled. "He was most helpful."

"Remind me to thank him."

He was apparently unmoved by what she'd said so far. Probably because it was all a matter of record.

"What other gems did you unearth?"

"You graduated from college with a minor in business. You've put your theories on cattle breeding to practice, with good results. You have plans to buy a hundred acres not far from here because you'd like to build a house there someday, and you have a soft spot for your Appaloosa stallion. Should I go on?"

He leisurely wiped his grimy hands on tissues. "Please do."

She had no idea what he was thinking, but she decided to go for broke.

"Native American Show Horses plans to name Cochise the Stallion of the Year, which is unheard-of for a young, unproven newcomer. In fact, Bill Stratton, who owns the current champion, refused even to talk about it on the telephone."

"You've been busy, I'll give you that. I've never known NASH to leak the name of the winner beforehand."

"That's my job," she replied blandly. "Any reaction from the recipient?"

"Nothing you can quote me on," he replied. "Any other secrets you can let me in on?"

"Well, I don't know how secret it is, but the citizens of Rio Blanco are evenly split in opinion as to whether or not Andrew Warren's idea of a mountain resort is a good one. The town could use some tourist money, but they're afraid he'd bypass them in favor of Concha Springs because there's an airport there."

Nick said nothing.

"What do you think?"

"What I think doesn't matter, because I'm not selling out."

For the first time, though he wasn't answering her questions, he was responding with more than a refusal to talk. Encouraged, but afraid to bring up the interview, she continued in the same vein while he turned back to her car.

"A friend of mine in the attorney general's office worked on the Warren case before it was dropped. He gave me a list of the witnesses involved."

Nick looked back at her curiously.

"They're a closemouthed bunch. In fact, some of them were openly hostile. I figure anyone that protective of their favorite son must be hiding something."

He leaned down, extending his arm into the bowels of the engine cavity. "You're probably right about that," he said, his words muffled. "I got the same feeling when he came at me with a pair of lawyers."

"You think he was trying to intimidate you?"

"Probably."

"Well, I did learn one interesting little tidbit."

"Which was?"

"Warren has a new girlfriend."

Nick brought his arm back and examined a greasy spot on his finger.

"Her name is Lynette Barlow."

He straightened abruptly, banging his head on the hood of the car. "Ow!" He backed up and stood upright, swallowing some pretty descriptive expletives, judging from the look on his face. "What did you say?"

Finally she'd gotten a reaction. "Apparently they're an item."

A parade of expressions crossed his face, but he said nothing. Instead he dropped to the ground and stuck his head behind the front tire.

Irritated at his refusal to react, she asked, "Don't you find that a little suspicious?"

"There's no law against dating."

"Damn it, Nick, don't you care?"

He slid out from under the fender. "About Lynette? Not at all. About the fact they're dating? They deserve each other."

He was certainly good at hiding his emotions. No one could hear news like that without feeling something. From the rumors she'd heard, their divorce had been nothing short of war. Curiosity was eating her alive, but it wasn't her place to ask personal questions about a marriage dissolved years ago. One thing for certain, she'd never learn about it from him.

"Don't you think it's a little too coincidental that your ex-wife is dating the man who's trying to coerce you into selling your ranch?"

"I doubt if it's a coincidence."

"Then you need to talk to the sheriff."

"I've already talked to him. Unfortunately, there's no proof that all this is anything but a string of bad luck. "

"So you're going to do nothing?"

"I didn't say that."

"Then what's your plan?"

He slid under her car, behind the front tire. "For starters, I'm going to see if I can fix this brakeline...."

Emma leaned against the car in frustration. How could the man learn his ex-wife was in all likelihood plotting the take-over of his ranch and calmly dismiss it without a word? He lay stretched out on the gravel as if fixing cars in the middle of the road was commonplace. In a thousand years she'd never understand him. And for all the talking she'd done, she had the feeling she hadn't changed his mind about the interview.

Then something about his attitude changed. A stillness. One leg remained flexed, the other stretched out beside it, but his body radiated tension that hadn't been there before. When he spoke, the lazy drawl was gone.

"Emma, I think there's a screwdriver in the glove box, too. Would you get it for me?"

Something in his tone of voice sent her scurrying for the tool.

Nick propped the flashlight between his teeth, thoughts of his ex-wife forgotten. There was something amiss here. The whole fender well was splattered with brake fluid, testimony to the hole in the line. From the looks of the hose, it was possible the thing had blown out, but something about the checked tubing didn't ring true.

The screwdriver was too large, and he succeeded only in knocking a chunk of dried mud into his eyes. "You don't have a smaller screwdriver, do you?" he asked.

"No."

The flashlight slipped and he gave up. The brakeline had to be replaced anyway. Slipping a small knife out of his pocket, he pried it open and sliced the hose off at either end. Sliding out from under the car, he blinked the dirt out of his eyes and sat up.

"You call that *fixing* the hose?" Emma demanded, the fury of a thousand injustices in her voice.

He almost smiled. "It had a hole in it."

"But couldn't you just have wrapped some tape or something around it?"

Distracted, he looked up at her. She was standing above him, hands on hips, looking as if he'd just passed a death sentence on her car. Unfortunately, the effect she was working so hard to achieve was negated by a smudge of dirt on her chin. Far from being cowed, he toyed with the idea of wiping that spot away for her. That and a few others. She'd never know there was only one.

Beyond looking more approachable, something else about her seemed different. True, she'd been frightened nearly out of her wits by the close call, but she'd recovered admirably. She'd given him the tools he'd asked for like a surgical nurse assisting a surgeon. How had the cultured woman she pretended to be learned that particular technique?

She still stood above him, looking somewhat less confident, and he realized he'd been staring. Shaking himself free of his thoughts, he turned back to the piece of hose. "Brake fluid eats through tape, Emma. It even corrodes metal. I wanted a closer look at this hose."

Her pique returned. "But now I have to have the car towed again."

Ignoring her as best he could, he eyed the hose critically. It was old. The surface was checked with tiny cracks, but the split where the fluid had erupted seemed suspiciously clean; it hadn't blown out. Bending the hose backward, he exposed the hole. His hunch was confirmed. The slice ran counter to the pattern of surface cracks. The hose had been cut.

Emma fell suspiciously silent. "What are you looking at?"

"How many times did you use the brakes before you got to the top of the hill?"

She gave him a bewildered look. "Once. Maybe twice."

"You didn't use them to turn off the highway?"

She shook her head, her gaze fastened on the piece of hose he held. "No, I downshifted before I turned."

She'd *downshifted?* Who'd taught her that?

"The car I learned to drive in was—unreliable. It was that or nothing." For some reason she sounded defensive. "Let me see the hose."

She reached for it and Nick let her have it. He needed time to think. Time to figure out exactly what was happening.

Lynette was seeing Andrew Warren. That didn't surprise him. Warren was the kind of man who'd capture Lynette's attention. He was a freewheeler, the sort who wouldn't be afraid to lavish his money on her.

Now Andrew Warren had set his sights on Nick's ranch. No surprise there. Given his history with Lynette, she'd probably sent Warren after him.

Then two unexplainable accidents had occurred. They hadn't been accidents, of course, but there was no proof. Nick had spent some time checking up on Warren in the past couple of days. Everything Emma said about him was consistent with what he'd learned.

But now Emma had suffered an accident, too. Where did that fit into the picture? She'd shown up on the scene less than a week ago. Could the cut brakeline be related to the ongoing chain of events, or was it just a matter of coincidence? No one here even knew her. And he didn't believe in coincidence.

"Wait a minute! The cracks in this hose all go in one direction. Why does the hole cut across them?"

Damn! He hadn't meant for her to find out until he'd had time to think it through. She was watching him for a reaction, the color slowly draining out of her face. Too late. She'd figured it out on her own. "Apparently not everyone finds you as charming as I do. What did you say to those people you talked to this week?"

"This is no time for jokes, Nick. This hose was cut, wasn't it?"

"It looks that way."

"Someone tried to kill me?"

The vulnerability in her voice got to him. She was beautiful and spirited, but in the face of someone who wanted to hurt her, what kind of defense could she offer? The attacks on him had been against his livestock. If they'd been successful, they would have proven costly, but they'd offered little risk to his safety. The attack on Emma, however, was another story. A car without brakes was a very real danger, both to the driver and anyone who might get in the way.

"Did anyone know you were headed out here?"

She shook her head. "I didn't decide to drive out until this morning."

"Then I doubt whoever did it wanted you killed so much

as warned." He hoped he sounded convincing, because he didn't buy it. None of the roads around here were without hills or dangerous curves. She could well have been killed. "Do you know of anyone who might feel threatened by you? How many people know you're here?"

She answered his last question first. "Anyone who wanted to find me could simply call my office."

"What about enemies?"

"I can think of several people who probably don't like me for one reason or another, but none of them have ever tried to get me killed."

All her answers seemed to point in one direction. The attack on her had something to do with him. None of this was a coincidence.

"When you talked with Warren's friends, did any of them threaten you?" he asked very softly.

She looked at him, her whiskey-colored eyes contracting to pinpoints. "No, but they made it clear they meant to tell Warren what I'd said."

"What, exactly, did you say?"

"I asked them if he was involved in illegal real estate transactions. Whether he used unlawful force to close the deals. I asked why the charges against him had been dropped."

"It might be time for you to go home, Emma."

She looked at him with the beginnings of stubbornness replacing fear. He could see her weighing her options, and he knew before she spoke what her decision would be.

"No."

He drew in a deep breath. "This isn't the time to dig in your heels. Obviously you've stepped on someone's toes here."

"You might as well be clear about it. I've stepped on Andrew Warren's toes."

"All right. You've stepped on Andrew Warren's toes, and

now he wants you to back off. You said yourself he was a dirty player.''

''Do you honestly think my leaving would change anything now?'' She shook her head. ''I don't have to be here to write about him. He could find me anywhere.''

What she said was true. She was scared, he could see it in her pale skin, her round eyes, but she wasn't about to run. In fact, he suspected nothing would change her mind now, regardless of the danger involved. Andrew Warren had underestimated her. But determined or not, she was vulnerable, particularly in a hotel room.

''I have a job to do. If that includes unearthing a criminal's activities, I'll do it. The only solution is for me to keep digging until I find proof.''

He hated to admit it, but she was right. The best way out of the situation for both of them was to expose Warren and his plans.

He took the hose from her. ''Come on, I'll give you a lift into town.''

She didn't look as if she trusted his calm acceptance of her declaration, but after a moment, she followed him to his pickup. ''What are you going to do with that?''

''For what it's worth, I'm going to show it to the sheriff. As old as it is, and as bad a shape as it's in, I doubt if he'll see things our way, but it'll be documentation, just the same.''

She fell quiet on the drive into town, giving Nick time to think. He didn't like the idea of her staying alone. She was too exposed in the hotel, with her car parked on the street and no one nearby to hear her if she called out.

She interrupted his thoughts, ''I've told you what I learned, and I know you don't want the publicity, but I think there's a real story here. Now it needs your input. It won't fly unless you cooperate.''

She'd just offered a solution to their problems, but he

needed a minute to think it through. In order to stall, he resorted to teasing. "It seems to me you've already found out all there is to know."

She ignored him. Speaking carefully, she built her argument. "What I found out is how others perceive what you're doing. Now I'd like to hear it from your viewpoint."

Realizing that he was opening a door that wouldn't easily be closed again, he finally gave in. "All right. You've got your interview. But on my terms."

She'd been prepared to argue further, and his surrender took the wind out of her sails. For a long moment, she stared at him in openmouthed surprise. Then her eyes narrowed. "What terms?"

"If you want to write about my ranch, I want you to see the operation firsthand. You come out and stay there—in the guest room, of course—and I'll show it to you personally."

"That's it?"

"No. There are a couple of other conditions."

"Such as?"

"One, you don't interfere. You'll be there just as an observer."

"Agreed. Anything else?"

"I get final say on the article. If I don't like it, you don't print it."

"I'm not sure if I can grant you that."

"Take it or leave it."

She didn't like being pinned down, he could see it in her face, but she'd accept his conditions. In doing so, she'd put herself under his protection. He'd be able to keep an eye on her, and working together, they'd get to the bottom of the mysterious happenings around them.

Under the circumstances, he'd found the best of both worlds. But already unwanted excitement was surging through him. Emma Reardon, with her red hair and freckles, her sexy little body and disturbing duality would be around twenty-four hours a day. Something told him he'd just made the biggest mistake of his life.

Chapter Five

*E*mma stood on the hill in the mist, the ranch buildings in the distance below her. She watched the fog rising out of the trees, remarkably similar to the mists she'd watched on the old farm. It gathered and thickened until the buildings dimmed and disappeared. If she closed her eyes she could smell the morning damp of her West Virginian childhood.

An eddy of wind sent the clouds swirling, and when they parted, it wasn't Nick's barn at all she saw. It was the barn she'd grown up with, weathered gray from long years of exposure to the elements, bits of moss growing in the sheltered cracks, fed by mists such as this.

Bittersweet memories fought their way to the surface, overwhelming the iron control that usually kept them buried. That old barn, with its leaking roof and sagging timbers, was the hallmark of a poverty-stricken farm, built on sterile soil long since leached of life-giving nutrients. Each decaying shingle that fell from the roof marked a faded dream turned to dust.

Each broken and rusty implement housed within gave proof that life and livelihood could not be pulled from the barren fields.

She'd grown up watching that old barn wither and die, proof to all the world that the farm, and the family trying to eke a living from it, were caught in a downward spiral from which there was no way out. The last time she'd seen it was in a mist like this, and she was struck now by the irony that the mossy, weathered boards were the stuff of picture post-cards and coffee-table books. "A building with character," the caption would say, and those viewing it would pause and wonder at the history of the place, unaware of the price in human suffering extracted from each character-building year that barn had endured.

The mists swirled again, and suddenly Nick was there. He placed his hand on her shoulder. "Why are you sad?"

She shivered, more from her chilly thoughts than from the cool morning air. Nick saw too much. "Sad? What makes you think I'm sad?"

He turned her toward him, his eyes telling her the ruse was wasted. "You looked lost," he said. "Defeated."

"It's the mist," she lied. "I've never liked the mist."

He pulled her close, wrapping her in his warmth. He smelled of fresh air and horses. The crisp finish of his denim jacket contrasted with the damp in the air. It felt good against her cheek.

"It was more than that, I think."

She didn't bother to deny it.

"On a morning like this," he said, "with the mist sur-rounding everything, I try to picture what my great-grandfather must have seen when he decided to homestead here. The land was full of promise. He put years of work into it, then passed it on to his son and his grandson. I think he'd be proud of what it's become."

She turned in his arms, trying to see what Nick saw. The

clouds lifted, and this time his barn appeared, a ghostly shadow in the distance. Nick took pride in ownership of all that lay below them, but try as she might, she saw only years—lifetimes—of backbreaking work.

"This ranch was his life. He said you have to give to receive. Even the land can't continue to give without nourishment."

"Neither can the people who live there," she said bitterly. "It goes both ways."

"Especially the people who live there."

For a fleeting moment, she wondered how he could have known what she'd been thinking, what he meant by those words. But then he turned her to face him again and pulled her against him. His warmth dispelled the gloom, and she looked up into his knowing eyes.

"Do you need nourishment, Emma?"

The intensity of his gaze forestalled any answer she might have given. She merely watched as his lips descended to hers, then closed her eyes and abandoned herself to the pleasure.

The kiss was nothing like the heated exploration that impulsive first kiss had become. It was tenderness itself. He held her close, protected her in his arms while he gave what she needed. Strength, warmth, security, all chased vulnerability away, asking nothing in return. That very generosity lit a spark deep inside her, a spark that grew and spread, igniting desire until she burned with it.

She pressed herself against him, pulling him closer until there was no room even for air between them. His hands roamed across her back, molded her to him until she wanted only to get closer, to take his strength into her. When kissing was no longer enough, she loosened his shirt, driven by the need to feel the warmth of his skin against hers. Together, they slipped to the ground.

Suddenly the world exploded in a riotous clanging of bells.

Nick and the mists evaporated, and Emma opened her eyes

to the ringing of an old-fashioned alarm clock on a nightstand near her bed. She reached for the alarm, knocking it backward in her haste. Eager to return to Nick's waiting arms, she chased it down and silenced it. But when she turned back to him, the bed beside her lay empty in the early morning light.

At first her sluggish brain refused to accept the obvious. She closed her eyes and lay back against the pillow, willing her breathing to slow, willing the tension out of her sexually charged body.

Reality came back into focus, and she looked around the room, tucked under the eaves of Nick's grand old log house. She'd jumped at his suggestion to come here, feeling exposed and vulnerable at the hotel surrounded only by strangers. Somehow staying here had seemed safer, with Nick and his levelheaded ranch hands all about. Even the sturdy logs in the house had seemed secure and impermeable to who or whoever wanted to harm her. But she hadn't counted on the enemy within. How could she combat old insecurities rising out of her past? How could she protect herself from her attraction to a man whose very life-style threatened her peace of mind? All things considered, she'd been safer back at the hotel, where the only opponent she faced was someone real, someone she could fight with facts and figures.

Sunlight filtered through the windows, dispelling the nighttime coolness as Emma tripped down the stairs a half hour later. Since waking, she'd tried without success to cast off the lingering effects of the too vivid dream. Fortunately, she hadn't met Nick in the hallway, dressed only in his bathrobe or still damp from his morning shower. She didn't think her rattled composure could have handled such an intimate moment so soon. But now she told herself, she was ready to face him across the breakfast table. It was only a dream after all, and no one knew about it but her.

Maria was humming to herself in the kitchen, setting a place at the table when she walked in. No one else was there.

"Good morning," Emma said, glad of the reprieve.

Maria turned and smiled. "Did you sleep well?"

"Very well." She spotted a coffeepot on the kitchen counter. Picking up a mug from the table, she poured herself a cup, savoring the aroma before she took a sip. "Am I late?" She'd intended to rise with everyone else, to follow their routine.

"No," Maria laughed. "Nick usually eats breakfast about now, but Lucy is foaling."

"Lucy? Isn't she the mare that—" she couldn't go on.

Maria nodded solemnly. "Yes. The baby's in a hurry." Then she brightened. "But our Nicky's a good midwife. Everything will be okay."

Emma hoped so.

"Are you hungry?" She was spooning out a dish of oatmeal.

Emma nodded, surprised to find she *was* hungry. After the turmoil of the dream she hadn't even thought of food. "Won't you join me?"

The older woman smiled and found a bowl for herself. When she was seated, Emma let her take up the conversation.

"Nick tells me you had car trouble again."

"Not exactly. Someone cut my brakeline."

Maria didn't seem surprised. Apparently Nick had said something to her about it. "You talked to the sheriff?"

"He said he couldn't be sure from looking at the hose."

"Nick has been having these accidents, too."

"So I understand. Have you seen anything unusual around here?"

Maria shook her head. "We're all watching, now. Nick will put an end to it soon enough. He'll watch out for you, too. You were wise to come here."

"Does Nick do this sort of thing often?"

Maria raised an eyebrow in question.

"Does he bring needy people home with him?"

Maria laughed. "No, you are a first. Harley Jacobson was having some trouble with a chicken thief last year, and Nick helped him out, but he didn't bring him home. Of course, Harley isn't a beautiful woman like you."

Emma felt her color rising. "I doubt if that's why Nick asked me to come here."

Maria didn't look as if she agreed, but she said nothing more about it. Instead, she changed the subject.

"You want to write a story about Nick?"

Emma nodded, glad to move on to a more neutral topic. "He's experienced remarkable success with the ranch in just a few years. My editor thinks he has some sort of secret formula that the rest of the world could benefit from knowing."

"I don't know about any secret formula. He loves his land and works hard."

She didn't think a love of the land necessarily had much to do with it. "Not many can claim such success these days."

"No. But not many are as smart as Nick. He'll always be successful."

She spoke with such profound assurance that Emma felt a twinge of guilt for her doubts. "You don't think luck is involved?" She could have bit her tongue before the question was even out. It was one thing for her to be skeptical, but critically unprofessional for her to voice her doubts. Now she'd cast herself as a disbeliever, something she'd never intended to do.

Maria eyed her thoughtfully, as if weighing her next words. "Is that what you think, Emma?"

Confused, Emma stammered, "I—I don't know what to think." Catching herself, she added, "Nick seems to be bucking the tide. He's not merely successful, he's a phenomenon. You live here. You see him at work. Tell me what *you* think.''

''I think Nick will show you what you need to know. But he won't blow his own horn. If you want to know the key to Nicolas Barlow, you will have to look deeper.''

Oh, how she wanted to do that. Beyond her personal interest, she wished she could write an article about the man behind the ranch. When she'd come here, Nick Barlow had been merely a difficult interview; a man who'd drawn attention to himself through his success, but who studiously avoided publicity. But since then, she'd seen a man who would lend a hand for no reason beyond simple friendliness. She'd seen a man who rode his horse as if he'd become a part of the animal. She'd seen a man who examined the facts and reacted, based on those facts, to protect not only his interests, but hers as well. There was far more to Nick Barlow than a financial success, lucky or otherwise, and she wished she could write her article about that man. But *American Business Monitor* cared only for the key to his bottom line.

Maria watched her cooly, as if to judge her reaction to her challenge. Hoping to dispel the mood, she asked, ''How long have you known Nick, Maria?''

''He hired me just over two years ago. I have a friend, Sophie Freeman, who told me he might be looking for a housekeeper. My boys were grown, and my husband was gone, and I needed something to occupy my time. Sophie invited me here and introduced us.''

''His old housekeeper left?''

''No. No one worked here after his wife left.''

The disdain in her voice was unmistakable. Was it for the condition of Nick's house? Or was it for Nick's wife?

''He said he didn't need a housekeeper—he never spent enough time in the house to make it dirty.'' Her eyes lit with humor. ''But he is a man. He likes a good meal.''

''So he hired you.''

"Yes. I cook for him and keep his house clean. And I tell him he's lived alone too long, but he ignores me."

Emma could believe that. But she suspected their relationship went beyond employer and employee. Maria spoke like a proud, protective mother. From what she'd witnessed between them, she deemed the feeling was mutual. "You like working here."

Maria swatted the air in a gesture of feigned torment. "He teases me constantly. I am glad you're here. Now maybe I'll get some work done." She leaned forward. "Don't worry, together we'll keep him in his place."

Emma found herself nodding in conspiracy. How quickly the woman had drawn her into some imagined inner circle. But, she reminded herself, she was here only for the magazine. In a few days she'd be gone.

Maria refilled their coffee cups. When she spoke again, she turned the focus toward Emma. "Why is a pretty girl like you not married?"

Emma choked on her coffee.

"These days I see young people everywhere all alone. They should get married and have children."

"Some would disagree with you."

She brushed Emma's comment aside. "Young people should be together. What are they waiting for? Look at you. You live out of a suitcase, moving from town to town to write about other people. Where are your friends?"

Emma sputtered, defensive despite herself, too aware that at least part of what Maria said was true.

"Nick is the same. He works hard all day, then he comes home and works some more. And for what? Who will take over when he gets tired of working? He should have a wife and family. Sons to help him when he gets old."

"He loves his work. It shows in everything he does." Somehow she'd been cast as Nick's defender. "Where would he be without his ranch?" To her surprise, she believed what she said. Regardless of her opinion of the security of his profession, she couldn't picture him doing anything else. But Maria's mind was set.

"A man needs more than land to make him happy."

"What about his horses and cattle? They're more than livestock to him."

"Horses and cattle won't keep him warm at night."

Emma couldn't help but smile. In her way, Maria was genuinely concerned about Nick, and Emma liked her for it. Why *wasn't* Nick married? He was handsome, personable, and by everyone's standards, except perhaps hers, successful. What sort of baggage was he carrying around that kept him single? Of the many bits and pieces she'd learned about him in town, nothing had ever been said about women in his life except for Lynette, his ex-wife. The idle gossip had raised her curiosity, and Nick's studied lack of interest in Lynette's activities had fueled it, but it hadn't seemed right to indulge in gossip about his private life.

"What do you know about Nick's wife?" The question slipped out, perhaps because she wanted to know what drove the man.

"I never met her," Maria said, but something in her tone said she harbored an opinion, just the same.

"They've been divorced for some time now."

Maria nodded, but remained steadfastly silent.

Against her better judgment, Emma tried one last time. "I understand the divorce was ugly."

To her surprise, Maria released a dam of pent-up emotions. "She was the wrong kind of woman for Nick. They should never have married. When she left, she left him screwed up in the head. Now he blames all women. He thinks all women want—" She caught herself.

"Want what?" Emma asked gently.

Maria's sharp eyes studied her carefully. "When I came

here," she said, "Nick kept to himself. He didn't talk. So I asked Sophie about him. She explained."

Emma said nothing, afraid an interruption would break the mood and she wanted desperately to hear what Maria had to say.

"Lynette liked money. Lots of money. She married Nick because he had a big ranch. But she didn't understand ranching. The money is tied up in livestock and equipment, and she couldn't spend cows or tractors. So they fought. She wanted to sell it off and live like a queen in Denver, showing off her rich husband. But Nick wouldn't sell. Instead he bought more land."

Emma didn't need a map to see where this story was going.

"That was the last straw for Lynette. If he had the money to buy land, he had the money to buy a house in Denver. So she left. She hired an expensive lawyer and sued him for half the ranch. For a while it looked as if she'd get it, too. But Nick fought back.

"The trial was ugly. For days everything about their private lives was aired like dirty linen. When it was over, Lynette got her settlement, and Nick kept his ranch. But he doesn't trust anymore. A pretty city girl like you probably scares him to death."

Emma almost laughed in her face. "I'm not a city girl, Maria. I grew up on a lowly little farm in West Virginia."

Maria gave her a speculative look. "Ah, well, maybe that's why Nick brought you home."

The sounds of men climbing the porch steps precluded any further exchanges. A moment later Nick and Pete walked into the kitchen.

"How's the coffee, Maria?" Nick asked as he hung his hat on a peg by the door.

Maria was already headed for the cupboard and a pair of

mugs shelved there. "Emma and I drank it," she laughed. "I'll pour what is left and make another pot."

At the mention of her name, Nick glanced over to the table, and Emma wondered guiltily whether she'd gotten Maria into trouble by taking up her time. But he only nodded and turned back to wash his hands at the sink. When he was finished, he took the coffee and the cookie jar, and joined her at the table.

"Emma, you remember Pete Malowich, don't you?" he asked as he pulled his chair out.

She tried to act nonchalant, but watching him wash up, the casual way he stepped across the chair, she recalled her dream in vivid detail. True, his kiss had been imagined, and his touch only a vivid fantasy, but the image was so clear she couldn't separate it from reality.

He was wearing a plaid shirt, not a denim jacket, but the blue in the plaid reflected the marvelous color of his eyes. The dimples in his cheeks appeared as if by magic with every expression, zinging an electric arrow into her overly vigilant senses. Her heartbeat accelerated.

Long, strong fingers pulled a cookie from the jar, and he looked up, catching her glance, reacting to it immediately. His expression changed from casual interest to pointed awareness to a slow, dazzling smile. Only when Pete cleared his throat did she realize the room had gone silent.

Pete was watching the two of them with a speculative expression. Maria, who'd been mopping up the countertop, looked from her to Nick and back again. Something akin to dawning light crossed her face, and she returned to the table with the washcloth in hand. Only Nick didn't drop his eyes.

"Did you sleep well?" he asked, taking a healthy bite out of the cookie.

"Ah," she cleared her throat, which had suddenly gone dry. "Very well, thank you."

Nick let his hand, which seemed suddenly shaky, fall to

the tabletop. He chewed resolutely and swallowed, willing his racing hormones to slow down.

He was mistaken. He had to be.

But he thought he detected a flush across Emma's cheeks. A nervousness disproportionate to the small talk making its way around the table. She was avoiding his glance, and there was a distinct flavor of the South in her voice. She, too, was shaken.

Had it been some kind of gratitude he'd seen in her eyes? The hero worship of a woman who'd been rescued in her time of need? Somehow that kind of devotion didn't fit with what he knew of Emma Reardon. The look she'd given him had nothing to do with gratitude.

Admittedly, it had been a while, but a man recognized that look. Eyes so large they were almost dilated. An unguarded expression revealing emotions too fundamental to put into words. No, he wasn't mistaken. For one perfect moment, they had connected at an elemental level. It had been the look of a lover.

But what did it mean?

In the short time since he'd met her, regardless of his own overactive hormones, there had never been anything loverlike about Emma Reardon. There was certainly nothing loverlike about her now. She was chatting inanely with Pete, though he noticed she still kept her eyes carefully focused on the untouched mug of coffee in her hands.

"So what did she have?"

When he didn't answer, she looked up at him. In his peripheral vision, he saw Pete watching him as well, barely containing his mirth. He'd been caught wool-gathering, and would, no doubt, suffer for it in days to come.

"I beg your pardon?" he said as blandly as he could.

"The mare. Did she have a boy or a girl?"

Frantically, he tried to recall the sex of the foal. Only ten minutes ago, he could have described her down to her last nose hairs. He had to get a grip. "A girl," he managed to reply, "a filly."

"Can I see her?"

"Of course. As soon as you've finished here."

Nick led the way out of the house a few minutes later, mentally lashing himself for getting into this situation. It was bad enough to have agreed to let Emma write a story about him without imagining some sexual undercurrent every time she looked at him. What he wanted was to saddle up Grayson and ride away for the rest of the day. But they'd gotten home too late yesterday to do anything productive, and he'd already put her off until this morning, promising she could accompany him wherever he went. Now, regardless of that ridiculous scene in the kitchen, he was committed to showing her around.

Instead of the pad and pencil he'd expected, she carried only a small tape recorder, which he planned to ignore. He hated tape recorders. Even a telephone answering machine made him freeze up inside. Talking coherently to Emma was going to be hard enough without knowing she was recording every word he said.

"Where do you want to start?" he asked.

"How about the general layout of the ranch," she said, all business. Apparently she wasn't bothered by sexy daydreams of him. "Then I'll be able to navigate without getting in the way."

Her comment reminded him of a point he meant to make clear. "I'll show you the outbuildings and introduce you to the boys. But I'd suggest you don't go anywhere alone. In light of what happened yesterday, I'd feel better if you stayed with someone." She frowned at that, but if he was to keep her safe, he meant to make her understand. "If I can't be with you, I'll make sure someone else can." She looked as if she wanted to argue, but he had no intention of backing down. Finally, she nodded reluctantly, but he suspected it was only to avoid a confrontation.

"What else do you want to know?"

"Could I see your breeding program?"

"It's on the computer. I'll show it to you this evening."

She nodded. "Then for now, I'd just like to fill in some background information." She turned on the tape recorder. "How long has the ranch been in your family?"

"Three generations." He knew he should have expanded, but that damn recorder robbed him of his tongue.

"You mean you're the fourth."

"No, I'm the third. My grandfather was the first."

"Not your great-grandfather?" She sounded so perplexed he forgot the tape recorder.

"No. You sound surprised."

"Didn't your great-grandfather homestead here?"

He laughed. "No, my grandfather won the place in a poker game. He used to love to sit me on his knee and tell me about it. Of course it wasn't much of a ranch then."

"Tell me." She sounded so genuinely interested that he elaborated.

"Grandpa was just home from the war in Europe. He was on his way to Denver to find work, and he stopped in Rio Blanco to spend a couple of days with an army buddy. There was a barn dance that weekend, and he met my Grandma there, so he decided to hang around for the summer.

"There wasn't much work to be had, so he worked odd jobs here and there, but after three or four months, he only had about twenty dollars saved up.

"In the army, he'd been a pretty fair hand at poker, so one night he decided to see if he couldn't speed things up a little. There was a game behind the general store, mostly penny ante stuff, but Grandpa was holding his own when Oscar Johnson showed up. Oscar homesteaded this place, for what it was worth. He wasn't much of a rancher. And he was drunk.

"To make a long story short, Oscar bet the ranch and Grandpa took him up on it. Next thing he knew he was the proud owner of a sod shack and a broken-down corral over there under that hill." He pointed to a grove of cottonwood trees. Emma followed where he pointed, as if she expected to see the old soddy still standing. He smiled.

"It wasn't much, but in a year's time he'd built a barn and added a few head of cattle. He and Grandma got married, and together they built it up, a little at a time."

"What happened to the sod shack?" She appeared transfixed, still staring into the cottonwood grove. She'd probably built up some romantic image of young lovers in a cozy little cabin. He hated to disappoint her.

"It wasn't much of a house. As I understand it, the thing was ready to cave in when Grandpa got it. He built a new house right after he and Grandma were married."

"So he built the log house?"

"No, it was a frame house. During the depression, they took in boarders to help pay the bills. One of them fell asleep smoking and burned the house down. The barn caught fire, too, and everyone but Grandpa moved to town. He stayed in the corncrib—claimed he'd lose the ranch if he moved to town."

He'd never considered himself much of a storyteller, but Emma paled at his words.

"What about your grandmother? The family?"

"She took in sewing and cooked for a soup kitchen. Dad worked after school shoveling coal for the neighbors." Emma didn't look well. "Are you all right?" If he didn't know better, he'd say she'd taken the story personally. "They were tight times, but they made it through."

"Once."

He had no idea what she meant by that, but something

about the faraway look in her eyes told him not to ask. Suddenly, she shook herself, then metamorphosed before his eyes. With a click of the button, she snapped the tape recorder off. He'd actually forgotten she was taping him. Then she strode ahead, her back ramrod straight. When she spoke, she was all business, clipped and impersonal. "We'd better get on with it. I have a deadline."

Her abrupt change in attitude rubbed him the wrong way. She'd asked, hadn't she? Did she think the history of the ranch was all sunshine and roses? Hell, he didn't need this. He might have known she wouldn't care about old family history. Well, he wouldn't open up to her again. She'd get her interview, but nothing more. The sooner she left, the sooner his life would return to normal.

Chapter Six

The tiny foal peered out at them from behind her mother's shoulder, staring at Nick and Emma with liquid brown eyes. Lucy nudged her gently, murmuring reassuring noises deep in her throat. Still cautious, the baby looked at them for another moment, then pursued more urgent matters, careful to keep the mare between herself and the strangers in the doorway.

Emma watched the pastoral scene, wishing the serenity of the moment extended to her state of mind. Behind her, she could feel Nick's eyes drilling into her back, chilling the atmosphere as surely as if the temperature had plummeted. She hardly blamed him. He'd opened up to her in a way she'd never expected, and her thanks had been to turn on him.

On top of that, his reminder to stay close had reawakened the sick feeling inside that Andrew Warren meant her harm. Without Nick's help, how would she fight him? No one else even believed Warren posed a threat. Her life was flying apart, and she'd responded by insulting the only person who seemed to care. Somehow she needed to apologize, but she didn't know how she'd pull it off without explaining why— and that she could never do.

"How long will you keep them in here?" she asked, unable to stand the brooding silence.

"Just for today," he said curtly. "Lucy's wounds are healing, and the foal seems to be healthy. I'll turn them out into the pasture tomorrow."

Forcing her fears into the background, she ignored the animosity in his voice, trying instead to find some common ground. "What will you name her?"

After a long pause, he finally answered. "Her name will encompass her lineage and combine something of the sire's name with the dam." The temperature dropped another few degrees.

The filly suckled her mother's milk, eagerly flicking her tail and blissfully unaware of their conversation. With her sorrel coat and spotted rump she was a already a beauty, but she didn't look large enough to support a name such as Nick described. "Surely you won't call her by that."

"No. If we kept her, we'd probably give her a nickname."

"You'd *sell* her?"

"I breed horses for profit, Emma. Isn't that why you're here? To dig out the secret to my success? Well, there it is all tied up in a neat little bundle."

He'd put her in her place, and unless she did something, his next step would be to toss her off the ranch. Turning to face him, she said, "I probably deserved that. In fact, I deserve it if you don't answer my questions at all. I cut you off out there, and I apologize. I have a habit of getting too involved in the wrong aspect of a story. Call it one of the drawbacks of writing for a financial magazine."

If the apology had any effect on him, it didn't show in his expression. "You don't like writing about finance?"

His emphasis on the *you* spoke volumes, and she couldn't stop the defensive note in her reply. "I think there's more to any story than the bottom line. Sometimes I find the other aspects more interesting."

She endured a long, skeptical silence before he replied. "Then why don't you write about them?"

"*American Business Monitor* doesn't agree."

"*American Business Monitor* isn't the only magazine out there."

"*American Business Monitor* pays the bills."

"But there's more to life than money. You just said so, yourself. If you want more, write for someone else."

"No one wants a full time human-interest reporter."

"Then go freelance."

He didn't know what he was suggesting. Permanent employment was her buffer between peace of mind, such as it was, and the cold realities of poverty and hunger. She'd grown up with destitution, and she had no intention of ever giving control of her future to anything less solid than a regular, substantial paycheck.

"I can't do that."

"Why not?"

She was saved having to reply by the muttered cursing of a man leading Nick's uncooperative stallion into the stable. When Nick looked up, she nearly stumbled backward, so strong had been the hold of his cold blue eyes. Tension had her neck in knots, and she reached up to massage it.

"I did what you said, but it ain't gonna do nothin' to help," the newcomer mumbled as he struggled to keep the horse under control. "That leg's gonna heal or it's not, and no horseshoe is gonna make any difference."

"Lead him around and let me see," Nick replied, ignoring the rancor in the other man's voice.

The man did as he was asked, and Emma watched, trying to decide what they were talking about. The man grasped the lead rope close to the halter and attempted to lead the horse around while the horse resisted by throwing his head. Nick watched closely, though Emma couldn't imagine what he'd see with the horse dancing like he was. Once, he made them repeat a turn, and she stopped rubbing her neck to try to see what he saw.

The horse favored his front leg. On that hoof, he sported a shiny new, oddly shaped shoe. "Orthopedic shoes?" she asked.

"Something like that," Nick muttered. His attention was wholly on the horse. Approaching the restive animal, he put a calming hand on his neck. Then, with gentle, knowing fingers he ran his hand down the leg, probing the knee joint carefully. Satisfied, he picked up the foot to examine the shoe.

At Nick's touch, the stallion calmed visibly, proof of Nick's affinity with the animal, and he submitted to the examination without dispute. His reward was an affectionate pat on the shoulder. Watching them, Emma suffered a momentary longing to feel those gentle hands soothing her own neck.

"I think it helps," Nick said. "He's not dropping his shoulder now."

He opened the door to the stall opposite the mare and foal. "We'll leave it on for a few weeks and see what happens."

The stranger spat into the dirt and mumbled coarse words into his chest. When he started into the stall, the horse resisted, laying his ears back. From the spate of cursing that erupted, Emma suspected it wasn't the first time this happened. Nick hurried in behind them with sharp words of caution. The two men emerged a moment later, and while Nick latched the gate carefully, the stranger leered at her. The way he looked at her left her with the urge to keep Nick between them, much as the foal did with her mother.

"Emma, I don't think you've met Frank Howell," Nick said. "Frank's the farrier hereabouts."

Unable to avoid it, Emma took Frank's proffered hand. Against the brilliance of the doorway, she hadn't been able to see him clearly, but she studied him now. He was big, muscular from his work, but his shoulders stooped, as if all the bending of his labors never allowed him to straighten fully. He wore a dirty shirt and three-days' growth of beard, and he smelled of stale sweat and cigarette smoke.

Thankfully, her article called for little interaction with the man who kept Nick's horses shod. She pulled her hand out of his grasp as soon as tact permitted, pretending to ignore his insulting perusal. Leaving the men to finish their business, she turned back to Lucy and her foal.

She'd met men like Frank before. She'd been a little girl when her father had taken her to the sour-smelling tobacco shed to witness the stripping of the leaves. Frank was every angry, dissatisfied laborer who'd worked in silent resentment that day. When she'd returned home, even young as she was, she'd felt the need to wash off the odor of discontent they all wore.

Nick apparently saw the distaste in her expression when Frank left. "Frank's a little rough around the edges," he said, "but he gets the job done."

But he didn't like doing it, she thought. Was that what she was destined to become? Would she one day let the bitterness of dissatisfaction take over her life?

Maybe Nick had a point. There was nothing to stop her from writing freelance, and she'd never get a better opportunity. Fear was holding her back. Fear of the unknown. Fear of Andrew Warren. Fear of letting herself care.

All the old rationalizations fought back. She'd weighed the pros and cons, and she'd made her decision. It was only watching a brand-new foal sniffing in wonder at an ordinary grain bucket that brought home the weight of antipathy she felt for her job. The purity of newborn innocence would affect anyone that way.

"I'd like to start over," she said. "I'd like to see the whole ranch. Would you show it to me?"

Something in Emma's voice made Nick take notice. This wasn't a bland attempt at smoothing ruffled feathers. The request, punctuated by the Southern accent he'd come to recognize, was sincere, and he felt his resolve against her melting away. Considering her stubborn streak, it must have cost her a lot to apologize. On top of that he knew she was genuinely frightened of Andrew Warren, regardless of the brave front she wore. When she looked up at him with earnest amber eyes, he couldn't make himself refuse her. She'd asked to see the ranch, and he wanted to show it to her. "Sure."

Her answering smile sent his heart skipping, and he took a quick, impulsive step toward her before catching himself. This sexy, tempting charmer was the same woman who'd cut him cold not a half hour earlier. Unless he was very careful, he'd find himself doing anything she asked, and he had no intention of falling under her spell. He'd protect her, he'd show her the ranch, and he'd give her the damned interview, but that was all.

But even as he thought so, he knew he was lying to himself. For reasons he couldn't explain, he wanted her to see the ranch as he saw it. He wanted to erase the vulnerability in her face and restore the sparkling, smiling woman he glimpsed too rarely. He wanted to explore the unexplainable attraction she held for him.

Behind him Cochise whickered softly, his temperament restored now that Frank had left. Emma started at the sound, and Nick experienced irrational anger at Andrew Warren for making her so jumpy. Tearing his eyes away, he turned to his impatient horse.

"Is this the proud father?" Emma asked, a husky note in her voice.

"In the flesh." His own voice sounded odd, and he cleared his throat. "Come on over here. It's time you two met."

Cochise nosed his chest impatiently, and he pulled a couple of carrots from his back pocket. "Emma, meet Cochise, my rotten, spoiled NASH Stallion of the Year."

He held a carrot out for the horse, who took it as if it were his due. Emma laughed, then surprised him by asking for the other one.

"May I?"

He gave it to her, and she held her hand out cautiously, as if recalling the stallion's temperamental display only moments earlier. Nick watched, ready to intervene, should the need arise. Cochise was gentle, but he was a stallion, and he reacted to people's moods.

His fears were unfounded. Emma held the carrot in her open palm, and the horse accepted it eagerly, his ears pricked forward. Emma scratched his muzzle and he stopped chewing long enough to breathe in her scent.

"You didn't tell me he was such a marshmallow," she said.

Her head barely reached Cochise's shoulder, and to hear her say such a thing about a fourteen-hundred pound horse was almost laughable. "Well, not everyone would agree with you. I think Frank would sooner nail shoes on the devil himself."

She chuckled. "That just proves Cochise has discriminating taste."

As if to prove her point, Cochise nuzzled her eagerly, plainly expecting another treat. Emma suffered his advances with good humor, even when he blew down the neck of her shirt.

Nick thought the horse indeed had discriminating taste. He'd considered doing the same thing himself. "You'll have to pardon his manners. Around here, Cochise is pretty much king of the castle. He has no concept of restraint.''

Emma laughed. ''Forget it. He's just being friendly.''

Yeah, right. He wondered what she'd say if the owner were as friendly as his horse. ''The two of you have a lot in common.''

''We do?''

She looked up, her eyes wary, as if she expected him to comment on her restraint, too. Though they'd outwardly buried the hatchet, he realized how tense she was. How tense he was. Weary of walking on eggshells, he was determined to lighten the mood.

''Yeah. You both have a heavy mane and freckles across your nose.''

Her gaze dropped to the stallion's speckled muzzle, even as her color deepened, but she came back with surprising alacrity. Giving her hair a toss for effect, she said, ''Well, we both may have freckles, but anyone can see he's a natural brunette.''

He laughed, forgetting the tension.

''Are freckles an Appaloosa trademark?''

''That and a few others. Here, I'll show you.''

He opened the door and held it for her. Thanks to the inquisitive stallion, she brushed against him as she passed, producing a whole new kind of tension. With heightened awareness, he steadied her with one hand while he discouraged the horse with the other. Her skin was warm beneath her shirt, with soft curves that brought to mind images best left unexplored. When she nimbly ducked through the opening, he caught a whiff of green apples, and hoped fervently Cochise would discern the difference between shampoo and his favorite treat.

Thankfully, the horse had satisfied his curiosity, and for the next few minutes, he stood quietly, giving Nick a chance to point out the striped hooves and white eyes common to

Appaloosas in general, followed by the points of confirmation that made him a champion.

Emma was an apt and willing student. She asked questions and made him clarify points that were unclear to her. She had a way of listening that put him at ease, and he relaxed again, comfortable in the knowledge that she was genuinely interested in what he had to say.

Interspersed in her comments were questions meant to draw him out, and he knew he was being subtly interviewed, though the topic of finance never came up and the tape recorder remained turned off. Watching her, he decided she was very good at what she did.

"Tell me about this new shoe," she said, indicating Cochise's front foot.

"Cochise still limps noticeably from the accident. I thought the shoe might take some of the strain off his leg while it heals."

"At least it's better suited for the corral than mine were that day."

"And not nearly as expensive as yours, even for four of them," he teased.

"How do you know mine were expensive?"

"My wife liked Italian shoes."

"Oh." She managed to put just the right amount of expression in that one word.

"Unlike you," he continued before she could question him further, "Cochise couldn't care less how tall he is."

"Pardon me?" she asked innocently.

"He knows height has nothing to do with intimidation."

"Is that a fact!"

"Do you think I'd let something as insignificant as an inch or two in height sway me?"

"Well, since they obviously didn't work in my favor, I'll try to remember not to wear my Italian heels in your presence."

"Actually, I thought they looked rather sexy." Damn. He hadn't meant to say that.

Color bloomed on her cheeks, but she had the grace to hide a smile before she turned away. "I'll try to remember that, too."

Thinking he'd just been outfoxed at his own game, he followed her out of the stall. If she'd been out to unsettle him, she'd succeeded. In one short hour she'd surprised him, angered him, offered an olive branch and beguiled him into saying much more than he'd intended. Regardless of his intentions, he couldn't seem to keep the upper hand.

"I heard that Appaloosas are easy-gaited horses. Is that true?"

Thankful for something to steer his thoughts away from his unexplainable hunger for her, he forced himself to focus. "They don't have a special gait, if that's what you mean, but as a rule they're easy riding."

"I'd like to—"

He waited, but she didn't finish. "You'd like to what?"

"Nothing."

Obviously it was something. "Would you like to go for a ride?"

"No, it's been years since I—"

"You've ridden before?"

"Well, yes, but nothing like a blooded champion."

He pictured her on a rental hack, bouncing on a horse concerned primarily with returning to the stable. It would be a pleasure to show her the difference a good horse could make.

"All you have to do is ask, Emma." Was that gratitude he saw in her face? "I'll make sure you get a chance before you leave."

"I'd like that."

They walked into the sunlight, and he gave her a quick tour of the rest of the barnyard, reintroducing her to Hank as he headed out to the hayfields and Bob Perkins, who took care of the horses.

The clear, bright morning brought ranch matters back into focus. Neither Hank nor Bob had seen anything out of the ordinary, but a nagging sense of urgency continued to plague him. Andrew Warren and his flunkies were still out there. Hoping to keep Emma close by, he decided to take her up to the summer pastures.

"I'm going up to check the herd this afternoon, Emma," he said. "Want to come along? It'll give you a chance to look around."

She agreed at once, and he congratulated himself for keeping his fears hidden. But later, when they climbed into his truck, he wasn't so certain he'd succeeded after all.

"You're nervous about the herd," she said.

"A little," he admitted. "Nothing has happened for several days now, and I'm thinking our developer friend is waiting for me to get complacent."

Though he tried hard to hide it, Emma heard the concern in Nick's voice, and it stirred up a ball of uneasiness in her stomach. She knew he'd brought her along to keep an eye on her. Normally, she'd never put up with such blatant protectiveness, but losing her brakes on that hill had frightened her. Badly.

She felt a kinship with him. Whether it was because he was the only person beside herself who believed something was afoot or because he seemed so sure of himself, she didn't know. She only knew he would keep her safe, and being with him eased the anxiety when nothing else would.

He drove in relaxed silence, with one hand on the wheel and the other arm hung out the open window, and though the width of the seat separated them, she felt a sense of closeness in the confines of the cab. The warm breeze ruffled his hair, inviting her to study his profile as he concentrated on the road.

He had a strong jaw, and though he'd shaved that morning, his beard was beginning to shadow his face. Tiny lines spread out from his eye where he'd squinted too many times into the sun, and the beginnings of a crease bracketed the dimple she found so distracting. There was a scar just at the base of his jaw, and a couple of silver hairs behind his ear. All in all, she decided, he had the kind of face that would be as handsome at sixty as it was in his mid-thirties.

Catching the bent of her thoughts, she looked away. The road climbed out onto an open hillside and she was treated to a view of the Uintah below her. Green pastures and hay-fields stretched down the valley, separated by the river threading between them with deceptive tranquillity. In one field, Hank was cutting hay, and across the river the displaced mares grazed peacefully in the sun. In a setting like this, it would be easy to forget the outside world. It would be easy to forget someone was out there waiting for them to get care-less.

Shivering, she decided she'd be better off concentrating on her work. Looking out at the sky, she said, "You've got good haying weather."

Nick nodded. "It's usually not a problem this time of year."

"How many cuttings do you get in a season?"

He looked surprised for some reason, but he answered am-icably, even when she asked his anticipated bale count per acre and his method of calculating how much hay he'd need for the winter. She was trying to get it all into her notes when he turned the tables on her.

"Correct me if I'm wrong," he said, "but you don't do many articles about ranchers, do you?"

Intent on her writing, she didn't look up. "No. I'm usually chasing down corporate presidents and factory managers."

"Then why is it you know about bale counts and haying weather?"

He caught her unprepared, and the truth slipped out. "I grew up on a farm."

"*You* grew up on a farm?" He laughed out loud. "Tell me another one."

"What's so funny?" She heard the Southern accent creeping into her voice, and the knowledge made her more defensive.

"Are you serious?"

"Of course I am! You don't see me laughing, do you?"

He sobered, but he obviously didn't believe her. "If you grew up on a farm, why didn't you have sense enough not to step in the water the other day?"

She felt her color rise. "We never used irrigation. For us, the problem was more what to do with all the water than how to get it onto the fields."

"Where was this farm?"

"West Virginia." When she looked up at him, he appeared perplexed.

"When did you leave?" His voice was so low she barely heard him.

"A long time ago." She hoped he wouldn't ask any more questions, because she had no intention of supplying any more answers.

Fortunately, a logging truck appeared in front of them, and he concentrated on his driving. When he picked up the conversation again, it was to point out the boundaries of his summer pasture and a road he said led to them.

"You're not turning off?" she asked when he passed it by.

"No. There's another road up here that leads to a vantage point on top of that cliff over there." He gestured to a precipice in the distance. "I want to go up there first."

He might have wanted to see over the ranch, but he also wanted to impress her with the view, she decided when they hiked out onto the rocks. The land spread before them, with aspen and pine trees covering the rolling landscape. Grass grew tall in the open meadows, dotted with the red-and-white Herefords that made the ranch famous. The hillsides channeled into a broad valley where a stream cut a lazy swath, broken into a series of lakes where beavers had dammed it. Looking out over the scene, Emma was justifiably impressed. It was beautiful.

"You see those rocks below us?" Nick asked. He pointed to a field of massive boulders where the cliff had given way in years past.

"The road I showed you before ends just below there. Jack and I used to sneak up and play in the rocks when Dad and Grandpa were moving the herd," he said. "I think Mom always thought the cliff was going to cave off again, and she told us never to play there, but we couldn't resist. Once you get into them, it's like being in a maze. We got lost so many times we finally learned our way around."

"Did your mom know that?"

"Probably. She had a way of knowing a lot of things."

Emma could picture the two boys hiding in the rocks, shooting at imaginary bad guys or sneaking up on unsuspecting animals. Given the number of ways a boy could get into trouble, she thought that one was relatively harmless. Her own mother had been the same about the creek bottom on hot summer days. "Moms are like that."

On a distant hillside, he showed her where his grandfather had sold timber to finance a new home. He even knew which slope had provided the logs to build it. Through it all, Emma heard the pride in his voice, and she began to understand something of his connection with the land. No wonder he refused to sell it to a man who would see it only as potential for profit.

Later, when they drove down into the meadows, she helped him set out salt blocks for the cattle, clear a fledgling beaver dam before it flooded the road, and doctor a cow with an inflamed eye. She found herself being seduced by the demanding, but satisfying work.

The sun was setting when they returned to the ranch. Maria had left a casserole warming in the oven for them, and it tasted like only hearty food could taste after a long, hard day. After dinner, Emma helped stack the dishes, then fell into a chair in front of the television, too tired to work any more that night. Feeling full and satisfied, she was only half listening when the evening newscast came on, but the lead story caught her attention and plummeted her back to earth with a thud.

Vesicular stomatitis was running rampant in New Mexico. An outbreak had just been discovered in Meeker, and the state veterinarian had declared a quarantine on all of the western counties. Until further notice, Nick's cattle business was at a standstill.

Chapter Seven

"I'm going to bed," Emma said, standing abruptly.

Nick started. A moment earlier she'd been half asleep in front of the television, looking far too relaxed and attractive for his peace of mind. Now she wore her impersonal, businesslike mask, as if daring him to contest her decision.

"I forgot about the computer tonight, Emma. I'm sorry."

Her expression said she'd forgotten about it, too. But if that wasn't it, what had caused the sudden change? When she answered, she sounded rattled. "We'll do it tomorrow. Good night." She disappeared up the stairs, and he listened to the rapid beat of her retreating footsteps without a clue what had just happened between them.

He still had no idea the next morning.

"What do you and your pretty little reporter have planned for the day?" Pete asked as they walked across the barnyard.

"What do you mean *my* pretty little reporter?" He winced inwardly at the tone of his voice. He hadn't slept well, having spent the better part of the night trying to make sense out of his houseguest's erratic behavior. Maria's matchmaking tactics at the breakfast table hadn't helped any, either.

Pete intentionally misunderstood. "You don't think she's pretty?"

"Of course I think she's pretty. I'm not blind."

"So what's your problem?"

"She's not *my* reporter. I don't even want a reporter. She doesn't want to be here any more than I want her here. In fact, I don't know what the hell she's doing here."

Pete seemed to see something humorous in his lengthy reply. "You invited her, as I recall. Though I must admit I don't blame you."

Ah, here it came. "What's that supposed to mean?"

"A pretty woman like that doesn't come along every day. Especially one who's interested in you."

He almost laughed. "She's not interested in me."

"She's not?"

"Hell, no. She's interested in money and how much of it the ranch can generate. I'd think you'd recognize her type by now."

"And what type would that be?"

"How can you even ask after what Lynette put us all through?"

"You think Emma is like Lynette." It was a statement, but Pete managed to make it sound incredulous.

"They came out of the same mold."

Pete took off his hat and scratched his head thoughtfully. "Well, they're both easy to look at, and they both look fine in strappy little high heels," he said. "But beyond that, I think you're wrong. Emma's real interested in this ranch. More than she wants you to know."

"Oh, she's hiding something, all right. But I've seen through her. Money is number one on her list." He related her comments about her job.

Pete listened thoughtfully. "Well, that's a puzzle, for sure. But I'd bet a year's wages it's not from greed." He paused to put his hat back on. "I like her."

Nick pulled up, astounded. Pete was only a few years older than him, and he'd always displayed uncommon sense when it came to women. Somehow Emma must have gotten to him. "She's got you bamboozled."

His foreman responded with an unflappable smile. "Aw, you're just afraid to admit you like her, too."

"What?"

"I saw the way the two of you looked at each other yesterday. You like Emma and you don't want to."

"Who would? Even if it were true, *which it's not,* who would want to go through all the hell of getting involved again?"

Pete grinned. "You're arguing pretty hard for a man who doesn't care."

"Hmph."

"If a woman like that gave me the eye, I'd go after her."

"Go for it," Nick muttered, all the while thinking he'd fire the man if he did.

"Naw. The lady's eye is on you. Why don't you give her a chance and see what happens?"

He'd already seen what happened. His hormones were on full alert without Pete's help, and the *lady* was working on her own agenda, whatever that was. "Yeah. Let's take her with us to castrate those calves we missed last spring and see how interested she is in that."

Pete gave him a disapproving glare. "Emma is a plucky little gal, but watching something like that makes *me* sick. What would be the point?"

"It's all a part of ranching."

"So's cleaning stalls. Why are you trying to antagonize her?"

To reveal the real woman. Maybe he'd see once and for

all what was hidden so carefully beneath the woman she pretended to be. Without realizing it, he voiced his confusion. "I don't understand her. One minute she's all curiosity, wants to know everything. Then, when I tell her, she backs off. It's like she's asking, but she doesn't want to hear the answer.

"I took her up to put out salt blocks yesterday, and she helped me all afternoon, acted like she was enjoying herself. Then, after supper she just—retreated. I'd promised to show her my computer work, but it was late and we were both tired. I even apologized, for all the good it did me, but this morning she's about as approachable as that wild-eyed mustang you were so bent on taming."

"That mustang was terrified. As you recall, with a little patience, he turned into a damned good horse."

"Are you saying Emma is afraid of me?"

"No, she's not afraid of you, though she ought to be," Pete added, not bothering to hide his irritation. "But who knows where she's coming from. You don't know anything about her."

And he never would, if she had her way. "Well, it's all academic anyhow. She won't be here long enough to find out."

"Unless you invite her back."

"I have a ranch to run."

"Aw, hell. Listen to yourself." Nick didn't think he'd ever heard such disgust in Pete's voice. "Not all women are going to disappoint you, Nick."

"I never said they would."

"But you're not willing to—"

"I've already promised to protect her from Andrew Warren. She's even got me carrying a rifle."

"Well, you'd better watcn out what you shoot. It might just be your foot." Pete turned away.

Nick's temper flared. He hadn't asked for Pete's advice,

and hearing the ring of truth in it only made it worse. "If you're so taken with Ms. Reardon," he growled, "you can escort her into town this morning and pick up her car. Joe called this morning and said it was ready."

Pete stopped and turned. "What about you?"

"I'm going to fix fence." Even as he said it, he knew Pete would recall how much time he'd spent "fixing fence" when Lynette was rampaging about some thing or other. How could the man think Emma was anything but trouble when he already needed time to think after spending only one day in her company?

Conscience reminded him that Andrew Warren wouldn't care about his mental health, but Emma would be safe with Pete. "Just make sure the car's fixed. And don't let her out of your sight." He wanted to add, make sure she comes straight home, to his list, but he already sounded like a nagging hen. "And, Pete—"

"Yeah?"

"Watch out for her, okay?"

Pete's mulish expression unbent a little. "I will."

There didn't seem to be much more to say. Slapping his gloves against his thigh, he turned away.

"Nick? What about Warren?"

Nick stopped. "I'm through playing cat and mouse. He went too far when he cut Emma's brakes." His statement sounded personal, and he guessed it was, but he meant what he said. "If he wants to play hardball, he'll have to play with me."

"You want to let me in on the plan?" Humor had replaced the stubbornness in Pete's voice, and Nick suspected he'd been waiting for Nick to come around.

"A stranger can't sneak in and out of here if we're all on the lookout, so he'll have to strike somewhere else. When he does, I want a close look before anyone touches anything.

You can't move around this country without leaving a trail, and we have the advantage of knowing the lay of the land.''

"It's a big ranch."

"I have a personal interest. We'll catch him."

With that, he went in search of Grayson and threw a saddle on him.

Emma closed her laptop computer when she heard a horse galloping out of the ranch yard. Glancing out the window, she saw Nick astride his gray horse, urging the animal to run. Pete approached from the other direction, and he watched Nick's departure, shaking his head as he went. Whatever Nick's rush, apparently it wasn't an emergency.

She'd spent a restless night, reminding herself over and over that Nick's problems had no effect on her. She'd fallen under the ranch's spell yesterday, but her eyes were wide-open now. Nick would cope somehow with the quarantine—with the disease, if it came to that. It was none of her affair. She simply had to keep her distance. She'd come to write a story, that's all.

Nick had been preoccupied at breakfast—from worry, no doubt. He hadn't suggested any specific activity, and she hadn't pushed the matter, retreating instead to her room with the excuse that she needed to work on her notes. Now, watching him ride out of sight, she wished wistfully she was with him, that she could match his skill with horses. He could teach her to ride like that. Given the inclination, he could do just about anything.

Great! She sounded like a teenager caught up in a serious case of hero worship. If experience had taught her anything, it was that no man was inviolable. Nick was human, after all. But if she'd ever met a man who came close to standing alone, it was him. And he had a way of making her want to join him, making even the most mundane task exciting. How else could she explain having enjoyed setting out fifty-pound blocks of salt all afternoon?

Maria's knock at the door brought her around.

"Pete asked me to find you," Maria said.

"Is everything okay?"

"As far as I know. Why do you ask?"

"Nick just went flying out of here on his horse—" She cut herself off, hearing the anxiety in her voice.

Maria merely smiled. "Nick is wrestling with problems he'd rather not face. He'll work them out."

The quarantine, Emma thought. Perhaps it was his way of working off stress. Maria seemed awfully calm about it, though. It was odd that she didn't appear more concerned.

Pete waited for her in the kitchen. "Nick said your car is ready. I'm headed into town now, if you'd like to come along."

"There's no need to make a special trip."

"I'm not. I need to get a part for the tractor."

"Okay, you can drop me off."

"That's all right. I'll only be a minute." His words were edged with gentle determination, and she realized he'd been instructed not to leave her alone. Surely Nick didn't believe Warren or his flunkies would be stupid enough to try the same trick twice, did he? Independence chafed against uneasiness, and irritable words bubbled up inside. But she swallowed them. Pete was merely the messenger.

"Just give me a minute and I'll be ready."

During the drive to town, Emma grilled Pete about vesicular stomatitis, but she still didn't feel any better when Pete reassured her Nick's livestock probably wouldn't be exposed to the disease. She couldn't help fearing that if it struck, Nick stood to lose everything. With her stomach twisted into knots, she turned her thoughts to her other problem.

Nick seemed certain Warren would send someone to do

his dirty work, but she wasn't so sure. A stranger in town would call attention to himself. It would make more sense to hire someone locally. Suddenly the friendly little community seemed a town full of strangers—any one of whom could be the person who'd tried to get her killed. But who? It might be easy to hire someone to sabotage her car, but which of these people would be willing to undermine Nick Barlow?

Whatever the answer, she felt exposed. Pete was friendly and capable, but he wasn't Nick. Her stomach twisted again, and she decided if she wanted to escape getting an ulcer, she'd better find some neutral ground.

"What's Nick doing this morning?"

Pete grinned. "Fixing fence."

His expression didn't match his answer, but the lightness of it helped unravel the knots. "He goes tearing out of the yard at a dead run to fix fence? How does he react when he hears a mare's in labor or the bulls are out?"

Pete burst into laughter.

She waited for him to explain.

"I gave him some advice this morning and he didn't care much for it."

"Apparently not."

"He'll get over it."

"So you say." Pete must be confident of his job to make his boss that angry. But then Nick had never been anything but fair, even when she'd pushed him. She wondered what they'd discussed.

Joe Burke, the mechanic who'd fixed her car twice now, had it parked in the second bay of his garage when they arrived. He assured them it had been locked up overnight and no one had touched it but him. He'd even taken it for a test drive that morning. Pete also went over it while she settled her bill.

Pete offered to drive her car back to the ranch, but she

decided she'd had enough. If Andrew Warren wanted her, she wouldn't hide behind Pete and put him in danger, too. She refused to let fear take over her life.

Nick was just walking out of the house, munching a cookie, when she drove up. He stopped outside the gate and waited for her, and the clear light of his smile lifted the shadow of worries that had dogged her morning. She pulled up beside him.

"I thought you were fixing fence."

He smiled, as if at a private joke. "Grayson threw a shoe."

"I see."

"Frank is here this morning, so I brought him back." With a teasing smile, he indicated her car. "How's the old car today?"

She ignored his jibe. "Good."

"No other problems?"

The edge in his voice belied the smile. "None. Everything's quiet."

"Good."

He expelled a breath, but she thought she saw a hint of a frown cross his face. He probably didn't like the waiting any more than she did. There was little to do until Warren made his next move, but the waiting wasn't easy.

"Where do you want me to park?"

He indicated an empty space behind a pine tree just outside the picket fence. "It'll be out of the way over there."

She parked the car and got out. He'd followed her around, and offered to carry a bag for her. When he saw a new pair of jeans inside, he lifted his brows and she felt compelled to explain. "Silk skirts don't seem to be the thing here."

He shifted his gaze to the linen slacks she wore, and she felt her face burn as his eyes traveled up her figure, but he didn't comment. "I thought I'd show you my computer model now," he said. "That is, if you don't have other plans."

Apparently the ride this morning had cleared the cobwebs. He was all friendliness and charm, and her heart leaped into her throat. Quiet or sullen she could handle, but charming was a whole different story. "Sure—" she cleared her throat "—now would be great." They walked inside together.

Nick poured them both a cup of coffee, then led the way into his office. While he cleared a place for them to work, she tried without success not to recall his kiss the last time she'd been in that room.

"I thought we'd work here," Nick said as he drew up a chair beside his in front of the computer. She slid in beside him, too aware of his nearness, and tried to concentrate. For the next two hours they worked elbow to elbow while he showed her the basis of his financial empire.

He proved what she'd known must be true. He kept detailed records of every aspect of the ranch from the cost of producing hay to the net gain he'd earned on the last sale of yearlings. Using current market prices, he ran a projection, estimating the cost of feeding calves through the winter and comparing it with the relative profit from selling them for less in the fall. His formulas were based on sound techniques, and she realized if he ever gave up ranching, he was well equipped to set himself up as a business analyst.

When they turned to the records he kept on his livestock, he moved aside to allow her access to the keyboard while he bent over her to show her the control strokes. Surrounded by his scent, awareness returned, and it took all her concentration to listen. Still, she couldn't help but be impressed by his expertise.

The detailed records he kept on his Appaloosas were just as impressive. With his help, Emma pulled up his file on Cochise. Even distracted as she was by Nick's touch, she could see why the horse was a champion, why the foals he sired would be champions. Nick had brought the breeding of livestock into the modern age. In fact, he'd almost convinced her raising livestock was merely a matter of studying computer printouts.

To clarify her theory, she picked out a cow at random. The cow had good conformation and coloring, and the notes implied she came from hardy stock. With it she matched a yearling bull that promised to be compact and strongly muscled. "So if I bred these two, I could expect hardy calves with heavy muscling."

Nick settled into the chair she'd abandoned earlier, giving her space to breathe separate from his proximity. "No. I'd never breed those two."

"Why not?"

"That cow comes from a line of aggressive, overly protective mothers. The bull likes to fight. Their calves would likely be unpredictable, and in a herd they'd cause trouble."

He owned more than five hundred cattle, and she listened skeptically. "You can't tell me you know both of these animals personally."

He grinned. "I know the bull."

"Then why do you keep them?"

"Because, with the right combination both will produce good beef." His voice lost the teasing quality of a moment earlier.

"What's the right combination? Isn't that what these records are for?"

"No. These records are proof of lineage. They're the buyer's guarantee he's getting what he pays for and the reason I can charge top dollar." He was all businessman, now. "You can't breed cattle on paper. You have to know the livestock, study them and then decide which direction to take."

As he explained his rationale, Emma began to understand, though if this were the secret to Nick's success, her article about him in a financial magazine would be short and sweet.

"I use the same theory matching people with horses," he

continued. "Take Cochise for example. He's gentle, but he likes to play. Before he settles in he needs a certain amount of time to burn off excess energy. As long as you understand that, you'll get along fine. But let's put Frank into the scenario. Frank doesn't like to play. He wants to wade in and get the job done, and he has no patience for funny business. When the two of them get together, the fight is on. You saw them yesterday."

She nodded.

"You, on the other hand, have a sense of humor." His eyes danced, and she wondered if he was teasing her again. "You're willing to put up with Cochise's little games, even play a few of your own. The two of you got along fine."

"So you think he'd be a good horse for me?"

He hedged. "I'd say you have compatible temperaments."

"But you wouldn't let me ride him." She felt oddly deflated.

"Let's just say I'd want to see you ride first. Cochise is a stallion, and everything you've heard about stallions is true. I think he'd be too much horse for you."

"I see. But you ride him, don't you?"

He nodded.

"He's not too much horse for you?"

He grinned. "No, we're pretty well matched. We're both stubborn."

She thought they had a lot more in common than stubbornness. She'd seen him ride. "So what horse would you set me up with?"

He leaned back in his chair to think about it, his long legs stretched out in front of him. One of his thighs brushed her knee, sending awareness zinging through her again. Whether it was by chance or design, she didn't know, but he didn't move his leg.

After a moment, a playful smile tugged at his lips. "I have

a little mare that's just about your size," he said. "She likes adventure."

Suspicious, she asked, "What do you mean by adventure?"

"She won't ever be the one who wants to turn back before you're ready. She's spirited, but fair-minded."

She was intrigued. "What's her name?"

"Vixen."

"Vixen. That's reassuring."

He grinned and shook his head. "You misunderstand. On Dasher, on Dancer, on Prancer and Vixen... She came early—Christmas Eve. The man I bought her from said she kept him up all night."

"Why didn't he call her Noelle?"

He shook his head and smiled. "Vixen is more fitting. She's not very angelic."

"But you'd put me on her?"

He leaned forward until their eyes were level and she could feel his breath on her cheek. "I think the two of you would suit perfectly."

All the oxygen in the room seemed to have disappeared. "You just want to see me sitting on my butt in the trail."

He shook his head almost imperceptibly. "I want you to know the pleasure of riding a good horse."

He released her gaze, and she gulped in air. But instead of pulling away, he reached forward, fingering a lock of hair that had escaped the clip at her neck. "Why do you always tie your hair back?"

She tried to shake off the tension. "My hair has a life of its own. I only try to keep it under control."

He smiled. "Some things aren't meant to be tamed." Instead of reverting to her gaze, he reached behind her, sending goose bumps sliding down her spine. She heard the click of the latch and felt a tug as he pulled the clip free. A moment later, his fingers swept up through her unbound hair.

"Some things," he said, "are meant to be free."

His hand on her scalp, with her hair cascading around his fingers, awakened a response deep in the nether regions of her body. When his eyes centered on hers again, she read a similar awakening in his expression. He brushed her cheek with the pad of his thumb, then slowly, inexorably, he pulled her to him. His gaze held her hypnotized until, just before their lips met, her eyes drifted closed.

His kiss was neither gentle nor harsh. It demanded response, stripping away her defenses. He stood, taking her with him and spinning slowly around. With his free hand, he brought her close, then sat down in the chair she'd just vacated, pulling her into his lap. He was lean and hard, and with every movement, she felt the flex of solid muscles. His hand on her thigh, settling her more comfortably against him, stirred the last thread of sanity.

"We shouldn't do this, Nick," she said, even as she ran her fingers over his beard-roughened jaw.

"Probably not," he admitted, "but it needs doing."

He covered her mouth with his to forestall any further objections, and she abandoned the struggle. It was only a kiss, after all. Delicious sensation slid over her. The world shifted, and she reached out to anchor herself. His heartbeat was strong and steady beneath her palm.

With a soft growl, he tightened his embrace, adjusted her against him and deepened the kiss. His tongue danced with hers, sending little arrows of pleasure darting through her body. The world grew curiously short of oxygen, and she wondered vaguely if one could die from pleasure. Then she forgot to think at all.

Someone cleared his throat in the doorway sometime later, setting time in motion again. When he spoke, she recognized Pete's voice, and the urgency of his tone brought her eyes open. "Nick," he said without apology for the interruption, "there's something out in the stable you'll want to see."

Chapter Eight

Emma hung in the background while Nick bent to examine the bale of hay, fingering the wire that held it together, paying special attention to the ties. "How many are there?" he asked.

"Four," Bill replied. "I found them when I was moving hay into the stable."

For the life of her, she couldn't tell what was so important about a bale of hay, but Nick, Pete and Bob all looked at it as if it were a product of the devil. Nick reached into a leather pouch on his belt and produced a fold-up tool, which he used to cut the wires. They gave way with a solid click, the wire springing up as the bale expanded. Methodically, he peeled the layers back until he found what he was looking for. Near the middle of the bale, the hay separated easily, exposing several large pockets of black residue. Powdery dust billowed up, and the pungent odor of mold sent her sinuses into spasm. Backing away, she sneezed. Repeatedly.

"When's the last time you pulled hay off this stack?" Nick asked.

"About three days ago," Bob replied. "I moved it into the stable along with a load of straw."

"So it could have been planted here anytime in the last three days," Pete mused.

Nick stood up. "Well, at least we have something to go on now." He pulled the wire from around the broken bale. "You see this funny crimp just below the knot?"

All three men peered at the wire. Emma tried to see, too, but her eyes had begun to water. "What is it?"

"It's like a fingerprint for a hay baler," Pete told her.

"It's not yours?" she asked as another sneeze threatened.

"We use twine," Nick said. "Horses and wire don't mix." He indicated the broken bale. "Get rid of this and take the other three bales into the storeroom. Keep your eyes open, but don't say anything."

They walked out together. "So you're saying someone put four bales of hay onto your stack," she said, still trying to sort out the facts.

"Four moldy bales."

She sneezed again. "Which would make the horses sick?"

"Which would kill them from the looks of that bale."

She felt the blood drain from her face. "What if they'd been baled with twine instead of wire?" Cochise stood watching them from the corral, his majestic head high, ears pricked forward. What if that magnificent horse had eaten that hay?

"I'd like to think we'd notice anyhow. Bob's been around horses all his life. He wouldn't let a bale like that get by him." He looked down at her, and the stormy light in his eyes retreated a little. Reaching into his back pocket, he produced a handkerchief. "Just to make sure, though, maybe you should go with him to feed the horses tonight. You could be our nose."

She grinned. If he could keep his sense of humor, so could she. "No thanks." By now, she knew her nose was red and her eyes swollen, and despite the significance of the discovery, she couldn't forget that ten minutes ago, time had been suspended in Nick's arms. Feeling like anything but the sexual creature she'd been then, she blew her nose in annoyance. Couldn't Warren's flunky, whoever he was, have chosen something besides moldy hay?

Nick watched Emma, charmed in spite of the anger boiling just under the surface. Far from repelling him, the sight of her blowing her nose into his handkerchief underlined the attraction she held for him. It made her more human, somehow, and he had to fight the impulse to put all of this on hold and finish what he'd started in his office.

"So does this really help?" she asked, indicating the wire he still held. "We don't even know for sure how long it's been here."

Drawing his mind back to the subject at hand, he grimaced at the wire tie. He was missing something. He couldn't put his finger on it, but there was a clue here he'd overlooked. He was sure of it. "Not much by itself, but it'll come in handy before this is all over."

"Is there any way of tracing where it came from?"

"My guess is it came from Paul Freeman's ranch. He got caught flat-footed last fall. I heard he lost nearly a thousand bales when the weather changed while his last cutting was down."

"Are you going after him?"

"No. He made no secret of the fact the hay got wet. In fact he stacked it out by the highway and sold it for a dollar a bale. I'll talk to him, but I doubt if he even knows who got the hay."

"Then we're back where we started."

"No, I wouldn't say that." He ground his teeth, wishing

the vague feeling would come clear. ''It tells me quite a lot about whoever left it here.''

''Such as?''

''For one thing, he's sloppy. Either he didn't know enough to check our bales or he didn't really care if his little ploy worked.''

''How could he have gotten hay into your barn without you knowing it?'' She sneezed again.

Nick was puzzled about that, himself. ''We weren't really watching that close until a couple of days ago. It's possible whoever it was could have sneaked in without our seeing him.''

''But not very likely. How many people travel around with hay in their vehicles?''

Too many. In the last three days alone, he couldn't count who all had been here. Neighboring ranchers stopping for a chat, a tourist asking for directions, Sophie Freeman selling cosmetics to Maria—those were just the people he'd noticed. How many had come by when he wasn't looking?

''It would really help if we could pinpoint when the hay was left,'' Emma mused. She'd abandoned his handkerchief and stared into the distance. He could almost hear her thoughts shift gears. She was on the scent now and she'd be hard to divert, but surprisingly, he no longer wished she wasn't involved.

''I have a plan,'' he said throwing an arm over her shoulder. ''If our culprit wants to show off, we'll give him a target.''

Three hours later, Emma steered the tractor around, shifting with the rhythm of bumps and hollows as the wheels crossed the corrugated creases in the hayfield. Nick had showed her the rudiments of driving a tractor, and she'd spent the time since pulling the baler up and down the field, her eyes on her work and her mind sorting and compiling the day's events. When the tractor was straight, she aligned it with the sun-dried alfalfa, and the machine behind her swept up the fragrant swath, compressed it, tied it and pushed it out the back.

At first she'd been nervous when Nick told her he meant for her to pull the baler, but after only a few minutes, she'd picked up the rhythm. To her surprise, he'd stepped off the tractor and motioned her to continue. Since then, he'd been driving the stacker, picking up bales dropped that morning, transporting them to the stack lot, and returning for another load. Each time they passed he waved or smiled, making her feel like an important cog in the wheel of his operation. She'd enjoyed every moment.

Maria appeared at the end of the row in front of her and waved to get her attention. Emma hoped she'd brought something refreshing to drink. Pulling up, she shut the baler down and climbed stiffly off the tractor seat.

"You're working hard out here," Maria said. She made the statement sound like a compliment.

"Well, not exactly, but it's fun and it gives me a feel for ranch life."

"You'd make a good ranch wife."

Emma hardly knew what to say. Certainly Maria's meaning was clear, but she had no intention whatsoever of taking up permanent residence here. She was merely living the life for a few days to give credence to her article.

Apparently Maria didn't expect an answer. "Not like that other one."

Emma jumped at the diversion. "I thought you never met Lynette."

"I didn't have to meet her to know she never drove a tractor."

Knowing that sent a wave of pleasure through Emma. Lynette's beauty and style had taken on heroic proportions in her mind, but in this small way, she knew she would come out the winner in Nick's eyes.

The stacker lumbered up behind them and Maria poured two tall glasses of lemonade. Emma turned to watch Nick's approach. He climbed gracefully down from the single seat and flashed her a smile. His teeth glowed white against his tanned skin, and his eyes looked almost gray in the bright light. For some reason her mind superimposed his expression with the look on his face when he'd kissed her in his office. Her heart fluttered in her chest.

"Ah, Maria," he said, "I think I love you."

"You waste your words on me, Nicolas Barlow. You should be ashamed of yourself."

"I should?"

"Emma is a guest in your home and look what you're making her do!" She gestured toward the tractor. "Not even a sunshade. You have her working like a farmhand in the sun."

Emma hid a smile. Maria's campaign to throw them together made her uncomfortable, but her tactics were worthy of a general directing battle. While Nick had been setting his trap in the stable, Maria had personally supervised the application of sunscreen on every exposed inch of Emma's skin. She'd even produced a ragged straw hat, which she'd insisted Emma wear. A full day of sun couldn't penetrate the barrier Maria had erected.

Nick merely smiled, pulled off a dusty glove, and drained the glass Maria offered him. "You're right," he conceded as he held the glass out for a refill, "but you told me you'd never drive a tractor again. I had to find someone to help out."

Maria never missed a beat. "You should take her out to dinner. She's earned it."

He nodded agreeably. "Want to go out for a burger tonight, Emma? My treat."

"Bah! You'd buy her fast food when she has earned steak? Never mind. I'll make dinner myself." Turning to Emma, she added, "Do you like lasagna? I'll make you a real meal."

Emma had a good idea just what kind of dinner Maria had in mind, and it had nothing to do with payment for driving a tractor. "That's not necessary, Maria."

"I won't hear any arguments. You're a guest here. It's time someone—" she glared at Nick "—remembered that." Without another word, she turned and strode back toward the house.

"Don't forget the garlic bread, Maria," Nick called out after her. He gave Emma a wink that brought his dimples to life and sent heat surging through her chest.

"Nick, you have to stop her," she whispered anxiously.

To her surprise, he shook his head. "She's right. You've earned it. I only meant to have you make a pass or two with the tractor to get the feel of the job, but you're a natural. You've been a big help, and I'm shorthanded at the moment."

His words reminded her of why his men were occupied elsewhere. Events were spinning out of her control, and Maria's determination to throw them together underscored all the reasons she ought to avoid the very scene Maria had in mind. Someone was proving over and over just how precarious Nick's position was. His livelihood, his ranch, his very way of life were built on quicksand, a ready target for Andrew Warren, who merely had to create enough tremors to crack the foundation. How much longer would Nick's luck hold out?

That same someone had drawn her into the web, threatened her until she had no choice but to get involved. To make matters worse, the barriers she'd created between herself and Nick were crumbling. She was beginning to care about more than the outcome of the devious games, and there was nothing she could do about it. She was a player now, with Nick cast as the protector who threatened her peace of mind. She could no longer deny that he made her forget her fears, that she enjoyed his company, that she longed for his kiss. She'd come to care about the ranch, the people on it, the outcome of Warren's ugly scheme. And in the end, she stood to lose everything.

Distance. Distance was what she needed, what she *must* maintain. Depositing her glass in the cooler Maria had left behind, she turned back to the tractor. "I can finish this field by tonight if I stay with it." Nick said nothing, and he didn't try to stop her, but she felt his eyes burning into her back as she climbed aboard. He didn't understand her abrupt change of mood. She couldn't expect him to. She only knew she had to get away.

Maria's dinner was all Emma feared it would be. She served it on a shaded patio in back of the house. The appetizing aroma of Italian cooking drifted through the open windows as Nick escorted her outside. A snowy linen tablecloth covered a small round table with two intimate place settings set side by side. Expensive wine chilled in an iced cooler, and birds singing in the trees above them gave note to the last rays of sunlight. Unable to disappoint Maria, she'd dressed the part in a cool, silken sundress, but she was afraid all of Maria's work had been wasted. Her stomach was in knots, and she found it hard to breathe.

Nick, likewise, seemed detached and thoughtful. He kept the conversation light, but the atmosphere between them radiated energy, and she wondered if, after an afternoon's contemplation, he regretted his impulse to kiss her.

Like actors, they played the parts handed them. Nick pulled her chair out for her, and when she was seated, he uncorked the wine. He wore black jeans and a Western shirt that emphasized his broad shoulders. Just as the scene demanded, he was all gentleman. Despite her misgivings about the evening, she couldn't keep her eyes off him.

"When Maria puts on an Italian feast, there's no better place to eat," he said as he poured the wine. "But if you'd like to go out to dinner, I'll be glad to take you when this is all over."

He'd given her an opening, and she jumped on it. Anything to distract herself from the turmoil inside. "Do you think I'm still in danger? Maybe the brakes were meant only as a warning. Everything else has been directed at you."

He looked up, his expression serious. "Don't count on it. It'll be harder to get at you here, but he'll try."

"I hate waiting."

He handed her a glass of wine. "I know," he said gently, his eyes soft in the evening light, "I hate it, too. But he's getting bolder, and more careless. It won't be long now until he makes a wrong move."

"So you think he'll fall for the trap you set?"

"If he's as cocky as I think he is, it'll work. The keys to every outbuilding are on a board on the back wall of the storeroom. Anyone interested in causing problems will have to have them. In the meantime, I have a ranch to run, and you have an article to write—unless you've changed your mind?"

Smiling, she shook her head. "Not a chance."

His voice filled with emotion. "Emma, do you have any idea what you've gotten yourself into? You should get out now, while you still can."

He was looking for a chink in her armor. "Look, Nick. The stakes here have changed. Andrew Warren crossed the line when he started this, and I won't be intimidated into letting him get away with it."

He studied her for a long moment. "Okay, if that's how you feel, we'll rout him out together. But any time you change your mind, just let me know and I'll take you out of the equation.''

She wondered how he planned to do that, but Maria chose that moment to bring them a tray laden with Caesar salad, steaming lasagna and a plate full of golden garlic bread. She bustled around them, putting the serving dishes within easy reach. Then, with a murmured good-night, she left them alone.

''You know we're being set up, here,'' Nick said when she left.

Emma nodded.

''Do you mind?'' For a fraction of a second, his eyes held hers, and he held his glass aloft, a smile tugging at the corners of his mouth. ''To Maria,'' he said, ''a woman with the best of intentions and all the finesse of a bull in a china shop. She's a hard woman, but her cooking makes it all bearable.''

As if to punctuate his words, Emma heard Maria's car starting and shortly, the sound of her engine retreating down the drive, leaving them truly alone.

The atmosphere became intimate and comfortable in the growing dusk, lit only by a lantern on the table. Emma touched her glass to his. Beneath the tablecloth she felt his knee brush hers. Both of them started at the contact, and his expression said he, too, was sorting through unexpected emotions. Their relationship was changing of its own accord. When the reassuring pressure of his knee returned, she allowed her uncertainty to unravel. Just for tonight, she vowed to forget her worries and enjoy herself.

''So, Cowboy,'' she said, ''what do you have in store for me, tomorrow?''

''Why don't you get on and I'll adjust the stirrups,'' Nick said the following morning.

Emma looked at the little mare waiting quietly. She couldn't believe she'd agreed to this ridiculous expedition.

How did one mount a saddle? She'd seen it a thousand times on television. It couldn't be that hard. Raising her left foot, it was all she could do to reach the stirrup. "I thought you said Vixen was just my size."

"She is." She felt his hands on her waist, and before she could gather herself to jump, he boosted her aboard.

Vixen snorted and shuffled her feet, but she quieted when Emma reached forward to pat her neck. Nick had been right about the two of them. It had been love at first sight.

Vixen was what Nick called a leopard horse—white with abundant black spots spattered over her entire body. The spots narrowed to freckles on her head and nose, and her intelligent eyes were almost black. She'd pranced into the corral when Bob led her in, but when Emma approached, she'd displayed nothing more than avid curiosity. Emma had given her an apple, which Vixen had taken, then she'd promptly dipped her head to be scratched.

"How do the stirrups feel?" Nick asked.

How were stirrups supposed to feel? "A little long, I think."

Nick released some hooks in a leather strap behind her knee and pulled it up. It was not an intimate gesture, but the brush of his hands against her leg was warm, and it distracted her. After doing the same on the other side, he asked, "How's that?"

Reeling in her imagination, she put her weight onto the stirrups. It was easier, but to be honest, she didn't know if they were short enough or not. "I think that's better."

"Western saddles aren't like English ones," he said. "You want to be able to clear the seat, but you don't want to stand too high."

It was time to confess. There was no disgrace in admitting the truth, and her ignorance would probably get her dumped. "I've...never used a saddle before."

He looked up at her, surprised, his eyes filled with questions.

Suddenly, from behind the door of the storeroom, the air was split by a bellow, followed by expansive, explicit cursing. The door rattled under the impact of an angry fist. "Somebody open the damn door!"

Nick smiled as Bob and Pete appeared from nowhere. "I think there's a fox in the henhouse," he said as he helped her to the ground. "Let's go see what we caught." He caught her hand and led her over to the storeroom.

With Bob to back him up, Pete already had his key out, but he stood aside when he saw them approaching.

"Let me out of here!"

"Hang on, we need a key." Nick nodded to Pete, who unlocked the door and pulled it open.

Frank Howell appeared in the doorway, red-faced, the veins on his neck bulging. He was still cursing. One hand was balled into a fist, and in the other he carried a tool of some kind. Emma had never seen one like it.

"What the hell's the idea of locking the door on me?" he demanded.

"What were you doing in the storeroom?" Nick asked coolly.

"I forgot my buttress so I borrowed yours. It's nothing I haven't done a dozen times before, but the lousy door never flew shut behind me like this. And there was never a stupid lock on it before."

"We've had some problems with thievery," Nick said smoothly.

"Well, you should warn a man when you put a lock on a door like that." He fired off another spate of cursing. "And another thing. Don't you have any lightbulbs around here? It's darker'n hell in there."

"Watch what you say, Frank. There's a lady present."

Frank hadn't said anything Emma hadn't heard before, but

she was struck by the edge in Nick's voice. Though his expression remained bland, his body radiated tension.

Frank gave her the once-over, acknowledging her presence. "Well you better watch who you go in there with, little missy," he said, thumbing over his shoulder. "You never know what you might trip over."

Emma thought Nick was going to hit him. He balled his hand into a fist so tight his knuckles turned white, but he kept his hand resolutely at his side. "Get back to work, Frank," he said. "And when you're through with the buttress, leave it on the bench over there."

Frank glared at him. "Yeah, well, if you want shoes on those half-grown stallions, you'd better send someone over to hold them. I ain't getting kicked again by one of your wild horses. You ask me, you ought to take a switch to every one of 'em."

"No one asked you." He nodded to Bob. "Give him a hand."

When they were gone, Nick went inside.

"Prop the door open," he said, disgusted. "It smells in here."

Pete lodged a rock in front of the door while Emma followed Nick inside. He was examining the rack of keys hanging on the back wall.

"Is everything there?" she asked.

He nodded and turned to the tools hanging on the side wall. Every peg was occupied except one. A shiny black mark on the wood below it roughly outlined the shape of the tool Frank had been holding. In the corner, the three bales of moldy hay were stacked against the wall. The rest of the storeroom was neat and orderly. Nothing seemed out of place.

"You think he was telling the truth?" Pete asked behind them.

Nick grimaced and turned around. "Probably. Nothing's

missing except the buttress. Fix the lock again, and we'll see
what happens.''

Outside, Nick apologized. ''I'm sorry you had to witness
that. Frank Howell's a hard man, and he doesn't pay much
attention to the niceties.''

''Don't worry about it,'' she reassured him. ''I've heard it
all before.''

He ground his teeth. ''I can hardly abide the man myself.
If there were anyone else who could do the work, I'd give
Frank the boot. But the honest truth is Frank's the only man
available right now, and despite his rumblings, he does a
good job.''

They walked back to the corral, where Vixen stood patiently waiting for them. Visibly controlling his anger, he
asked, ''You think you can ride her?''

She smiled up at him with confidence she wished she felt.
''It's been a while, but I won't have a problem.''

''Take a couple of turns around the corral, just the same,''
he said. ''I'll saddle up Grayson, and by then Maria should
have a lunch of some kind packed.''

Emma recalled the luscious meal Maria had prepared the
night before and wondered what she had in mind for them
today. There were advantages to being targeted by a match-
maker, but she decided it was good she was working hard
here. Otherwise, by the time she left, she'd have a real problem fitting into her clothes.

Under Nick's watchful eye, she patted the mare on the
neck, set the reins and, using what she'd learned earlier,
mounted and urged Vixen into motion. The saddle was stiff,
much different than riding bareback, but the horse responded
to the pressure of her knees just the same.

After a brief period of trial and error, Emma caught the
rhythm. Using her legs and the stirrups to absorb the shock,
she was soon cantering comfortably around the corral.

Nick acknowledged her mastery with a smile and a nod, then opened the gate and went in search of his own mount. Fifteen minutes later, with Maria's lunch tied behind them, they were on their way.

Chapter Nine

"So, Emma, why is it you've never used a saddle before?" Nick had been watching, and she was no tenderfoot. Though it had taken her a few minutes to learn to use the stirrups, she was a natural-born horsewoman, and the sight of her moving fluidly in the saddle sent his suppressed libido into overdrive.

She didn't answer his question, though he knew she'd heard him. Wondering what she was hiding this time, he nudged Grayson up beside her. For once, he meant to get some answers.

"When you mentioned riding before, I pictured a rental hack with an English saddle, but I was wrong, wasn't I?"

She nodded, looking straight ahead.

"Why didn't you use a saddle?" he repeated.

"I liked riding bareback." At least she'd answered him, short though it was. Her drawl was a sure sign the subject made her nervous.

"I like it, myself. But it's not very practical on a working horse." His words brought a fleeting smile, but she still didn't look at him. "You haven't answered my question."

She turned on him abruptly. "We didn't have a saddle, okay?" The words were spoken in pure Southern brogue, and given the passion behind them, he wondered if he'd pushed her too far.

"You had your own horse?" he asked gently.

She looked away, but nodded. "Pal."

Apparently he was going to have to pry it out of her word by word. A gentleman would let it go. But they had two hours before they reached the herd, and her constant secretiveness left him feeling anything but gentlemanly.

"A pony."

She sighed. "He was a plow horse. Daddy used him in the fields until he traded some fence posts for a run-down old tractor."

She'd learned to ride like that on a *plow horse?*

"Pal was more reliable than that tractor ever was, but Daddy claimed a tractor would solve all his problems."

She didn't elaborate, but then he hadn't expected her to. He could tell this was something important. Maybe even a clue to the real Emma. "Tell me about Pal."

It took her so long to reply that he thought he'd reached another dead end.

"I used to sneak out to the barn at night and feed him treats," she said, her voice filled with affection. "All the time I was growing up, he was my best friend. My brother caught me once, but he never said anything."

She continued, "I was ten when Daddy brought home the tractor. At first I thought it was a slap in the face for Pal, but after a few days, I realized it was my lucky break. I found an old bridle in the barn. The reins were broken, but I talked my brother into fixing them. When he finished, I showed it to Daddy and asked if he'd let me ride. We had to stay in the barnyard until I proved myself, then we were free to go wherever we wanted.

"From then on, I groomed him every day after my chores were done, then we'd head out together."

Nick listened in silence. For the first time he thought she spoke the undiluted truth. Whatever had made her into the cosmopolitan woman she chose to be, her early years were spent on a simple, poor farm in West Virginia.

"For the next two years, Pal and I went everywhere together. We rode the farm roads until we got to the hills, then we'd take off cross-country. He was old, but he was sure-footed, and I think he must have resented all those years harnessed to a plow, because he loved to run."

"You never fell off?"

She chuckled again. "Lots of times. But I learned to hang on because it was so hard to get back on again."

He pictured a wiry red-haired girl galloping through the underbrush. "Why haven't you mentioned him before?"

Her smile faded. "There was a flood. It washed the crop out, and there wasn't enough money to make it through the winter. Daddy sold him at the auction barn."

"You never got another horse?"

She laughed, a hollow, brittle sound. "No."

Apparently family finances hadn't improved after that. "I'm sorry, Emma."

She looked at him. "Don't be. It was a long time ago."

But she'd been hurt. They rode in silence while Nick decided whether or not to push her any further. The last thing he wanted was to stir up painful memories, but this was his first glimpse behind the contradictions that made him so crazy. He needed to see more.

"So, how did a West Virginia farm girl come to be a feature writer for *American Business Monitor*?"

"It's a long story."

"We've got all day."

She didn't answer.

"Come on, Emma. You're learning all my dirty little secrets, and I know almost nothing about you."

She looked almost frightened.

"Is it so hard to talk about it?"

"You won't like what I have to say."

Her voice quavered, making him want to hold her, to reassure her somehow. "Try me."

Still she hesitated. "What do you want to know?"

Everything. "Tell me about the farm. I get the distinct impression you don't care much for farming."

She grimaced and turned her face away. "It wasn't much of a farm. Daddy always said it was on bottom land, but the truth was, it was in the flood plain. We were at the mercy of the Saint Croix River, and half the time the crop never made it to harvest."

"What about the other half?"

"You name it," she said wearily. "If we planted sorghum, the price of sorghum dropped. If we planted grain, the rain knocked it down. One year everyone around us made a killing on tobacco, so Daddy planted tobacco the next year. That was the year of the tobacco hornworms. The tractor broke down, and by the time we got it fixed, there wasn't money for spray. We picked worms from before daylight to after sunset, but the crop was ruined." She shuddered. "Every year it was the same. We'd get our hopes up, then something would happen. It was almost a relief when the bank finally took over."

"What did you do then?"

"We moved to town. Mama died that spring and Daddy went to work at the mill. My brother finished school, then joined the navy. He never came back."

Nick didn't care much for the picture she was painting. "What about you?"

"I was too young to leave, so I got a job at the grocery

store. It didn't pay much, but it was my first taste of a regular paycheck. Half my wages went to pay off our bills, and I saved every cent I could out of the rest.''

What she told him raised more questions than it answered. There was no disgrace in being poor, yet she'd all but erased her roots. There had to be more. ''Why do you hide where you came from?''

''I don't hide it so much as I don't mention it.''

''Isn't that the same thing?''

She shook her head vehemently. ''My journalism teacher in high school said he recognized something in me, and he helped me land a scholarship. I was so proud—I was going to college! But when I got there, every time I opened my mouth people looked at me like I didn't have a brain in my head. It didn't matter how smart I was or what I knew. With a name like Emmaline and an accent thick enough to smother pancakes, I never had a chance.''

Nick grimaced. ''That was their problem, not yours.''

She turned toward him. ''No, it *was* my problem. She hesitated. ''There was one girl from Indiana I admired because she seemed so classy. So I copied the way she acted and dressed, and I practiced talking like her. I even tried to fix my hair like hers.'' She pulled at a curly lock, and he was glad she hadn't succeeded. ''After a while, I found a job at a nice restaurant bussing tables. It gave me a chance to study the way rich people acted in public. By the time I was a senior, no one ever suspected where I came from. As far as I'm concerned, they never need to know.''

But what had it cost her? The woman he knew was proud and stubborn. She wouldn't make such drastic changes she described lightly. ''Do you ever miss it?''

She angled him a glance. ''The farm?''

''The way of life.''

''Are you kidding? Those years were the worst of my life! We lived from hand to mouth, never sure where the next meal was coming from. Our lives weren't even our own. We were there at the whim of the weather or the mood of the banker when Daddy talked to him in the fall. I still have nightmares of insect infestations, or that the neighbor's pigs get out and eat the crop before we can stop them.

"Our lives balanced on the mood of Mother Nature and the stock market. Every time the telephone rang—when we had one—my heart was in my throat for fear it was the bank calling to foreclose. We left, but it was too late. It killed my mother and nearly killed my father."

With a sinking feeling, Nick knew what she was going to say next.

"When I left, I promised myself I'd never go into debt again, no matter how much I had to do without. My future is in *my* hands, and my security, such as it is, is under *my* control." She stopped, as if she realized how vehemently she spoke. More calmly, she finished, her words laced with bitterness. "There. Now you know what I think of farming and anything else dependent entirely on outside forces."

Like ranching. Well, he'd asked for it. Suddenly it was all clear to him. The dilapidated old car she drove, the cosmopolitan image, her overconcern about the state of his ranch, the way she'd cut him off when he'd described his grandfather's struggles during the depression—everything except why she'd chosen to get involved with the Andrew Warren affair, which would surely spell the end of his ranch should Warren win.

And in her way, she was right. Every decision he made was a gamble. If prices dropped, if the hay crop was destroyed, if his cattle went out of favor, or if Cochise didn't prove out as a stud, he stood to lose—big. That's why he'd spent years in school, learning better ways to safeguard his heritage, and he'd succeeded. But even if worst came to worst and he had to start over again, he could do it. It was the life and the land he loved, not the success or the money, though he'd never be able to explain that to Emma. She wouldn't understand. "Why did you come here?"

She spoke candidly. "The series I'm working on was my idea. But in all honesty, the only reason I'm here is my editor wouldn't let me finish it without an agricultural angle. But if you don't think I can write an honest article now, I'll understand."

Regardless of her personal convictions, he knew she was a professional. She'd given him an opportunity to back out of their agreement, and though he still wasn't hot on the idea, she needed his trust now. "Don't tempt me," he said.

"You still trust me?"

"Is there any reason I shouldn't?"

Emma was thankful for the saddle that held her in place. She felt as if she'd just run a gauntlet and somehow managed to survive. Although he disagreed with her, Nick still believed in her ability to do her job.

Not once in the past ten years had she told anyone what she'd just told him, and the relief of sharing the load left her almost light-headed. He understood. But deep in her heart, she'd known he would. That's why she'd told him. There would be no more passion between them now, but it was better this way.

"It *would* be nice if you held off until October, though."

She was so caught up in her thoughts, the words didn't sink in for a moment. "I beg your pardon?"

"I might as well tell you I had every intention of holding the article up for a few weeks, anyhow."

"And you weren't going to tell me?"

"That's what I'm doing now."

Semantics. He was better at them than she was. "Why, exactly, don't you want it published until October?"

Shaking a finger at her, he said, "Uh-uh. I have the right of refusal, remember? No one mentioned anything about explanations."

"No one mentioned stalling the story, either."

He hesitated, giving her imagination time to spin off in a dozen different directions. "If I tell you, it's off the record. Agreed?"

"That depends."

"On what?"

"On why you want it off the record." She pulled closer to him. "What are you trying to hide, Nick?"

"Nothing. Let's just say your timing bothers me." He urged Grayson to a trot. "It's my way or not at all. You decide."

She spurred Vixen after him. "Oh, no you don't, Nicolas Barlow."

"Do you trust me?"

Implicitly. "Of course."

"Then what I say is off the record."

He was honest and fair. Whatever his reasons, they were important enough for him to make an issue of it. "Okay. Off the record. What's happening in September?"

He took a deep breath and looked away, and she realized whatever he had to say was hard for him to put into words. Unconsciously, she steeled herself.

"By now, you've probably gotten an earful about my divorce," he said. "It's to your credit that you haven't asked me about it." He slowed his horse to a walk again.

"Lynette didn't understand ranching. As you're well aware, it takes money to run a ranch, but she thought the money should be spent elsewhere. She wanted a modern house and a new car every year. When we split, she sued for what she considered her due. We'd been married five years, but she expected half of everything I owned, everything that had been in my family for three generations." He ground his teeth. "Of course her attorney was all for it, but I wasn't prepared when the judge seemed to agree.

"For a while, it looked as if she would win. Finally my

attorney hired an independent CPA to testify that splitting the property would break the back of the ranch. In the end, the judge ordered a cash settlement in five installments, with annual reviews to update my financial status.

"I mortgaged the land to pay her off, and after the last review in September, the settlement will be final—unless something changes the judge's mind."

Emma's heart jumped into her throat. He was in debt. Just like her father, he was forced to go to the banker each year with his hat in his hand. Just like her father, his life, his very existence was at the mercy of a man behind a desk, a man who had no idea what it took to pry a living from the land. She swallowed hard and forced herself to listen.

"Let's just say I don't want my picture plastered on the cover of a national magazine proclaiming me some kind of financial wizard when the judge looks at my case."

She grasped the gist what he was saying, but her thoughts snagged on details. "But your net worth has improved in the last five years."

"The judge is aware of that. I'm expected to do what it takes to pay Lynette off. I just don't want anyone getting the idea that I've fooled them somehow. I don't want to end up back in court again." He turned to her. "I'd like to hold the article until this is all over."

Still, her mind grasped at straws. "That's why you've been expanding so quickly? To pay off the debt?"

"Something like that. The ranch will finance it, but with luck, Cochise will pay it off."

And he'd come within a hairbreadth of losing him.

"Can I count on you, Emma?"

What he was asking was reasonable. Her deadline was less than a week away. It would cost her nothing to delay, and no one ever need know why. Her editor wouldn't like it, but this story had been chancy anyhow. Nick wouldn't ask unless he felt it was important. For him, for the trust he'd shown her, she couldn't refuse him. "All right. I'll hold off."

The terrain turned upward and the trail became rocky. Emma fell in behind, making talk difficult, and they settled into a thoughtful silence. Telling him about her past lifted a weight off her shoulders, but she had the sick feeling she'd destroyed the comfortable rapport they'd created in the past two days. It hurt. After their cozy dinner last night, she'd felt a closeness with him, but in the light of day, she realized she'd only been fooling herself. It was better this way. Now they both knew why it couldn't work between them.

Nick, too, seemed pensive. He rode with his eyes down, as if deep in thought, and for once she knew what he was thinking. The day had lost its beauty, despite the scenery and the exquisite mare she rode. Knowing she wouldn't get another chance like this, she tried to recapture the magic. Vixen was a joy to ride. Surefooted and responsive, she followed Grayson up the trail, alert to the surrounding countryside. When Emma patted her on the neck, she listened almost as if she understood, and Emma was tempted to pour out her problems to Vixen's friendly ear.

They found the herd in a clearing near a salt block. The yearling bulls lazed in the morning sunshine, flicking flies indolently with their tails, unconcerned with the appearance of strangers. They were a handsome bunch, with straight backs and thick, muscled shoulders.

Nick did a quick head count. "They're all here but two," he said. "See that one standing over in the shade? He's the one you picked out on the computer the other day."

Emma studied him. The curly hair on his back ruffled in the breeze, and his dark red coat made his white face look even brighter in the shade. Half-grown, weighted horns grew down in stylish crescents. "Well, I'd say I have good taste."

Nick nodded. "The other two are probably around here somewhere. Want to stay here or come along?"

"I'll come if you'll tell me what to do."

They found the missing bulls in the brush on a hillside above the rest of the herd. Unlike the animals below, both eyed them suspiciously, and Vixen pricked her ears forward at full alert. Nick turned his horse to get behind them.

"Give Vixen her head," he said. "She knows what to do. Just remember to—"

One of the bulls bolted. Vixen planted a foot and spun out after him, and Emma felt herself go airborne. A heartbeat later, she landed in an undignified heap on the ground. Her hat settled in a bush beside her head, and dust filtered off the leaves into her eyes. Swallowing a curse, she put a hand out to ward off the onslaught.

Nick was beside her in a flash, not bothering with the stirrups as he dismounted. "Emma?"

She looked up at him, his grim frown, the unmistakable worry in his eyes. "You were saying?"

A smile tugged at his lips, and dimples danced in his cheeks. He offered her a hand up. "Just remember to hang on when she turns. She's the best cutting horse I own."

The bulls disappeared into the brush, their tails in the air, and Vixen, true to Nick's prediction, waited apologetically a few feet away. "So I see."

He reached for her hat, still hanging in the bushes, and held it out for her.

She smiled. Her dignity was gone, and the best she could hope for was a sense of humor. "I'll—ah—try to be ready for her next time."

He coughed, his dimples deepening. "I probably should have warned you sooner."

"You might as well let it out," she said as she brushed herself off. "It's a sight you won't see again." She hoped she wasn't lying.

"Then I wish I had seen it," he said, letting the laughter out. "All I heard was a crash and something that sounded suspiciously like blasphemy."

She looked up at him innocently.

"When I turned around, Vixen was herding cattle and you were nowhere to be seen."

"Better luck next time." She walked over to Vixen, gave her a friendly pat to show she didn't hold a grudge, and mounted again. "Come on, little lady, I'll get the hang of this yet."

An hour later, Nick closed the gate behind the last of the bulls. For all their languorous behavior, they'd resisted moving to the fresh pasture with surprising stubbornness, and Emma had a new respect for working horses—and the cowboys who rode them. Nick was tenacious, even-tempered despite the uncooperative cattle, and always one step ahead of the game. Seeing his operation had been impressive, but nothing compared to watching him in action. Now, as he turned and smiled up at her, she was struck by the thought that not only did he love his land, he loved his work. He displayed none of the weary futility she'd seen in her father. He was in his element.

"Hungry?"

As if in answer, her stomach rumbled. "Starving."

"There's a good place to rest not far from here," he said. "From the sound of things, you'll just make it if we hurry."

He'd heard her. "Then be quick about it."

"Yes ma'am." He mounted Grayson. Horse and rider lunged forward. To her credit, Vixen waited until Emma gave the go-ahead, then sprang after them. Nick checked over his shoulder to see that she was coming, then spurred Grayson to a gallop. Emma followed, determined to keep up. Old reflexes returned as if she'd used them only last week. With the wind in her face, she abandoned herself to the joy and freedom of riding headlong aboard a horse bred for the sport.

Nick pulled up in a glade surrounded by aspen trees and bisected by a stream of clear, gurgling water. Dropping the reins, he untied the bag containing their lunch from the back of his saddle, along with a blanket, and dropped them on the ground. Then he showed Emma how to loosen the cinch. That done, he slapped the horses on the rump, and they trotted off toward the water.

Three hours in the saddle and an unexpected landing in the dirt had taken their toll. She followed stiffly while Nick led the way into the shade.

"I always thought this would be a great place to build a little getaway cabin," he said. "I usually stop here when I'm up this way." He spread the blanket on the grass in the mottled shade of the aspens, and she fell upon it. "Tired?"

"Stiff. I don't remember feeling like this after I fell off Pal."

He smiled. "Just relax for a minute while I get us some water to drink from the spring. I'll be right back."

She lay on the blanket, staring up at the cloudless sky through the shimmering leaves. Water gurgled in the rocks nearby, and a bee made its way from flower to flower. Below her, the horses had drunk their fill and began to crop the grass along the creek bank. Nick was right. All the problems and worries of the past few days seemed only a distant memory here.

He returned with dripping canteens and handed one to her. The icy water tasted sweet and refreshing. Hunger returned, and she helped him unpack the lunch.

"Say what you will about Maria," she said when she saw the crusty bread and big chunks of cheese, "but she knows what's good to eat."

Nick unwrapped a bag of fat, juicy grapes.

And she knew how to put together a romantic lunch. Laughing, she added, "Where's the wine?"

His look made her realize what she'd just said. "I'll talk

to her. She must be slipping." He sliced off some cheese and handed it to her.

His touch sent a jolt of awareness through her, and she jerked back. Their eyes locked, and shaken, she turned away. There was no room in their relationship for this kind of re-action to him now. Somehow she had to get control of her emotions.

Behind her, she heard him drop the knife. "For what it's worth, I find your Southern accent appealing."

Surprised, she turned to him.

"It's fun to tease you until it comes out."

"It's mellowed a lot since I left home."

"Maybe other things have, too."

What did he mean by that?

"Have you ever been back?"

"No. Dad died a couple of years ago. There's no reason to."

"What about the farm?"

"It's gone now." She pictured it in her mind. "My mom kept a bank of irises outside the back door. When I saw yours that first day, it made me think of them."

"And uncovered some long-buried memories?"

"Yeah." Surprisingly, they were pleasant now. "Your screen door sounds the same, too."

He reached out to her, and the threads of her control began to unravel. "Times on the farm were hard," he said softly. "But the story you told me this morning about Pal was a fond memory."

She couldn't answer him.

He dropped his hand. "I remember my first horse. He wasn't a pony, but the next step above one. I was about five, I think, and I sneaked out to the barn to feed him, too." He paused. "Feel free to ride Vixen for as long as you're here."

It was a simple gesture, but it drove an arrow straight into her heart. They both knew she'd be gone soon. She couldn't stay.

"What I said to you must go totally against your grain," she said. "Why haven't you tried to convince me I'm wrong?"

"Would it do any good?"

She shook her head.

"Emma, you endured a lot and reacted the only way you could. I don't blame you for feeling the way you do."

"But you don't feel that way."

He shook his head. "This ranch is as much a part of me as eating and breathing. For you, the farm was a burden. For me, the land is my heritage. I can't imagine doing anything else."

And he would never leave it.

"So, what are you going to write about me?"

She took her cue from him and smiled. "I thought I'd write about how you lock the hired help in the storeroom."

He chuckled. "And my hands-on way of teaching you to herd cattle?"

"Now that you mention it, yes."

"I always said experience was the best teacher."

"What about your housekeeper's efforts to marry you off? Should I include that?"

He hesitated. "Well, you have to admit she has good taste."

"What?"

"If Maria hadn't set her sights on you, I'd have gone after you myself."

"But—"

He leaned toward her, his eyes smiling. "Does that surprise you? It shouldn't."

No. It didn't. He meant to kiss her again. But he couldn't, not after what she'd told him. "Nick, this isn't a good idea."

"You said that before." She could feel his breath on her cheek. "And what did I say?"

"You said it—"

"—needed doing," he finished for her. "It still does."

She couldn't escape his blue, blue eyes.

"Do you want me to kiss you, Emmaline?"

Her old-fashioned name on his lips sounded sexy and appealing. She did want his kiss. She wanted it more every day. When his lips touched hers, her resistance melted.

"I thought so," he breathed, and together they sank back onto the blanket.

Chapter Ten

Nick swept their uneaten lunch out of the way, cushioning Emma's fall as they slipped backward. He stretched out beside her and raised his head to study her face, afraid that if he allowed himself to continue kissing her, he'd never stop. She looked up at him, her amber eyes wide and dark. If he looked close enough, he was sure he'd see her soul. But they had no future, only a bittersweet present that tempted him to the very limits of his control.

But he couldn't pull away entirely. He settled for running his fingers through the soft curls in front of her ear. Leaning on one elbow, he reached behind her and released the clip she wore, giving him access to all of her silky tresses. In the mottled light, the sun painted each strand with fire, and he spread the shimmering mass on the blanket around her, combing it with his fingers until it formed a halo of color around her head.

''I like your hair,'' he said, smiling as he removed a broken leaf left over from her fall. "I like the way it shines in the light." He lifted a handful, letting the strands sift through his fingers.

She didn't answer, but merely watched him, her eyes darkening even more.

Playfully, he brushed her cheek with the pad of his thumb. "I like your freckles, too."

At this she grimaced. "No one likes this many freckles."

He shook his head, loving the softness of her. Drawing a finger down the length of her nose, he said, "I like the way they're sprinkled here."

She twitched, fighting a smile.

"And I like how they spread across your cheek." He drew a grapevine that angled from the corner of her eye to her lips, captivated by the way she shivered at his touch. Dragging his eyes away, he caught her hand and studied it. "I like the way they disappear into your sleeve, and the glimpse of them I get when you wear a dress like the one you wore last night." Recalling the golden vision she'd made in the soft light of dusk, he smiled. "They're like you—a mystery. You show just enough to make me wonder how many more you keep hidden."

He kissed her hand and let go, but instead of dropping it, she brushed the backs of her fingers along the line of his cheekbone, and the margin of control he'd gained evaporated. Stunned by the power of his need, he caught her hand again. Her fingers trembled, and when he raised his eyes, he saw her confusion.

She tried to pull away, but he wouldn't let her. Pressing her hand hard against his cheek, he closed his eyes. He was playing with fire. There was no room for this kind of need in his life.

Emma wasn't the woman for him. If anything, her honesty this morning had only underlined the fact that she carried too much baggage to enter a relationship with him. Even if they overcame his problems, she'd never be able to live here. She knew too well the insecurities of ranch life. She'd lost her home and everything dear to her once, she'd never be able to risk losing so much again. Hell, she couldn't even bring herself to borrow money for a decent car. Her fears would eat away at her until she hated the ranch—hated him. But in this place of quiet and peace, her softness urged him to cast reason aside.

His body remembered the feel of her molded against him, and the taste of her lingered on his lips. But it wasn't fair to push this any further. His heart was hardened—encased in five years of bitterness—and she wasn't the type for an explosive affair destined to end before it even began. He didn't want that, either. He didn't know what he wanted from her. He only knew he wanted—needed—to hold her close, to kiss her until their worlds blended into one. To love her.

One by one, the reasons to release her, to back away before it was too late, drowned in the current of desire surging through him. He was drowning, too. They may not have a future, but they had now. It had to be enough.

Emma felt Nick's restraint in his iron-hard grasp, in the steely tension of his body, in the tortured expression on his face. His seductive tenderness had her feeling weightless in the wake of his attentions, wanting only to touch him the way he touched her. But he'd stopped her, and some unnamed fear took hold. Her life-style didn't leave room for many scenes such as this, but she knew enough to realize Nick was fighting a crucial inner battle.

He didn't want to want her. He didn't want her to touch him. How ironic that he'd broken down her defenses only to repulse her when she would have done anything he asked. She felt the tightening of his jaw against her hand, and only his unyielding grasp kept her from pulling away. But when he opened his eyes, she saw such raw desire in them that she froze.

Something in her expression must have stopped him.

He released her hand and slowly reached out to her, wiping an errant tear from the corner of her eye. "I'm sorry," he said. "I shouldn't have pushed you like this."

Another tear followed in the path of the first.

"I heard what you said this morning. There's no future for us. There never has been." He looked away, focused on some distant point as he drew in a ragged breath. When his gaze returned to hers, his eyes were dark, wide black orbs surrounded by clear, perfect blue. "But when I look at you, when we're alone like this, I want you. I wanted you the first time I saw you, and I want you more now." He brushed the second tear away. "When I touch you like this, the future doesn't matter."

She reached up to him, traced the lines that bracketed his mouth. God knew she'd fought it, but she wanted him the same way. When he looked into her eyes with such total honesty, it didn't matter how he made a living or that his livelihood was under attack. It didn't matter that he owed money or even that he'd just admitted they had no future together. She couldn't help the way she felt about him.

His skin was warm and firm. The shadow of his beard beneath her fingers invited her caress. For once she allowed her hands to wander over the planes of his face as she'd dreamed of doing countless other times. He clenched his jaw, but his eyes never wavered. He'd put the decision in her hands, but there was only one choice. With gentle pressure, she pulled him to her, meeting him halfway.

"I want you, too," she whispered against his lips. Then she kissed him with all the hunger stored up inside her.

Nick took over from there, rolling to his back, not breaking the kiss, but dragging her eagerly with him. He groaned once, a satisfying sound of long-suppressed desire set free. With strong, insistent hands, he lifted her until she lay atop the length of him. His chest was firm, with pliant muscles that flexed with every movement. His arms formed a solid circle of strength around her as he ran possessive fingers through her hair with one hand, while he caressed the curves of her body with the other. Beneath her, as he pressed her closer to him, she felt the unmistakable proof of his hunger.

Every heated inch of him burned into her, and sensation blended into hazy, all-encompassing awareness as he unleashed the passion in his kiss. She felt as if she were floating, free of earthly bonds, with Nick's touch and his kiss the source of all things in the universe. To touch him was to touch the sun, and suddenly, she couldn't get close enough.

Her body came alive with want, with need. Where his fingers passed, he left a burning trail, and the spiraling sensation gathered and centered deep inside, erupting in a fountain of passion. His kiss, the insistent touch of his lips, the deep searching duel of tongue against tongue was not enough. Chills skittered down her spine when she felt his hand against her breast and the answering siren call of her nipple against his palm. The world shifted.

Suddenly she lay on her back on the blanket. The welcome heat of Nick's body disappeared, along with his kiss. Opening her eyes, she cried out in protest. But Nick was there, watching her with passion-filled eyes so blue they burned a hole into her soul. He gave her a reassuring smile, then brushed her lips leisurely before moving on to the sensitized realm of her neck. Satisfied that he wasn't leaving her, she welcomed the weight of his body and the heat of his touch sliding up beneath her shirt. Giving passion free rein, she sought the warm skin beneath his.

Fabric became a barrier, and with clumsy fingers she fought the buttons that held his shirt together while he worked magic with his tongue in her ear. She needed to hurry, to run her fingers through the soft curling hair on his chest, but he'd slowed nearly to a stop, exploring, tasting, setting her senses afire. When his shirt wouldn't give way, he obligingly pulled it free of his belt and threw it off. Just as quickly, he drew hers over her head, then returned to his pursuits, skin against skin, and time ceased to matter. Her urgency disappeared, soothed by contact, and she abandoned herself to the pleasure of his attentions.

With soft touches and whispered praises, he fueled her passion, making her feel free and beautiful in his arms. Piece by piece, her clothing fell under his determined onslaught, and with each new revelation, he paid homage to her body with a look, a touch, a kiss.

When there was nothing of her left unexplored, she followed suit, searching out and tasting the hills and hollows of his body, learning every inch of him as he had her. At last he held himself above her, and as they came together, she looked into his eyes and saw the passion there. Slowly, thoroughly, he kissed her and set the final tribute into motion. Sensation spiraled until there was no awareness but of him, no desire but to please, no more pleasure than to receive.

"Open your eyes, Emma," Nick whispered. "Look at me."

His eyes riveted her gaze. The blue sky framed his face in brilliance, and the dam holding the tide back began to crumble.

"Let yourself go. Let yourself fly and take me with you."

He kissed her, demanding nothing less than everything she had to give. She felt herself slipping, gaining speed, sliding headlong. For one perfect moment she balanced on the edge of ecstasy, then she let go. With a cry of unqualified pleasure, she wrapped herself around him while sensation exploded through her. Nick gave one last mighty thrust and followed. He collapsed above her and together they flew, soaring in sweeping circles, round and round, until he brought her safely back to earth.

Nick lay with his eyes closed, replete. Little by little awareness returned. The tranquillity of water cascading over rocks, the call of birds in the trees, the rustle of leaves as a breeze stirred in the aspens above them. Beneath him, Emma lay peacefully, one finger idly tracing his shoulder back and forth.

He shifted, taking the brunt of his weight off her, but he didn't roll away. He wanted to savor the soul-deep satisfaction of her lying with him, languid from his loving. Everything about her felt right, from her long, perfect legs to her soft, gold-flecked skin, to the way her breast fit perfectly in his palm. Making love to her had been an exercise in giving—and receiving—and though his body still trembled from the exertion, he felt desire growing again.

He lay with his head pillowed between her breasts, savoring the soft beat of her heart, the gentle rise and fall of her breathing. It would be easy to spend the rest of the day, the rest of the week, here alone with her. Reaching up, he traced the curve of her breast and watched her nipple bead in reaction. He was contemplating doing the same with his tongue, when below his ear he heard a different sound—the protesting rumble of an empty stomach. Emma stilled, and he raised his head, smiling.

"Was that a hint?"

She smiled back. "I guess so. You promised me food an hour ago."

He pulled the bunch of grapes close. Choosing a fat, juicy one from the middle, he plucked it and held it for her. She reached for it, her lips brushing his fingers, reawakening the last of his sleeping passion. Sliding up even with her, he kissed her, tasting the sweet flavor of the grape on her tongue and the sweeter taste that was uniquely hers. But her stomach growled again, and he reeled in his desires. First he had to feed her lunch.

Sitting up, he looked around for her clothing. Most of it he found in a pile nearby, and he tossed it to her. "Better put these on before you get a sunburn on that perfect little body of yours.''

She blushed with self-conscious reserve that belied the temptress she'd been only a few minutes earlier, and he had to turn away before he ravished her again. While she dressed, he pulled on his pants and walked over to the spring. When he returned, she was clothed and gathering her hair at the nape of her neck.

"Leave it," he said, stepping up behind her. "I like it down."

Holding her hair back with one hand, she reached for the clip with the other. "If I do, I'll never get a comb through it tonight."

He kneeled behind her, taking the clip from her with one hand and combing through her tangled locks with the other. "I'll brush it for you." He'd welcome the opportunity. "Leave it down."

She turned with an expression that said she, too, could imagine the scene he envisioned, and for a moment he forgot everything but the sight of her, aroused and pleasantly disheveled in front of him. Recalling himself, he leaned back on his heels, and began gathering together the lunch they'd abandoned earlier.

Emma stood stiffly and walked toward the spring, undoubtedly trying to ease sore muscles. He shouldn't have brought her so far the first time out, but he wouldn't change a moment of this day if he could. She had an ugly bruise on the back of one thigh, but he had plans to ease the pain of it shortly.

When she returned, he was leaning against an aspen tree. He'd cut fat slices of cheese and bread, and arranged them with the grapes on a napkin beside him. "Your meal awaits."

Emma laughed. He liked the sound of it. There hadn't been nearly enough laughter between them. Patting the blanket in front of him, he assumed the role of waiter, but when she hesitated, he pulled her down between his knees, settling her against his chest. He wanted her where he could touch her.

"Comfortable?"

She leaned back. "Very."

"Good. Now tell me what you'd like to eat so I can feed you."

A half hour later, Emma lay with her head in his lap and the half-eaten cluster of grapes on her chest. She plucked one, examined it and held it up to him. He took it, nibbling at her finger, trying to capture it with his teeth. The horses grazed in the midafternoon sun, and a soft breeze played with tendrils of Emma's hair. He couldn't remember a time when he'd felt more at peace.

The silence was broken by the muffled sound of his cellular phone. He grimaced. "There are times when modern conveniences get in the way of old-fashioned solitude," he said. "Ignore it."

"It might be important," Emma replied. She reached for his shirt.

He knew no one would be calling unless it *was* important, but he still resented the intrusion. "Ignore it anyhow."

She smiled, pulled the telephone from his pocket and answered it. A second later, she handed it to him, chuckling. "It's for you."

He took the offending phone from her. Next time, he'd leave the damn thing at home. "This is Nick."

"Hey, Nick," Pete replied. "How's it going up there?"

"Fine. What's up?"

"Martin Johansen called a few minutes ago. He's headed up here with his mare. Should be here in a couple of hours."

Darn! Johansen was the first breeder to contact him about stud services. He'd offered a hefty fee, and Nick knew he should be there when the man arrived. "His mare's been tested?"

"Healthy as a horse." Pete chuckled at his own joke.

Nick looked down at Emma. Her very presence, so relaxed and close invited his touch, but the outside world beckoned. For the moment at least, their time alone was over. "All right, we'll head out in a few minutes."

"Problems?" she asked when he tossed the phone onto the blanket.

"I've got a horse breeder on his way here with a mare in season. We have to get back to the ranch."

Disappointment colored her face, but she sat up, resigned. "Then we'd better get packed." She began gathering the remains of their lunch together.

Her calm acceptance popped the rosy bubble coloring his world for the past hour. With the return of the real world came the return of the very real problems in it. Who did he think he was kidding? Making love with her had been exquisite, the best he'd ever experienced. But it changed nothing. They'd foolishly allowed themselves to taste the forbidden fruit, and now they must live with the knowledge that it would forever be out of their reach.

Emma tossed his shirt at him, turning his words against him. "Better watch out, cowboy. You're liable to get sunburned."

He caught the shirt, fighting back the certain knowledge that he'd live to regret making love with her. He wanted to stop time at the one perfect moment when she'd opened her heart to him, the one moment when the rest of the world couldn't get between them. Catching hold of her hand, he pulled her to him. "Not so fast."

She looked up, and her sad smile said she was caught in the same tide of emotion.

"There's something else I wanted to say."

"What's that?"

She would leave, but she wasn't gone yet. "This." He wrapped his arms full around her and kissed her.

*   *   *

The sound of Cochise's trumpeted challenge greeted them when they approached the ranch yard. It was followed by the answering challenge of a second stallion and a third. Something wasn't right. Uneasy, Nick spurred Grayson forward.

He found a chaotic confusion of dust and noise. Cochise was pacing inside the corral, snorting, his ears back. Not far away, a strange truck and trailer were parked, with a nervous sorrel mare tied to the back. Around her, the three young studs Frank Howell had shod that morning fought for one-upmanship, all three of them aroused and ready to fight. Pete was swinging a lariat over his head while Bob and Martin Johansen tried to herd the three horses away from the mare.

"What's going on?" Emma asked as she caught up with him. Cochise began pawing at the corral poles.

"Trouble," he answered, untying the rope on his saddle. "Stay here. I'm going to help Pete." Thank God he was riding a gelding. Kicking Grayson into motion, he dove into the melee.

Pete's rope lashed out and caught one horse around the neck. Turning to the other two, Nick swung his own rope over his head, but before he could take aim, they spun around. Pete had his hands full with a kicking, snorting stallion, and Nick moved out of his way before he tried again.

What happened next seemed to take place in slow motion. The two remaining horses made a break for the front of the pickup, but Emma and Vixen cut them off. The second horse turned, but the first screamed and reared, pawing the air only inches from Emma's head. Nick watched helplessly while her hands flew up to protect herself. Vixen backed away and swung out, ready to bolt. Emma held her seat, and in a heartbeat it was over, but Nick's heart lodged in his throat, and he found it hard to breathe. Damn it, he'd told her to stay back!

Emma caught the reins and brought Vixen under control while the panicked stallion broke free. The second horse circled around the horse trailer, and the mare tied there struggled against the rope. Cochise trumpeted again, and the mare swung around, snorting in fear.

Nick pushed Grayson between her and the young stallion and reached for the rope holding her in place. Jerking the knot loose, he dragged her away while Bob and Johansen circled behind them. Emma was at the point of following when he turned.

"Take this mare into the barn," he shouted above the noise. "I'll get the other two."

She nodded and reached for the lead rope. She was pale, but appeared all right.

Behind him, Cochise fought at the corral poles. Bits of wood flew out from under his sharp hooves. Catching Bob's eye, Nick motioned toward the angry stallion. "See if you can get a lead on Cochise and tie him down before he breaks a leg."

Bob nodded, and Nick turned back to the others. Swinging the rope over his head again, he went after the horse nearest him. This time he caught the errant stallion neatly in his loop. Minutes later, it was over. The three young studs were safely corralled, and Cochise was tied where he couldn't harm himself.

Turning his sweating gelding over to Bob, Nick raced toward the barn. "Emma?"

"In here," she called to his immense relief.

Not only had she taken the mare inside, but she'd judiciously pulled the enormous doors closed. He threw one open and peered inside.

Emma had the mare tied to a ring on a support post. Vixen was secured to the gate of a stall. Emma stood at her head, her hand buried in the horse's mane. The other mare jerked her head when he appeared, but she'd calmed enough not to shy at his intrusion.

"Are you okay?" he asked when he saw Emma's enormous eyes.

"I'm fine," she reassured him. Her voice quavered only slightly. "Is everything out there okay?"

"It is now." In two strides he reached her, and in the third she was in his arms.

"What the hell kind of operation is this?" Johansen followed him angrily into the barn. He went straight for his mare, running anxious fingers over her shining coat. "I didn't bring this horse here to be trampled by three half-grown, hormone-crazed stallions. You'd better have a damn good explanation, Barlow."

Emma bristled at the angry tirade, but Nick held her silent with the pressure of his fingers on her arm. Outside, Cochise voiced his dissatisfaction with the turn of events, and the mare snorted and tugged against her lead.

It took fifteen minutes to soothe the angry breeder. Finally, when he was assured his mare was unhurt, Johansen agreed to proceed. Nick let Johansen supervise, and after seeing to his horse, the man left, saying he'd return in the morning to complete the transaction.

Nick found Emma tending to Vixen. She'd left, red-faced when Johansen led his mare into the corral. Under other circumstances, he'd probably have teased her about her retreat, but the image of flying hooves only inches from her head wouldn't leave him.

"Bob will take care of Vixen," he said. "I want to talk to you."

She shook her head and stood her ground. "Bob has plenty to keep him busy."

He caught her hand. "This is important, Emma."

She stilled. "I know what you're going to say. You told me to stay back, and I didn't."

"You could have been killed."

"But I wasn't, and you needed the help."

"That's not the point."

"What is the point?"

The point was he'd brought her here to protect her, and he'd done a poor job of it. The point was Andrew Warren had the upper hand. The point was somehow Emma had come to mean far too much to him, and he'd only been able to watch helplessly when she needed him.

"I'm okay, Nick. And right now you have much bigger problems than whether or not I follow orders."

His protest died. She was right, though he hadn't finished with her yet.

"What are you going to do?"

"Pete is calling everyone together. While we wait, I'm going to have a look at the corral where those three horses were penned."

"I'll go with you."

"All right," Nick said when everyone had gathered together. "I want to know what happened." Emma stood in the background, listening. He was anxious for her take on the matter.

No one answered.

"Pete?"

"You saw almost as much as I did," Pete answered. "We were unloading Johansen's mare when the three studs jumped out from behind the stable like the devil himself was on their tails. They caught scent of the mare and all hell broke loose. You got here about a minute later."

"Who's been here today?"

"Nobody. Johansen's was the first truck down the driveway since Frank left."

"When did Frank leave?"

"Around three," Bob filled in. "We had trouble with Red, and it took the better part of the morning to get his shoes on.

When Frank finished this afternoon, he said something about having to be somewhere and left.''

''And no one else has been here?''

''Nobody.''

''Then how did that gate get open?'' The gate hadn't merely been ajar, it had been propped wide-open, just as the one in the pasture had been. And like before, Nick hadn't been able to make any sense of the confusion of tracks in the soft dirt.

No one knew.

A sick feeling settled in the pit of his stomach, and he looked over at Emma. Her expression said they were thinking the same thing. There was a traitor on the ranch, and it was one of his own men.

Chapter Eleven

Nick needed time to think. Turning to Bob, he said, "Get those three horses out to the east pasture until Johansen leaves with his mare. We don't want any more scenes like this one."

Bob nodded and left. Was he the one? Nick hoped not.

To the rest of the hands, he said, "Wrap it up for tonight. It's getting late." The men disbursed. Was it one of them?

Pete waited quietly. When only Emma remained in earshot, Nick gave his final instructions. "Lock this place down, Pete. No one comes in or out. No one."

Pete nodded, his expression grim. Could it be him?

Emma waited until Pete left. "How well do you know your men?"

He knew all of them, and until this moment, he would have staked his life that every one of them was trustworthy. "Apparently not well enough."

She slipped a timid hand around his waist, and he completed the embrace, drawing her close. She was worried. Given what she'd told him this morning, she must be beside herself. "Don't worry, Emma," he reassured her. "We're going to win this one." He only wished he knew how.

The sun was sitting low in the sky, casting long shadows across the barnyard, the same sun that had shone so brightly on them earlier that afternoon. He felt as if the shadows extended across his soul. At the rate they were going, it was only a matter of time until one of Warren's schemes worked. Today, luck alone had saved him. If Johansen's mare had been injured, he'd be discredited forever as a horse breeder.

But how could he keep watch on an entire ranch when he couldn't even trust the people who worked with him? Somehow he had to flush out the traitor. He had to protect his land and his animals, and he had to keep Emma safe. Up until now, he'd done a poor job of it. Frustration had him tied in knots. Only Emma's warm touch felt right. He looked down at her. She wanted to help. But how could he ask her to, knowing what all of this must be doing to her?

"Let's go inside."

Emma detoured to her car. "I was looking for some papers this morning," she said. "Go ahead, I'll catch up with you."

She trailed her hand down to the tip of his finger before letting go, and regardless of what the next days brought, he thought having her around made it all bearable. He decided to wait for her.

She opened the car door, still smiling back at him, but when she bent inside, she backed out as if she'd been stung.

"Nick!"

He strode over to her, his imagination conjuring a dozen frightening possibilities. Looking where her gaze was directed, he stopped short. Hot air escaped the open door, accompanied by the plastic smell of a closed car. The seat cover had been slashed, repeatedly, until the vinyl was gone.

Emma began to shake, and she literally fell against him.

Thank God she wasn't hurt. The damage to the car was minor, but this was no harmless prank. First the brakes and now this. But this seemed so much more violent than the incident with her brakes. Was this a warning that next time she—and not her car—would suffer the attack?

Nick muttered an expletive. Backing away, he took her with him. "Don't touch anything. This time the sheriff will listen."

"I'd like to help you more, Nick, but you just haven't given me much to go on."

The sheriff signed his report with a flourish—the consummate politician, Emma thought irritably. He'd been called out here to see *her* car, but he'd addressed all his comments to Nick. She wondered if he'd have enough to "go on" if it were an election year.

"I'll admit you've got a problem here. But I need more than three moldy bales and an act of vandalism to arrest Andrew Warren. There's no proof Warren had anything to do with any of this. You don't even know when the car seat was slashed. It could have happened any time since Ms. Reardon arrived."

Nick looked as if he were ready to take the man's excuses and shove them down his throat. "What do you propose, Sheriff?"

The man shifted uneasily. "You're gonna have to keep your eyes open. I can send a couple of boys out here on patrol, but this is a big ranch. I don't have the manpower to cover it all."

"That's it?"

"Give me something substantial, and I'll do more. I've done some checking around town, and to be honest, the only person who's been asking questions about you is this little lady here." He gestured toward Emma, making her want to remind him that she was adult and literate and very much able to talk herself.

Nick's voice grew dangerously soft. "Well, since she's been the object of two attacks, we can safely eliminate her from the list of suspects, can't we?"

"Now Nick, don't get your hackles up. I'm only saying we don't have much to go on. I can't arrest a man because you have a gut feeling about him."

"I have more than a gut feeling!"

"But I need evidence." He tore off one copy of the report and handed it to Emma. "I'll send somebody out here to-morrow to dust the car for prints, ma'am. For now, that's all I can do." Tipping his hat at her, he climbed into his cruiser.

Emma watched him until he drove away. "We're on our own."

"Yes." Nick nearly spat the word. He looked at her, two deep lines etched between his eyes, and took a deep breath. "Maybe you should head out behind him. You're not safe here."

She'd been waiting for that. "We've already been through this, Nick."

He sighed. "I agreed to bring you here to keep you safe. Obviously I can't protect you."

Stubborn fury rose up. "I'm not the 'little woman' to be protected, and I resent being treated like I am. I haven't been harmed. I thought we were working together."

He looked at her with tired eyes. "It's gone too far."

"Well, I'm sorry to ruin your macho image of yourself, Nick Barlow, but I can take care of myself. I came here to do a job and I'm not leaving until its done."

"You've got your interview."

"Yes, I've got my interview. But Andrew Warren is trying to intimidate me, and I won't let him get away with it."

"But we both know you could be in danger."

"I could be in harm's way at home, too. Warren obviously

thinks I know something about him, something big enough to risk warning me off. Frankly, I'd rather have you at my back."

He didn't answer.

Frustrated, she went on the offensive. "What about you? You can't cut and run."

"No, but that's no reason for you to stay. I'd feel better if you left."

"I'll feel better when we expose Warren for what he is." She reached out for his arm. "You can kick me off the ranch, but I won't stop until I get to the truth."

He pinned her with his eyes. "Why are you doing this, Emma?"

For you! The brash answer sprang to her lips, but never quite made it past them. Why *was* she doing this? Her job? If anyone else had insulted her in the myriad of ways Nick had, she'd have sliced him to ribbons with her contempt. From the beginning, it had been more than her job. She had what she'd come here to get, but she couldn't bring herself to leave. The very thought sent panic racing through her.

They'd started something this afternoon, and she needed for it to mean more than a cheap thrill in a wooded glade, even though it had no chance of ever becoming anything else. If she left now, it would end here. Even a faceless enemy posed less threat to her peace of mind than leaving Nick behind. *She was in love with him.*

No! She couldn't be in love. Not with a man whose very life-style represented everything that frightened her most. His whole future balanced on the top of a mountain being eroded an inch at a time until it caved in, right into Andrew Warren's hands.

"Answer me, Emma. What do you expect to gain from staying here?"

She had to think. Alone. Pressing shaking fingers to her

temples, she drew a ragged breath. ''I can't talk about this now.'' Without waiting for a reply, she brushed past him.

Nick watched her break into a run and felt like a first-class jerk. Why hadn't he seen how upset she was? The last thing he wanted to do was push her away, but she wasn't safe here as long as that bastard was out there.

She ran into the house, looking tiny and frail, and it was all he could do to keep from following her. She was gutsy and smart. He *wanted* her around. But he wouldn't let her stay at the risk of losing her. *Losing her?* She wasn't his to lose. She never would be.

His own head began to ache. Following at a slower pace, he went inside. It was less than an hour until sunset, and by the time darkness fell, he meant to be outside where he could keep an eye on things personally.

Emma slid neck-deep into the water. Her fingers were beginning to pucker, but the luxuriant suds clung to her skin, and she couldn't make herself get out of the tub yet. It was calm here, quiet. Lifting a foot, she toyed with the water drop clinging to the old-fashioned faucet and wished fervently that the hot water would ease her troubled thoughts as easily as it did her aching muscles.

In the hallway, she heard Nick's footsteps. He paused outside the door, and she waited, scarcely breathing, for him to say something. Her body remembered what her mind wanted to forget, and it called out to him. But after a moment he continued on his way.

Disappointment warred with relief. If she closed her eyes, she could picture the blue of his eyes, the way his dimples teased his cheek, his long, powerful body striding toward her. She could almost feel the reverence of his touch when he'd made love to her, and no matter how many ways she tried to neutralize her feelings, she ached to make love with him again. If only she were free to let the love flow.

But how could she? Even if Andrew Warren disappeared this minute, Nick still ran a ranch with all the pitfalls she knew only too well. At best, his way of life was a gamble, and the mere thought of returning to that kind of insecurity sent chills down her spine. She loved him, but they had no future together, even if he asked her to stay.

Maybe he was right. Maybe it was time for her to leave. She'd been of no help so far. And if Nick felt he had to protect her, she was more of a hindrance to him than a help. But she couldn't leave it this way. She needed closure.

Nick's footsteps returned in the hallway, but this time he passed without slowing. She listened dispiritedly until his confident stride faded down the stairway. Unlike her, he faced his problems. He didn't retreat behind a closed door to dwell on what could not be changed.

Daylight was fading, and the water beginning to cool. Wearily she rose out of the tub.

The house was deserted when she went downstairs. Maria had gone for the evening and Nick's office was dark and still. She wandered the empty rooms until the silence grew too loud, then turned on the television. After a restless hour, she went to bed.

After another hour of tossing and turning, she realized that Nick wasn't going to come to her. He meant to spend the night outside, keeping watch. But he was only one man, and he couldn't be everywhere at once. He needed help.

The night breeze filtering in the window beckoned, and she gave up trying to sleep. Slipping into some clothes, she went silently downstairs and out the door.

With only the light of the stars to guide her, she wandered toward the stable. Nick was out here somewhere, listening to the night noises. Waiting.

A black form loomed out of the blacker doorway of the storeroom. She jumped backward, her voice caught in her throat. The attacker was here, and she'd walked right into his arms. Her feet turned to lead when he reached out for her.

"It's all right, Emma. It's me." Nick's reassuring voice broke through her terror. Air rushed into her lungs and she weaved dizzily before he caught her by the shoulders.

"Nick?" she gasped, her heart hammering in her chest.

"What are you doing out here? You went to bed more than an hour ago."

Weak with relief, she muttered, "I couldn't sleep." Some help she'd be in a crisis.

She thought she saw him smile, and he relaxed his grip. "Come in here and sit down before you fall."

She might have felt more perturbed at his words had she not stumbled over the doorstep. When he caught her again, she let him guide her in the gloom. Just inside, her toe bumped into something solid. He turned her and pressed her down. "What is this?"

"Those three bales of hay," he answered as he sat down beside her. "I figured I might as well put them to good use."

He had. He'd stacked them, thrown a heavy blanket over them, and made a comfortable chair.

"Where were you headed just now?" he asked close to her ear, his breath brushing her cheek.

Feeling foolish, she whispered the first thing that came to mind. "I wanted to visit Vixen."

He leaned back against the hay bale, supporting himself with his elbows. "In the middle of the night?"

"I told you, I couldn't sleep."

He chuckled silently. "Well, you'll need a key, then. Help yourself. The keys are on that back wall there."

He was on to her, and she might as well drop the ruse. "Well, maybe I'll just visit with you."

"Good idea."

The seat was small for two people, and she felt the heat of his leg burning into her thigh. She shifted.

"Sore?" he whispered.

The hot bath had eased most of her soreness. "Not bad."

"How's the bruise on your leg?"

Heat flooded her cheeks. The bruise was closer to her bottom than her leg, and she'd forgotten that he'd seen it very clearly that afternoon. "It's fine."

He chuckled again, but said no more. Uncomfortable with the silence, she searched for a new subject. "Have you seen anything?"

"Nothing until you came strolling by."

"Is anyone else out here?"

"Pete's out by the barn somewhere."

"You don't think it's him, do you?"

He seemed to think about that for awhile. "I don't want to believe it's *any* of my men. But no, I don't think it's Pete."

"We need to make a plan."

"Yes." But he said nothing else.

She tried to think of something, but anything that came to mind seemed implausible. Unless they could figure out who they were up against, they might as well be shooting in the dark. Nick had already set a trap, and she couldn't think of anything more productive than that.

He shifted once, making her more aware of his proximity, and distracting her from her ponderings. His nearness erased all the nervous energy that had kept her wound up earlier. She felt herself relaxing, and the problems of the afternoon gave way to more pleasant memories of the day. A yawn escaped.

"Tired?"

"I could hardly deny it after that, could I?" She chuckled.

He slipped an arm around her, pulling her against his chest.

Snuggling against him, she said, "You must be tired, too. How long do you plan to stay out here?" His heart beat steadily against her ear, and she heard him take a deep breath.

"I thought I'd play it by ear."

"Then I'll keep you company."

Nick leaned back against the hay, settling Emma more comfortably against him. She smelled clean—of green apples and scented soap, and he had to resist the urge to bury his nose in her hair. She hadn't bothered with a bra when she'd dressed, and he liked the unbound feel of her breast against his arm. He liked the way she leaned against his chest so trustingly. Hell, he liked holding her, regardless of the circumstances.

He'd been sitting here rehashing the day's events when he'd heard the screen door open. It hadn't been his intention to have her join him when he'd stopped her in the yard. He'd merely meant to keep her from stumbling into something—or someone—but now that she was here, he was glad. He didn't really expect anything more to happen tonight, but he'd always found the night sounds of the barnyard made thinking easier.

She said nothing more, and before long her breathing slowed and deepened. Smiling in the dark, he wrapped his other arm around her while she slept. She wasn't dressed for a night in the open, certainly not for sleeping on a bale of hay, but for now she felt too good to send away.

He turned his thoughts back to the problems dogging them both. His plan to wait and watch wasn't working, and he hated the idea of how it was scaring Emma. So far he'd managed to hold his own, but how much longer could he expect to be so lucky? And why couldn't he shake that feeling that he was missing something?

One by one, he went over each of the mishaps, from the hours before the wheel came off his horse trailer to the minutes following today's fiasco. Try as he would, he couldn't come up with a common denominator. Whoever was doing this was very familiar with his operation. He still thought the key to catching the guy lay in the rack of keys behind him. Only he and Pete and Emma knew of the trap he'd set, unless that bumbling fool Frank Howell had tipped his hand. It was still his best bet.

An hour passed, and then two. Everything remained quiet, with only the sound of Emma's breathing. The moon rose over the eastern horizon, and Nick was ready to call it a night when he thought he heard something.

Footfalls. Heavy ones, grating on rock.

Pete wouldn't be so careless as to let himself be heard.

"Emma," he whispered, his lips just above her ear. "Wake up."

She jerked awake, and he touched her lips with his finger. When he was certain she wouldn't cry out, he loosened his hold on her. "I heard something. You stay here, and I'll go see what it is."

She nodded, and he stood, draping his jacket over her shoulders. Then, walking noiselessly, he slipped outside.

He met Pete inching along the side of the barn. "Did you hear something?" Pete whispered when he drew near.

"Yeah. Sounded like someone walking on gravel." That meant he was in the driveway. Pointing toward the house, Nick motioned for Pete to take one side of the yard while he took the other. Together, they worked their way from shadow to shadow until there was no cover left. But they found nothing.

Pete pulled off his hat. "This is the only gravel around here," he said, scratching his head. "He can't have gotten past us."

Unless they'd been mistaken, Nick thought. But he knew what he'd heard. They split up again, working their way around the house. *Emma!* His heart skipped a beat. If the intruder *had* gotten past them, she was alone and unprotected in the very building the prowler was likely to hit.

He turned back, moving as quickly as he could without giving himself away. If she was in trouble, he needed the advantage of surprise on his side, but it took everything he had to keep from running headlong.

Everything seemed quiet, just as he'd left it. But when he reached the hay bales stacked inside the door of the storeroom, they were empty. "Emma?" He chanced a whisper, hoping against hope that she'd merely moved for some reason.

"Nick?" Her answering whisper came from a dark corner.

Relief so intense that he nearly collapsed flooded his senses. "Where are you?"

"Over here." Walking blind, he moved toward her voice. His foot ran up against a box of some kind, and he stumbled sideways. A moment later he felt her hand probing the space in front of her. She grasped him, stepped over something and into his arms.

"Are you all right?"

In her free hand she held a club of some sort. Apparently she was better off than he was. Her hand was steady, but he could feel his shaking. "I'm fine."

"What happened?"

"I heard someone moving around out there, and I thought it was you, so I called out. Whoever it was stopped and dropped something—it sounded heavy. Then he took off running. I wasn't sure if he'd come back or not, so I found this board and hid behind the workbench. But I didn't hear anything else until you came in."

"He didn't try to come in here?"

"I don't think he was headed this way. It sounded more like he was aiming for the stable." She paused. "I'm sorry I scared him away…"

"Don't be," he said wryly. "Pete and I missed him entirely. I shouldn't have left you alone." He gave up whispering. Whoever had been out there was probably long gone. "Let's go see what he dropped."

They worked their way back to the doorway. Pete met them just outside.

"Where'd you disappear to?"

Nick explained. With the aid of Pete's flashlight, they found a bag of feed lying in the dirt outside the feed room door. Kneeling, Nick examined it.

"What do you make of it?" Pete asked.

The bag appeared to be intact. "I don't know," Nick answered. "The seam looks okay."

"What about the bottom?"

Nick ran his fingers along the bottom seam. It was rough. "Shine that light here," he directed.

Emma held the light closer. The binding was crooked, and when he pulled it away, a second set of stitch marks showed in the paper.

Pete muttered and stood up.

"What is it?" Emma asked.

"We won't be able to find out until daylight," Nick answered. "But my guess is there's more in this bag than horse feed."

"He must have meant to put it in the stack with the rest of the feed," Pete mused.

"But he didn't try to get the key." Emma said thoughtfully.

Nick grimaced. "Either he already has one, or he planned to set the bag down and come back for it."

"Can you trace the bag?"

Satisfaction took hold. "Yes, as a matter of fact, I can." Heaving the bag up, he shouldered it. "Let's all get some sleep. Tomorrow we'll find out whose bag this is."

"I sold that bag to you, Nick." The clerk didn't even bother to look up his records. "Everyone else who buys horse feed uses a different formula."

Tension knotted Emma's stomach. She knew Nick hated

the idea of one of his men turning traitor, but more and more, the evidence pointed toward someone working on his ranch.

As soon as Johansen left, they'd driven into town, stopping first at the sheriff's office, making certain he saw the altered bag. From there, they'd driven with the sheriff to Jack Wyatt's office, where they'd opened it. Jack had promised to send samples of the contents for laboratory analysis. Now they were trying to identify who'd purchased the bag.

"What about the extra bags I returned from the last delivery?" Nick asked. "Has anyone bought any of them?"

The clerk punched in some numbers on his computer. "We brought back a hundred bags, and my inventory says that's what we have on hand. We could count them if you like."

He led them to a corner of the warehouse behind the store. The bags were stacked on pallets in the back. Emma counted them twice, hoping somehow her first tally had been inaccurate, but every bag was there.

With grim lines bracketing his mouth, Nick thanked the clerk and ushered her out. Deep in thought, he walked her to his truck, opened the door and held it for her, apparently unaware that he'd steered her to the driver's side—something he hadn't done before. Their relationship had changed subtly.

She climbed in and scooted across the seat. Even though she knew he wasn't aware of what he'd done, the intimacy felt good to her. Natural. Then he found her hand and squeezed it.

"I guess that answers that."

"Someone tampered with your own feed," she said unnecessarily. "You wouldn't have caught that bag as easily as you caught the moldy hay, would you?"

"No."

Wishing for a way to reassure him somehow, she squeezed his hand. "Well, since Pete was with you last night, at least you can eliminate him from the list. Is there some way we can confirm where everyone else was?"

Nick nodded thoughtfully. "If you called for me, he knows both of us were out there. But I doubt if he knows about Pete. I'll have him send out some feelers."

He started the truck and backed out while Emma puzzled over what she knew.

"You're sure you heard the guy walking on gravel?"

"Positive. That's why Pete and I were circling the driveway."

"Then when we get home, let's look at it in daylight. Maybe we can figure out how he got past you."

"And how he got back again without running into us." He checked his watch, then smiled down at her, the worry in his expression softening as she leaned against him.

Nick stopped the truck abruptly when they rounded the tree marking the ranch yard. Lost in thought, Emma looked up. He was staring hard at a gold sports car parked in front of the house, but she couldn't be certain what she read in his expression. Curious, she looked closer as he put the truck back into gear. A woman got out of the car, a strikingly beautiful woman who seemed to be waiting for them.

She was the woman Emma had always wanted to be. Her golden hair cascaded down the back of an expensive silk dress designed to reveal every flawless curve of her body. Tanned, shapely legs extended from her fashionably short skirt to elegant Italian sandals. Behind oversize glasses, she peered at Nick and Emma, her expertly made up face set in a pouty mask. Slowly, she removed the glasses, exposing eyes every bit as blue and penetrating as Nick's.

Emma's confidence evaporated. Nick's subtle attentions had made her feel pretty and feminine, but with this model of perfection in front of her, she was painfully aware of her frazzled appearance, like an ugly duckling, conspicuous in the presence of a swan.

Swallowing hard, she searched out Nick's reaction to finding a perfect specimen in his own backyard. But his expression remained carefully neutral. He stopped the truck even with the sports car, and the woman approached.

"Hello, Lynette."

Chapter Twelve

The temperature dropped ten degrees with those two words. Nick's voice was edged with cold steel, and for the first time Emma saw the contempt he held for his ex-wife.

Lynette's expression hardened. "Now, Nicky, you're not still holding our divorce against me, are you?"

"No. I have a whole new list."

She seemed startled at that, but refrained from commenting. Instead, her glance strayed past him to Emma, fell to the seat where Emma's leg touched Nick's, then rose to meet her eyes. Emma wanted to cringe. But years of practice served her well. She returned the glance with poise.

Nick must have felt her tension. He broke the silence. "Emma, this is my ex-wife, Lynette. Lynette, Emma Reardon."

From somewhere deep inside, Emma mustered the courage to greet the woman amiably. She smiled, murmured her greeting with assurance.

"What can we do for you, Lynette?"

Emma heard the "we" in Nick's words and glanced up at him. Whatever he thought about her continued presence in private, he'd apparently decided to present a front of solidarity toward others.

Lynette smiled. "Oh, I think you'll be glad to see me today."

Nick was noncommittal.

"I brought some papers for you to sign." She held up a manila envelope, unmoved by Nick's stone-faced silence.

"Lynette, you know I don't sign anything unless my attorney's seen it first."

Lynette frowned. "This is different, Nick." She looked around. "Can we discuss it inside? It's hot out here, and that housekeeper you hired refused even to let me in your office."

The beginnings of a dimple danced in Nick's cheek, but he didn't allow the smile into his voice. "Be my guest." Nick shut off the engine, opened the door and slid out, then turned and pointedly waited for Emma.

She followed, still uncomfortably aware of her dowdy appearance. Lynette was tall, and with the advantage of her spiked heels, she towered over Emma. When the woman's glance casually drifted from her windblown hair to her wrinkled shirt to her untidy shoes, Emma could well imagine the impression forming in her mind. Just when her courage was deserting her, she felt Nick's reassuring hand on her shoulder.

"Relax," he whispered when Lynette turned up the walk ahead of them, "you're taller than you think you are." She looked up in time to catch his wink and flushed, wondering what other thoughts he'd read in her expression. But the knowledge that he supported her refueled her tottering self-esteem.

When they reached the kitchen Nick asked Maria to brew some tea.

"I'll leave you two to…" Emma trailed off awkwardly.

Whatever Lynette had come to discuss was clearly none of her business, but she *was* curious. Why had Lynette come here—especially now?

"Have some tea first." Nick's hand on her arm held her fast. "I'm sure Lynette won't mind waiting another few minutes."

Lynette's eyebrow curved up expressively, but she said nothing, and Nick gestured toward the living room. Emma started to follow, but she needed time to gather her scattered thoughts. With a murmured excuse, she detoured to the bathroom.

Why was Nick baiting his ex-wife? After seeing her, Emma found it hard to believe any man could remain unaffected by Lynette Barlow, but his greeting implied there was no love lost—or was there? Maybe he used contempt to cover deeper feelings.

Nick saw her insecurity, but she'd be damned if she'd let Lynette see it, too. Safely behind the closed door, she leaned against it and took three deep breaths. When she opened her eyes again, she caught her reflection in the mirror and studied it critically.

The frightened little girl was there. But so was the woman that girl had become, the discriminating reporter who covered billion-dollar business transactions for a national magazine. The woman who had successfully hidden her painful past for ten years. In the past few days, the two had blended together somehow. Their sharply defined differences had softened at the edges, until she wasn't sure where one ended and the other began anymore. She wasn't quite comfortable yet with the woman emerging, but Lynette need not know that.

Maybe Nick was right. Maybe she should give herself more credit. Taking a brush from her purse, she smoothed the worst of the tangles from her hair, then splashed some water on her face and tucked her shirt in. Whatever Lynette Barlow's unexpected visit meant, she was ready to face her.

Lynette had taken a chair near the fireplace, and Nick sat opposite her on the sofa. Apparently they'd taken advantage of her absence to discuss the business Lynette had brought with her. The manila envelope lay on the coffee table with several legal-size papers strewn across it, and they were talking almost amicably.

Both of them looked up when she walked in. "I'll come back if you'd rather—"

"No need," Nick replied. "We've finished."

Emma slipped into the chair opposite Lynette's, feeling ill at ease despite Nick's welcome. She felt Lynette's curious eyes on her again, and dug deep into her limited store of poise.

"Lynette is getting married," Nick said offhandedly.

Emma's eyes flew to him, then to his ex-wife. Lynette smiled brilliantly.

"To Andrew Warren?" The words slipped out, and she barely masked the doubt that accompanied them.

"You know him?" Though Lynette tried for a veneer of indifference, hope underlined her words, almost as if she were looking for someone to side with her in the enemy camp.

"Only by reputation."

"Emma is a feature writer for *American Business Monitor*," Nick said.

Lynette arched an eyebrow. "Then you know what a clever businessman he is."

Clever was hardly the word Emma would have used. "Yes, he's been in the news quite a lot."

Lynette's expression hardened. "I assume you're talking about those charges leveled against him last year."

"I didn't cover the story," Emma replied.

"Have you ever met him?" The challenge in her voice was unmistakable.

Nick stepped in. "As it happens, *I* met him about a month

ago," he said. "I don't suppose you know anything about that?"

If Lynette was hiding something, she was a very good actress. She turned to him, undisturbed. "Yes, Andrew had some idea of building a resort in the hills above here. I told him he'd never pry the land loose from you, but he insisted on giving it a try."

"How, exactly, did he find out about the area?" Nick kept his voice pleasant, but it was accusing just the same.

"A friend of his drove through here last summer. Larry spotted it and spent the winter drawing up plans. It's all he talked about for weeks," Lynette replied smoothly.

"You didn't add your two bits' worth?"

Lynette remained unruffled. "Andrew and I don't discuss business as a rule. We have other things to talk about."

"I find that hard to believe."

"That's your prerogative, of course. Andrew knows about you and me, but I had nothing to do with the project. I knew about the proposal only because Larry would talk of nothing else. He got to be rather tedious about it."

"Come now, Lynette. Since when did the prospect of making money bore you? As I recall, you spent a great deal of money trying to 'pry the land loose' from me. Don't tell me it wasn't for profit."

Lynette's composure slipped a notch. "I only want enough money to live comfortably, Nick, though I don't suppose I'll ever convince you of that." She seemed to have forgotten Emma's presence. "Believe it or not, other things mean much more to me."

"Like that flashy car outside?"

"Like love and companionship! God knows, I never got that here. You were too busy with your cows."

"Cattle."

"Whatever." Her eyes narrowed. "Why are you asking

me all these questions? I told Andrew you wouldn't sell, and you didn't. So what's the problem?''

"The problem, Lynette, is the method he's been using to try to change my mind.''

"Change your mind?'' Lynette looked truly bewildered. Emma had always found it easy to see through feigned surprise, and Lynette's seemed genuine.

"You heard me.''

"Are you implying that Andrew is trying to coerce you into selling to him?''

"Exactly.''

"Andrew wouldn't do that.'' She reached inside her purse and pulled out a gold cigarette case. "Oh, I'll admit he was in an ugly mood when he got back. I assume he ran into that impenetrable wall of yours.'' Pulling a cigarette free, she put it to her lips and lit it with a matching lighter, then blew the smoke into the air above Nick's head. "He and Larry didn't drop their plans immediately, but the project is dead.''

Nick waved the cloud of smoke aside. "Why do you say that?''

"They lost their financial backing. That's the reason I'm here.''

She paused, as if her presence explained itself, but try as she would, Emma couldn't see the connection.

Apparently, Nick couldn't, either. "I beg your pardon?''

Sighing, Lynette elaborated, but her eyes lit as she spoke. "We were planning a December wedding, but now that Andrew is unexpectedly free, we've decided to move the date up. Who knows when he'll be without a pet project again. We're leaving next week for Europe.'' A delicate flush crept into her cheeks.

Nick shoved an ashtray across the coffee table at her. "When did all of this happen?''

"Two days ago.'' Her voice sang with anticipation, and she forgot herself in her excitement, even stubbed the half-smoked cigarette out distractedly. She played a very convincing role of a woman in love. "I'm not taking the chance that something else steps in before we leave. That's why I brought these papers to you personally. I want to clear up the loose ends. I didn't think you'd mind."

Nick chuffed a mirthless chuckle. "Hardly."

Emma looked again at the papers strewn across the coffee table. What were they for?

"You're on the level, aren't you?" There was doubt in Nick's voice.

"Why else would I make that miserable long drive? Certainly not to commune with nature."

He seemed torn, as if he were weighing his options. Lynette frowned again. "You might show some emotion, Nick. Offer your felicitations. I'd think you'd be glad to be rid of me."

He came to a decision. "If you're going to marry the man, then you'd better listen to what I have to say." He outlined the happenings of the past few weeks. In detail. To her credit, Lynette didn't interrupt, but Emma could see her temper simmer.

"I'm surprised you'd go to such lengths to ruin my happiness," she said when he finished. Her voice seethed indignation. Her words bespoke feminine outrage—a woman whose man has been unfairly accused. "You've already tried and convicted Andrew, haven't you? Just because someone else leveled some charges at him, you think he's guilty. But the charges were dropped. No one ever seems to remember that. Well, he's promised me he won't deal with those people anymore, and I believe him."

She stood up. "If you have problems, find another scapegoat, because Andrew isn't involved." Turning toward the door, she added, "Just sign those papers, and have them back to my attorney by Wednesday. I wash my hands of this ranch and everyone on it."

She stalked out of the room, nearly running down Maria, who carried a tray laden with glasses of tea. The door slammed, followed shortly by the door of her automobile outside. A second later, the luxurious car roared to life. Gravel sprayed from beneath the tires as Lynette spun it around and out the driveway, and then all was silent but the clink of ice settling in a glass.

"Come in, Maria," Nick said, hastily making room on the coffee table for the tray she carried. "Lynette changed her mind," he added unnecessarily.

Maria muttered something under her breath and set the tray down. Emma could only watch, bemused. For some reason, she focused on the glasses. No sprigs of mint decorated them, and the idea that Lynette didn't warrant that extra something struck her as funny. Reaching for a glass, she saluted Nick.

He waited for Maria to leave, then patted the sofa beside him. "What's so funny?" he asked when she joined him. "Watching me and my ex-wife battle it out?"

She smiled. "No. I just noticed Maria didn't put any mint in the tea."

He looked at his glass, distracted, then chuckled. "So she didn't." He slid an arm around her shoulder, pulling her close. Touching his glass to hers, he said, "Here's to Lynette. May she and Andrew have a long and happy life together."

His wry words carried no wistful notes, and Emma's heart warmed with unspoken love. After all Lynette had put him through, he'd still had to the decency to warn her about Warren. It was more than most men would do under the circumstances.

"What do you think?" Nick asked.

"I think you made her mad."

He smiled. "Not the first time. Do you believe her?"

She recalled Lynette's excitement, her sparkling eyes, her breathlessness when she spoke of her honeymoon—emotions that came close to paralleling her own feelings when she thought about Nick. Unlikely as it seemed, Lynette was in love with Andrew Warren. "I believe she believes Warren's hands are clean."

He thought for a moment. "I think you're right. But do *you* believe it?"

She shook her head.

"Me, either."

He propped his feet on the coffee table. "Careful," Emma warned him, reaching for the papers under his boot. "Mind if I ask what these are?"

"A release."

Emma thought she must have heard wrong. "A release?" As in financial obligation? She didn't know the dollar value of the final installment, but it had to be substantial. If Lynette was giving up any portion of the settlement, she must truly be committed to Andrew Warren.

Nick nodded. "Under the terms of our divorce agreement, if Lynette remarries, she gives up any unpaid balance."

Ramifications rolled over Emma, one after another, until she felt light-headed. A sizable amount of money had essentially just been handed to Nick on a silver platter. He could use it against his mortgage. He might even be able to pay it off. His future, for the moment at least, was secure, yet he spoke calmly, as if he were talking about the weather. In his place, she would have been ecstatic. The papers in her hand probably represented his financial freedom.

Unless Lynette was lying.

"Would she give up that kind of money to trick you?"

"There's one way to find out."

Three phone calls and an hour later, Nick hung up the telephone and leaned back in his chair. He looked dazed. "The planning commission received word this morning. The project has been dropped, and the request for a zoning change withdrawn. Apparently Lynette was telling the truth. It might be by default, but we won."

Emma had thought she'd gained control over her unsteady emotions, but Nick's words proved her wrong. Tension inside her unraveled, and she wouldn't have believed until that moment how tightly wound she'd been. There would be no more attacks on Nick's ranch. No more threats to his security. No more sabotage to her car.

As quickly as it came, exaltation metamorphosed into pain. Heartbroken, she looked into Nick's eyes, but if his thoughts followed the same vein, he hid them well. Feeling small for allowing selfish thoughts to tarnish their victory, she forced a smile.

"You did it."

"*We* did it." He held out a hand. "Come here."

She stood from where she'd been sitting on the corner of his desk and put her shaky hand in his. His touch was warm, his callused hand comforting in an unsettled world. When he pulled her into his lap, she didn't resist.

A bleak future loomed on the horizon, but it wasn't here yet. She had this moment, and she wouldn't destroy it with what was to come. Recalling his words from yesterday, she focused only on the now. Now he held her with gentle strength. Now he looked into her eyes, searching her expression. Now his fingers delved into her hair, sending goose bumps sliding down her spine. Now he dropped his lips to hers, and now she needed his touch like never before. Closing her eyes, she gave up thinking.

Nick shifted Emma's weight, fighting the confines of his office chair. He'd meant only to kiss her, but she'd answered with an urgency that sent desire spiraling into lust. When she lifted languid eyes to meet his, sense all but deserted him.

"You're a bad influence, Emmaline Reardon." He shifted again, easing the suddenly snug fit of his jeans. "You make a man forget where he is."

Her reaction was comic. She gasped. Her eyes opened wide and flew to the doorway. "Maria—"

He couldn't help laughing. "Relax," he said, "I heard Maria leave a half hour ago. I think she was headed for the store."

She grinned sheepishly, and he gathered her close again. "Besides, I don't think Maria would mind if she found us here like this. Do you?"

"Pete already caught us," she said, snuggling against him. "My reputation will be in tatters."

"Then I'll have to marry you." The words came from nowhere, and they hit him with the force of a sledgehammer. He'd never marry again, never consider it. Not once in five years had he even joked about it. Oh, he'd like to keep Emma here for a few more days, weeks even. But marriage? It was out of the question.

Strangely though, with her sitting warm and pliant in his lap, the idea of permanence with Emma wasn't all that uncomfortable. He'd been jesting, of course, but—

"That's a lot to ask of someone for a kiss. Maybe I should just move."

She made no effort to follow through, but she'd gone still, and he wondered what her stillness meant. Surely she didn't think he'd try to tie her to him, did she? Would she find life with him that abhorrent?

The problem was, he was beginning to think life without *her* might be abhorrent. Desolate. Having her here felt right. He kissed her again, and his next words, he realized, came from the heart. "If we could stay like this, it wouldn't be a burden at all."

She smiled, but the mood was broken. She pushed away, and he let her go. "Just the same, I don't want anyone marrying me at the end of a shotgun," she said. "Somehow I think it would take the romance out of it." She stood up, leaving him cold where moments before her warm body had sung in tune with his.

He followed her up rather than endure the bereft feeling.

"As I recall, I promised you a dinner out." He checked his watch. "I have to talk to Pete, but I can be ready in a couple of hours. Why don't you get cleaned up, and we'll go out to celebrate?"

Finally, she met his eyes. "I'd like that."

"Where are we going?" Emma broke the silence when Nick steered the spotlessly cleaned truck away from Rio Blanco.

"There's a little roadhouse up this way," he answered. "I think you'll like it." In truth, he'd chosen it partly for the atmosphere, but mostly because he didn't want any interruptions through the evening, which would have been all but impossible in Rio Blanco. He'd read her expression very clearly in his office. She'd be leaving soon, but until she did, he wanted her all to himself.

She wore a dress that seemed to float over her body, clinging to her tiny waist and making the most of her slender legs. The silky, apricot-colored fabric illuminated her creamy skin and the golden flecks strewn there, and she'd smoothed her hair until it fell in soft waves around her shoulders. Everything about her was bathed in color, from her remarkable eyes to the fiery causes she championed.

Impossible though he knew it to be, once the idea of permanence had occurred to him, he couldn't get it out of his mind. It had taken root, infiltrated his thoughts, beaten down his resistance. Emma's scent filled the cab of the truck, and he found it intoxicating. Searching out her hand, he laced his fingers through hers. What would he do when she left?

By mutual consent, they spoke of anything—and everything—but the topic uppermost in their minds. The prospect of saying goodbye to Emma was too difficult for him to contemplate.

For Emma, the evening passed too quickly. She refused to think about tomorrow. With Nick it was easy. They dined, they laughed, they danced, and too soon, they drove home. The moon bathed the summer night in surreal radiance that she thought might forever remind her of this single perfect evening.

At the back step, he stopped her, like a schoolboy walking his date to the door. Laughing, she turned in his arms, bent on making a standard good-night speech for his benefit. But one look at his face in the half-light sent her intentions flying. She stood on the step above him, her eyes level with his.

He didn't kiss her. It would have been easier if he had. Instead, he brushed her hair away from her face, traced her cheekbone with the pad of his thumb. His face was shadowed, but he looked as if he were memorizing everything about her. She couldn't endure that kind of scrutiny without breaking down. For most of the evening, she'd managed to shelve reality, but here, so close to him, reality wouldn't be denied. None of it.

"I love you." The words spilled out.

He said nothing. He didn't move, and for an endless moment, her heart stopped beating. *Why doesn't he say something?* Then slowly, relentlessly, he pulled her to him. She felt him shudder, and suddenly, his lips burned her with a searing kiss that rocked her to her soul. Her heart jumpstarted, and the next thing she knew she was clinging to him.

Without raising his head, he swept her up and climbed the last steps. At the door, he paused to fumble with the handle, then they were in the darkened kitchen. He pushed the door shut with his foot, then carried her past the living room to the stairs. One by one, he climbed them, holding her effortlessly. He didn't stop until he stood above his bed. Then he let her slide, inch by inch, down his aroused body. By the time her feet touched the floor, her own body was strung with need.

"Wait here," he whispered. "Don't move."

He left her there, feeling awkward and suddenly shy, and giving her too much time to think. If they did this again, she'd pay a thousand times over in the days to come. She couldn't stop time. Just as surely as day followed night, she must leave. But would there be any harm in taking this night with her to keep her warm on the cold nights alone? Would she hurt any less if she denied herself this one last chance to hold him?

Tonight would be her closure. Tonight, she'd say goodbye.

Where had he gone? He'd said not to move, and she didn't. But she looked around the room she'd never permitted herself to observe until now. It lay mostly in shadows. The only thing she saw clearly was the quilt on the big bed. A wedding ring quilt. One that would never be hers.

Nick's footsteps returned up the stairs. He paused in the doorway, as if to see if she'd waited for him. In his hand he carried something, but she couldn't tell what it was in the gloom. Then he shut the door behind him and turned the lock.

Nervously, she waited.

He advanced on her slowly, soundlessly. When he reached the bed, he paused to kiss her. "You waited."

"You asked me to."

She thought she saw him smile in the dark. But instead of taking her in his arms, he turned away and fumbled with something on the stand beside the bed. A moment later she heard the rasp and flare of a match struck against something, and the room was bathed in the glow of candlelight.

He turned to her. "I want to see you when we make love," he said. "I always will."

Nervousness vanished, and she stepped into his arms.

Chapter Thirteen

Emma awoke slowly, stretched luxuriously in the comfortable bed. When she opened her eyes, she studied the unfamiliar room in sleepy luxury, recalling her night of lovemaking with Nick. She turned to greet him in the morning light, but the bed beside her was empty. The pillow he'd used still held the impression of his head, and in that small hollow lay a piece of paper. Disappointed, she reached for it.

Good morning, sleeping beauty. I was tempted to wake you with a kiss, but you looked so peaceful, I didn't have the heart. I'll see you in a while. Love, Nick.

Smiling, she recalled the long hours before dawn, the words he'd whispered in the velvety night. Her body came alive again just thinking about his hands sliding across her skin and the way his kiss made everything else disappear. The glow of the candle had cast soft shadows on his face. She'd never see candlelight again without recalling the look in his eyes when the world had exploded around them. The night had been a marvelous, sensual dream too good to be true.

But she was awake now, and the dream was over. In the velvet darkness, she had ignored the future, but now there could be no more pretending.

She had to leave. Today. Putting it off would only make it harder. Glancing at the clock beside the bed, she was appalled at the late hour. With the return of reality came the ugly truths that went with it. Her editor had already assigned her to a new story—one that took her far away from Rio Blanco. Though the thought of leaving threatened to rend her in two, she could put it off no longer. Sliding out of the bed, she gathered her clothes.

The hallway was deserted, and she dashed into her room for a change of clothes before she took a shower. She'd never be ashamed of having made love with Nick, but she didn't want to advertise the fact to Maria. Maria wouldn't understand why she had to leave.

It wasn't until she was dressed and had her heavy suitcase open on the bed that her hopes for a quick getaway were dashed. The pile of dirty laundry in the corner was gone. The room had been straightened. Maria had been there. She'd cleaned her room, taken her laundry. She knew where Emma had spent the night, and she was probably downstairs right now, making plans for the wedding.

With her old-fashioned logic, there was no way she'd ever understand why Emma couldn't stay, even if Nick asked her to, which he hadn't. She'd see only that Emma was leaving, just as Lynette had left. And that Nick was still alone. In Maria's eyes, that would be the biggest sin of all.

When Emma went downstairs, Maria greeted her with a beatific smile as she folded clean clothes. A pile of Emma's underclothes lay folded neatly beside Nick's. In the laundry room, piles of sorted clothes waited their turn for the washer. She recognized one of her T-shirts amid Nick's work shirts.

Unless she made a scene, she had no choice but to wait until the laundry was finished.

"Good morning," Maria said over the drone of the dryer. "Did you sleep well?" The light in her eyes asked a much different question.

"Very well. Thank you." Needing something to mask her agitation, she poured herself a cup of coffee.

"I'll make you some eggs as soon as I finish here," Maria said as she picked up another item of clothing.

"No hurry," Emma said. She wasn't hungry. She doubted if she'd ever be hungry again. "You didn't have to do my laundry."

"It's nothing," Maria assured her, oblivious to the problem she'd created. "I do Nick's wash every Friday."

"At least let me help, then." Emma grabbed a piece and started folding. It was a pair of Nick's jockey shorts, and a wave of intimacy flowed over her just folding his clothes. She caressed the garment, unaware of what she was doing until she saw Maria's expression. "I used to do this for my dad," she explained hastily, but she knew Maria wasn't fooled.

"It's good to fold your man's clothes. One of the little things a woman does to keep him comfortable."

Emma closed her eyes against sudden tears. Maria meant well. She couldn't know how deeply her words wounded. Pressing the folded underwear into the pile, she turned away. "I'll be leaving this afternoon. Will you bring my clothes up when you're finished?"

She didn't look to see Maria's expression. She didn't wait for her reply, but ran blindly up the stairs.

It could have been minutes or hours later, she didn't know which, but she sensed Nick's presence in the doorway.

"You're leaving."

She couldn't face him. "Yes."

"Will you come back?"

She turned to him, fighting back the tears. "I can't."

Nick felt the knife edge of those two words slice through his heart, effectively popping the rosy bubble that had colored every moment since waking. Last night had made him think there was a chance for them. After what she'd told him, he'd allowed himself to believe they had something worth fighting for. But in the cold light of day, it was plain he was wrong.

"I thought we'd take the horses out again this afternoon. Will you stay for the weekend? You can't turn the story in until Monday, anyhow."

She didn't even hesitate. "No. I can't."

The little candle flame of hope flickered and died, and he felt himself harden. "Why not?"

The pain in her eyes was palpable. He would have loved to take her into his arms, to tell her everything was okay. But it wasn't, and if she wasn't willing to fight, it never would be.

"That's it then? You're just going to walk away?"

"I have to."

He couldn't accept that. "You said you loved me."

She looked down. "I do."

"Then fight for us, Emma."

She wouldn't meet his eyes. "I don't know how."

But, damn it, he thought, she did. She'd fought all her life. She'd fought her way out of a nowhere future. She'd fought her way through college. She'd fought for a good job, and once she'd gotten it, she'd fought her way to the top. Why was she quitting now?

"You're just going to give up?"

She blinked and dashed a tear from her cheek.

"You don't give me much credit, Emma. This isn't the same battle. You're not the same person you were before."

She looked up at him, her tears forgotten. "But I *am* the same person, and the battle never ends. The past haunts me every day. I can't change it, and it's tying me in knots." As if to prove her point, she clutched her stomach. "I can't live like this."

"Then let it go."

"Let it go?" She leaned toward him. "Look what's happened to you, just since I've been here." Holding up her fingers, she ticked them off. "You nearly lost Cochise. You almost lost a mare *and* her foal. You've been threatened with stomatitis, you've had someone trying to discredit your ranch, poison your herd." She threw her hands up. "The problems never end."

He didn't understand her twisted logic. Did she think he'd never suffered a setback? Did she think he was so weak as to buckle under the strain of opposition? "Everyone has problems. I didn't lose Cochise. The mare will recover and her foal is fine. I'll weather the outbreak, *if* there is one. Someone might have tried to poison the herd, but he didn't succeed. *I'm still here!*"

She turned away, but he reached out and turned her toward him again.

"You had it tough when you were a child, Emma, but this isn't the farm you grew up on. I won't roll over and let someone walk over me."

"But you can't control everything," she insisted. "What will you do when the price of beef drops? Or the snow comes early? Or the bank calls up its loans?"

"I'll face it when the time comes." He dropped his arms. "But I won't live in fear of the future."

She backed away, as if he'd slapped her. "You've been lucky so far, but luck turns around. I can't go through it again."

Luck! Did she think he'd gotten where he was by *luck?* Did she give him no credit at all for business sense? Education? Knowledge of what he was doing?

She wrapped her arms around herself again and continued

backing until the wall stopped her. Her eyes seemed to focus on some unseen memory from the past, and her voice shook. "I watched my mother work herself into an early grave. I watched my father fight and scheme and fight some more, but it was never enough. That farm broke his spirit. It drove my brother away. It tore our family apart!" When she focused again, she looked pale, haunted. "Piece by piece everything I ever loved disappeared before my very eyes—and there was nothing I could do to stop it."

"You were a child, Emma."

She shook her head. "This ranch is a paradise, but if I stayed, I'd end up hating it. I'd end up hating you."

Paradise? The word stopped his explosive rebuttal. She thought the Uintah was paradise? "What are you really afraid of?"

The question seemed to throw her. She looked at him as if to ask if he'd even been listening. But she didn't reply. He let her think about it, then asked her again, gently. "What do you need?"

"Security," she blurted. "I need security. I need to know my future is in safe hands."

He nearly laughed. The woman who came here without the faintest hope of getting an interview lived only for security? The woman who drove into the wilderness in a car that was literally falling apart around her worried about her future? The woman who refused to leave when Andrew Warren all but drew a knife on her couldn't handle the thought of not making the rent? She might want to believe she needed security, but he didn't buy it.

"Where, exactly, do you think you'll find this security?" he asked for the sake of argument. "In a boardroom?"

She looked down, and he knew he'd struck a nerve. He'd been right all along. She thought unless money was made in a sterile, sanitary office atop some high-rise tower, it wasn't real somehow. Irrational anger boiled up inside him. Money was money, regardless of what it took to make it.

"I hate to disappoint you, Emma, but boardrooms are political hotbeds that make ranching look like a walk in the park. You're on top only as long as the climate suits the board of directors, and there's someone hiding behind every corner, ready to step in if you stumble. At least on a ranch you know who your enemies are."

She didn't answer.

"Even in stable corporations, the people in those boardrooms risk everything every time they make a decision. If you think their employees are secure, talk to all the midlevel managers out there looking for a job these days."

She still didn't reply, and her silence angered him further.

"Do you think you're secure in your job? What if the advertisers didn't like what you wrote? How secure would you be then? What would happen if you refused your next assignment?"

At last she raised her head, but the fire was missing from her response. "You're turning my words around."

"Get your head out of the sand, Emma. There is no security. Only calculated risk. You live with it every day of your life. Why can't you see that?"

"I do what I have to do."

"Unless you stand to lose a dollar or two. Then you freeze up inside. Maybe you should ask for a crystal ball. Then, if you didn't like what you saw, you could crawl into your cocoon until it passed."

She glared at him. "How dare you—"

"You run on fear. You work at a job you don't like because you're afraid to lose your paycheck. You won't take a chance on freelance work because it doesn't pay regularly. Hell, you even drive an old wreck of a car because you won't borrow the money to get a new one."

"That's easy for you to say. Try stepping into my life and see how it feels! I promised myself never to borrow—"

"You're willing to risk your well-being for a measly few thousand dollars?"

The question stopped her.

"You've got your priorities backward, Emma. You want guarantees, but the only guarantee any of us have is that we'll all die someday." He turned to leave. At the door, he paused. "I've got news for you. If you let fear control your life, you might as well be dead already."

Maria stood at the bottom of the stairs, dust cloth in hand, and she didn't even bother to pretend she hadn't heard. He stormed past her, unwilling to hear her plead Emma's case. Outside, he met Pete coming in, but he strode past him, too.

Unlike Maria, Pete didn't take the hint. He fell into step beside him. "What's on the agenda this afternoon, boss?"

"I'm going to put water on the south pasture as soon as Hank gets the bales in."

"Bob told me you asked him to saddle the horses after lunch."

"I changed my mind."

"Emma doesn't want to go riding?"

"Emma's leaving."

Pete stopped short, and Nick strode on, hoping he'd stemmed the flow of questions. He was wrong.

"When's she coming back?"

Nick stopped. Turned. "She's not."

"Why not?"

He glared, but Pete didn't back down.

"Did you ask her?"

Of course he'd asked her. Hadn't he? Well, not exactly, but she knew what he meant.

"Do you want her to come back?"

"What do you think?"

"Did you tell her that?" Pete pressed him.

Not in so many words. But he'd shown her last night. And this morning. That should be enough.

"A woman likes to hear the words, Nick."

He'd be damned if he'd beg. "Mind your own business, Pete." Changing his direction, he stamped back into the house, past Maria's disapproving glare, past the piles of silk and lace on the kitchen table, into his office, venting his frustrations on the door as he slammed it behind him.

He should have listened to his common sense the moment he met Emma. He'd known from the first that she was trouble. She was just like Lynette, only worse. Lynette made no bones about wanting her share of the pie. But Emma was sneaky. She dressed in the guise of wanting to help, and he'd fallen for it. Now he'd pay. He'd let her get close to him, and for thanks she was cutting his heart out. Just like Lynette...

But his mind conjured a picture of Lynette, with her constant demands for more. More money. More social life. More attention.

Who was he kidding? Emma was nothing like Lynette. She was kind, caring, witty, single-minded. Stubborn. And she was the sexiest woman he'd ever met. She was sneaky all right. She'd sneaked up behind him, pried her way into his life, refused to leave him alone until he couldn't imagine living without her.

And now she was leaving.

She admitted she loved him, which was more than he'd done. And she was strong enough to know she couldn't stay. The anger inside him moved over, making room for a more uncomfortable emotion. None of this was her fault, yet he'd vented his frustrations, never once considering the consequences, and now she'd leave with the echo of his words forever ringing in her ears.

Emma heard the slam of Nick's office door, felt the house shudder with the impact, and stared at her reflection in the mirror. For ten years she'd been running, hiding from the past. But Nick had exposed the ugly truth she'd refused to recognize. She was afraid. Fear controlled her life, and she didn't have the courage to take control back.

Nick had all but asked her to stay here on the ranch with him. But could she do it? Could she live here day and night, waiting for the worst to happen? Could she ignore her fears, pretend they didn't bother her? How long would it be before the tension started taking its toll? How long before Nick began to resent the anxious silence, the haunted look in her eyes? How long before he began to hate her?

She could endure anything but that. Nick was angry with her now, but bearing his anger would be a thousand times easier than watching him withdraw a moment, an hour, a day at a time until they became strangers. No, she couldn't stay here. Her scars ran too deep to erase, the past had been too heavy a burden for too long. She had no choice but to leave. She should have left days ago. She should never have come here in the first place.

Suddenly the room was too small. She couldn't breathe. She needed space, to let the sunshine burn the cold out of her. Swiping at the tears on her cheeks, she almost ran down the stairs.

Hot summer sunshine shimmered over the ranch. In the drive, Hank drove by on the stacker loaded with hay. He smiled and waved as he passed, unaware of the storm inside her.

In the pasture, Lucy grazed peacefully, swatting flies with her tail while her foal frolicked nearby. The little filly ran with her head aloft, snorting and kicking at some imagined foe, her red-and-white coat shining in the sunlight.

In the corral, Cochise whickered a welcome and hung his head over the top rail of the fence. When she offered only a friendly pat on his arched neck, he turned and trotted round the enclosure, plainly wanting to cut loose with some real exercise. Nick would put him back to work soon. His limp was barely noticeable anymore.

All around her, life moved on, unmindful of her passing.

Vixen greeted her with pricked ears and dark, intelligent eyes. Emma scratched her freckled nose and smoothed her velvety muzzle. In one short week, these people, these animals had become family to her. Even with all the difficulties, the ranch had become a haven of peace and tranquillity.

All her adult life she'd come and gone, drifted in and out of people's lives, and never had trouble saying goodbye. But leaving here would cost more than she had to give. With a strangled sob, she buried her face in Vixen's warm neck.

Frank Howell's raspy, belligerent voice wrenched her out of her self-pity. He appeared outside dragging a reluctant filly behind him, polluting the air with his profanity. Emma watched in distaste. For a man who made his living with horses, he showed no patience, not even the inclination to try to understand them. When he raised the end of the lead rope to strike the unfortunate horse, she intervened.

"Do you think hitting her will help?"

Frank spun around. Then, recognizing her, he let his gaze drop and linger on her breasts, an insult meant to put her in her place. He spat on the ground and started toward her. "I ain't never seen a female yet who couldn't use a little 'attitude adjustment.'" He laughed at his joke. "What about you, missy? You look like you could use a little male companionship. What's the matter? Doesn't Nick know how to keep a pretty little filly like you happy?"

Emma backed up in spite of herself. Revulsion crawled up her spine. "If you want the horse to cooperate, give it a reason to want to."

Frank's expression hardened. "You mean like this?" He reached for her arm.

"Let go of me!" She tried to sidestep, but the stall gate blocked her escape.

"If you want me to cooperate," he mimicked her words, "give me a reason to—"

"That's enough, Frank!" Nick's voice stopped him.

Frank turned, and Emma's legs nearly buckled in relief.

"Hell, Nick, I was just havin' a little fun."

Nick ignored his sputtered protest. "Pick up your tools and get out of here."

"But you said you wanted these fillies—"

"I said get out. Now!" His voice was steely, unbending.

Frank glared, but apparently decided not to argue. "I'll leave, all right. And I damn sure won't be back!"

"You've got that right."

"You owe me for—"

"Pete will give you a check. Now get out, and don't set foot on this ranch again."

Frank dropped the rope and spat again, then disappeared back where he'd come from. Nick grabbed the lead before the nervous horse could escape, then ran gentle fingers down her neck. Emma wondered if he meant to ignore her.

"I should have run him off years ago." He didn't turn.

"You shouldn't have sent him away on my account."

"The man is a cretin. He's insulted you every time he's seen you."

"But you need him."

"He has no business around horses. Lately, he's done more harm than good whenever he's gotten near them."

"What will you do now?"

He turned. "I'll get by." He was recalling their argument, just as she was, waiting to see what she would do.

She refused the challenge. He was a survivor. There could be nothing gained from picking up where they'd left off. The line between them was drawn, and nothing would change it.

"I need to finish packing." She would have brushed past him, but he stopped her with a hand on her arm.

"I came out here looking for you."

His touch was gentle, and his eyes, when she looked up, entreated her to listen. "Walk with me."

She couldn't refuse.

He led the horse toward some pens where three other horses huddled together, frightened, no doubt, by Frank's heavy-handed methods. Nick led the filly inside. When Bob appeared, he told him briefly what had happened, and directed him to turn the horses out until another farrier could be found.

Emma waited quietly, sensing Nick needed time to compose his thoughts. When he finished, he led her to the grove of cottonwoods that had stood over his grandfather's original house. To her surprise, someone had built a wishing well among the trees, and near it a bench invited a visitor to rest awhile in the shade. Nick led her to the well, but stood with his back to her, his hands in the back pockets of his jeans.

She chose to lean against the craggy bark of one of the imposing old trees. A passing breeze ruffled the leaves above her, and a pair of magpies scolded them from high among the branches. The rough bark of the tree dug into her shoulder. Pushing against it, she waited to hear what Nick had to say.

Nick had no idea how to begin. He only knew he couldn't leave things as they stood. "My father built this wishing well when he married my mother," he began. "They used to slip out here at night after I went to bed. I followed them once."

She didn't reply, and he didn't look her way.

"They just sat on that bench there and watched the stars. At the time I thought they'd lost their minds. All the best shows on television came on after my bedtime, and I couldn't believe they weren't watching them."

Emma still said nothing, though he thought he could feel

her gaze burning into his back. He needed to apologize—for his anger, though he still thought she needed to face reality. "I had no right to shout at you," he said suddenly. "I was angry, and I wanted to strike out, but it wasn't fair of me. I'm sorry."

He turned around. Emma stood with her head back against the old tree. Her eyes were closed tight, and her knuckles were white—whether from anger or grief, he couldn't tell.

"Emma?"

She opened her eyes. They looked black against her pale skin.

He swallowed. "I love you. I'm asking you to come back here. I don't need a commitment, I only ask that you—"

She shook her head slowly. She closed her eyes and shook it again, looking as if he'd just asked her to face a firing squad. He'd bared his soul, and she hadn't even waited to hear him out before she refused.

Before he knew it he was reaching for her. Shaking her. "Damn it, Emma! Look at me."

She did, but her eyes were lifeless. Resigned. She didn't fight back even when he tightened his grip. "I just told you I loved you," he said between gritted teeth. "But I can see now that I was talking to the wrong woman. I mistook you for someone I thought I knew. The woman I love is filled with passion. Courage. She never gave up on anything. You're only an impostor." He dropped his hands.

When it came, her reaction was explosive. "Don't you talk to me about courage! Don't talk to me about passion—"

He pulled her to him. Wrapped her in his arms. Silenced her with a brutal kiss meant to siphon off his overcharged emotions. But she'd unleashed a tigress. She clawed at him, hammered his chest with her fists, kissed him with staggering ferocity. She took control of the kiss, and she didn't give it back until his breath came in ragged gasps, until he could barely stand.

When the storm passed, she raised unguarded eyes to his, and he saw her love shining through. Gathering her up, he carried her to the bench where his parents had sat as lovers, and when he kissed her again, his heart reached out for hers. She hid nothing from him. He felt her love flowing through him. He sensed her sadness.

She would leave. She would never return. She was telling him goodbye.

He stayed there by the wishing well long after she returned to the house. Only when the flurry of activity in the driveway told him she was ready to go did he retrace his steps.

Emma stood in the advancing shadows of the tree above her car, watching his approach. Apparently she'd told Maria goodbye in the house. No one else was in sight.

"I'll send you a copy of the article for your approval," she said when he drew near.

"There's no need." He trusted her.

"But I will," she said. "It was part of our agreement." When he nodded, she continued. "The magazine will want artwork. They'll send a photographer out, probably within the week. Will that be all right?"

He nodded again.

There was nothing else to be said. He opened her door and held it for her, and she climbed behind the wheel. He steeled himself against the inevitable, then bent to her level, his hands on the open window.

"Be well, Emma."

She smiled a tenuous smile and looked up at him, blinking against unshed tears. He backed away.

She turned the ignition. The car roared to life, but instead of the reassuring purr of a newly tuned motor, the engine coughed, shuddered. Frowning, she gunned it, but it choked and died.

"Not now!" he heard her mutter. She started it again, but to no avail. The car shook in deathlike throes.

The irony was inescapable. This was where they'd begun. Leaning down again, he asked, "Car trouble, ma'am?"

Chapter Fourteen

Nick hoped to lighten a tense situation, but his words backfired. Emma burst into tears. She switched off the ignition and leaned her head onto the steering wheel. He opened the door.

"Emma? Sweetheart, don't cry."

But she wouldn't be consoled.

"It's not your fault."

"You don't understand." She raised her head and looked at him. "This car is *reliable*. I've never had a moment's trouble with it until I came here."

He reached for her, pulled her gently from behind the wheel and wrapped his arms around her, damning the whole miserable situation. "I'll look at it for you."

But first he meant to somehow soothe her frustrated tears. The strain of the last couple of days was taking its toll on her, and everything he did seemed to make things worse. Not knowing what else to do, he let her cry into his chest while he whispered reassurance into her hair.

She was trying so hard to do the right thing, frustrated at every turn, and demonstrating with every smothered sob how much it cost. If only she'd admit it—she wanted to stay with him.

Finally her tears slowed to an occasional hiccup. "Okay now?" he asked.

She still hid her face, but gave a watery chuckle. "Your shirt is wet."

"All in the line of duty." He'd gladly donate a thousand shirts if he thought it would help change her mind. But wishing wouldn't make it so, and he couldn't bear watching her cry. Like it or not, he'd give her what she wanted. Gently, he put her away from him. "Why don't you climb back in and pop the hood? When I tell you, start the engine. Okay?"

She nodded, and he tore his attention away from her. Trying to concentrate on the aging motor in front of him, he looked for obvious problems. Nothing seemed out of the ordinary. Hoses, belts, everything looked normal. "Try the ignition." When she did, the motor rocked and sputtered.

"Turn it off," he said when it became obvious the motor wouldn't settle in. An inkling came to mind, but he dismissed it. It couldn't be that. It couldn't be.

She joined him. "What is it?"

"The timing's off," he replied, still doubting the obvious. "I doubt if it's firing on four cylinders."

"What does that mean?"

"Trouble?" Pete came up behind them.

"You could say that." He looked at his foreman's innocent expression—too innocent. "You wouldn't know anything about it, would you?"

"Me? No. What's the problem?"

"Unless I miss my guess, someone's been messing with the distributor wires."

Pete's eyebrows lifted. "Switched them?"

Nick nodded, and Pete's expression changed from mild

concern to amusement. "Well I'll be damned," he said. "She did it."

"Who did what?"

Pete refused to elaborate, but he'd said enough. Nick's temper, already on a short fuse, boiled. "Maria. Tell me what you know, Pete. And make it fast."

"I don't know anything," Pete said, sobering.

He put an ever-so-slight emphasis on the word *know*. "Did she ask you to help her?"

Pete's eyes reminded him of a cornered horse who knew he was caught. "No. But you've seen her this afternoon. She doesn't want Emma to leave."

Neither did he, Nick thought, but he hadn't stooped to this. "She must have said something…"

Pete gave it up. "I told her I thought the only way Emma would stay the night was if her car had four flat tires," he admitted, "but I didn't think she'd take me seriously."

Emma couldn't believe it. Pete was saying Maria had switched the distributor wires on her car. Did the woman honestly think this would make a difference? Did she care that much? Up until now, her tactics had been embarrassing, but endearing in their own way. But not this. "Just switch them back," she said.

Nick sighed. "It's not that easy. We don't know which wires were switched." He turned toward the house. "But I'll soon find out."

He strode purposefully toward the house.

Turning to Pete she asked, "Isn't there a diagram or something?" Not that she harbored much hope. If there was an easy way to fix the car, Nick would have done it by now.

"Not here," Pete answered. "We'd need a manual."

He said no more, but leaned against the fender and waited for Nick's return. He looked as if he were enjoying all of this, and it occurred to Emma that for a powerful man, Nick had very little privacy. Neither, for that matter, did she.

After what seemed like an hour in the tense silence, Nick came back outside. He took the steps slowly, with his head down.

"What's the verdict?" Pete asked when he reached them.

Nick frowned and looked at her. "She doesn't remember which wires she crossed."

Out of the corner of her eye Emma saw Pete check his watch. "It's five o'clock. The parts store is closed."

"Yeah." Nick still looked at her. "We can't fix it tonight, Emma. I'm sorry."

No! Her courage floundered. "I can't—"

Frantically, she tried to think rationally. Eight wires and eight places to put them. Her heart sank. There were *thousands* of possible combinations. Still, her mind revolted. She couldn't stay here another night. She couldn't go through this all again tomorrow. Weak, undignified tears blurred her vision, and she shook her head. "I can't—"

The screen door flew open and Maria appeared on the porch steps, calling out to Emma in an unintelligible mixture of pleas and apologies. She hurried through the gate toward them.

"I'm sorry. I'm sorry," she repeated, gesturing frantically. She ended with broken bits of prayer muttered between sobs. "Forgive me, Emma, I only meant to help—" A look from Nick stopped her short.

Nick reached into his pocket. He pulled the keys to his truck out and extended his hand. "Take my truck," he said quietly. His words effectively silenced Maria's sobs. "I'll bring your car to Denver next week."

Emma looked into his dark-blue eyes, eyes filled with painful acceptance. He was offering her a chance to leave while she still had the strength and dignity to make a clean getaway. But knowing she'd see him again in a few days would only prolong the agony, give her days to torture herself with dreams of a different ending when there could be no other outcome. She couldn't endure that. Besides, he needed his truck.

"Take *my* car." Maria broke the silence. "Keep it. I'll trade with you."

Emma turned away from them both, shielding her aching temples with her hands. Across from her she saw Pete's bemused expression. Everyone waited expectantly for her answer, and in the silence, the raspy call of a magpie echoed around them.

This couldn't be happening. "No," she said miserably. She'd endured this endless day. Another night wouldn't make that much difference.

Turning back to Nick, she met his eyes above Maria's, telegraphing her thanks, hoping he understood. "You need your truck. You don't have time to be driving my car to Denver when in a few hours I can drive it myself."

"Take my car," Maria offered again. "I'll give it to you." Her tearful, openhearted plea dissolved Emma's anger. In her way, Maria had only done what she thought was right.

"You need your car, too," she replied gently. "I'll wait until mine is fixed."

Emma thumped the rumpled pillow, toying with the idea of smashing the old-fashioned alarm clock. Each tick echoed loudly in the darkened room, wearing on her nerves. And the sheet was tangled around her again. Irritably, she pulled it free.

Three-forty-five. Ten minutes since she'd checked the last time. Two hours until she could rise and resume pacing where she'd left off the night before. The parts store would open at eight, and no amount of tossing and turning would move the clock any faster.

This had been the single longest night she'd ever spent in her life. Not even twelve hours had passed since she'd loaded her car, since hopes of a clean break had been dashed. It felt like a lifetime.

Sitting up, she tugged at the nightshirt that seemed to be knotted under her arms. She fluffed her pillow and unwound the bedcovers, then lay down again. But sleep wouldn't come.

Until now, she'd thought this bed luxurious. Tonight it was hard, unforgiving. Tonight it tortured her, kept her awake. Last night she'd slept like a baby. But then last night…

Hot tears filled her eyes. Last night she'd slept in Nick's arms. Tonight, thanks to her awkward handling of an awkward situation, they slept apart, separated by a gulf they'd never bridge. Now she lay in her lonely bed counting the hours until she could crawl away and lick her wounds.

In the distance, a bell sounded. It was loud, and she wondered who slept so soundly that he used an alarm loud enough to wake the dead. Suddenly she heard Nick's door thrown open, followed by the hurried, uneven steps of a man dressing on the run.

It took a moment longer to figure it out. The bell wasn't meant to wake a heavy sleeper—it was a fire alarm, and it was coming from the stable.

Pete and two others were converging on the corrals by the time she ran out of the house. Smoke billowed from under the shelter that housed the massive haystack, and in front of the doors to the stable, another smaller pile of hay smoldered. Inside, even above the deafening alarm, she heard the frantic screams of Cochise and the other horses.

Nick was pulling the smaller fire apart with a shovel, spreading the burning hay across the ground in his efforts to get to the door. With the inrush of oxygen, each layer he peeled off ignited, lighting his shadowy form in the smoke.

Even with the open flames, the smoke was so dense she couldn't see. And if she couldn't see, neither could the men fighting the fire. She recalled a master switch near the stable doors. If she could light the area, even a little, maybe it would help. Already the smoke burned her eyes and threatened to choke her, but she fought her way through it until she found the box she was looking for.

Opening it blindly, she found the lever and pulled. Light flooded the barnyard, but it served only to illuminate the horror of what was happening. She turned back in time to see Nick throw his shovel aside and pull the stable door open.

Trying not to think of all the stories she'd heard of people lost in burning buildings, she focused on the fire spread across the ground. If Nick got the horses that far, they'd balk at the flames. There was a standpipe with a faucet next to the storeroom. She thought she remembered a hose curled at its base. Smoke boiled off the bigger fire, enveloping her and everything around her, but she stumbled through it until she ran into the storeroom wall.

Fear for Nick's safety made her hurry, and she nearly tripped over the faucet. With panicky fingers, she attached the hose, praying she didn't cross-thread the coupling in her haste. Not bothering to tighten it, she pulled the lever on the faucet and grabbed the other end. The hose uncoiled behind her as she ran, and as the force of the water moved through it, it bucked and hissed like a snake, aroused and angry, pulled from its nest. Water exploded through the nozzle, nearly tearing it from her hands, but she held on. Just as a capricious breath of wind cleared the yard of smoke, she put the full force of the spray on the burning hay in front of her.

She had time for one clear lungful of air before a sickening cloud of steam boiled up around her. Her vision was long since reduced to a watery blur as she struggled to keep her eyes open. With one arm, she covered her mouth and nose, and with the other, she tucked the hose against her side, using her body to spread the lifesaving water in an arc across the flames.

Nick should have been back by now. Had the fire gotten

inside the building? Was she out here extinguishing incon-
sequential flames while he was suffocating inside? The din
of the alarm rattled inside her head, and it was all she could
do to keep from blindly running in search of him.

Suddenly, a shadowy form loomed out of the smoke, almost on top of her. She jumped aside in relief as the form
took the shape of Nick, fighting to control a terrorized horse.
He'd taken off his shirt and thrown it over the frightened
animal's head. The muscles bulging in his arms and shoulders gave testimony to the effort he put into simply holding
on.

Emma turned the hose away, afraid that if the spray hit
the horse it would bolt. When Nick was safely past, she
turned her efforts back to the fire. A moment later, Nick
touched her shoulder, startling her. When she turned, he held
his shirt out in front of the hose. His face was smudged, and
a sheen of sweat shone on his skin.

"How many more are there?" she shouted above the din.

He held up three fingers as he pulled the soaked shirt up
to his face and dove back inside.

What seemed like hours later, Nick pulled the last struggling horse free, slapped it on the flank and turned back to
her. The fire was reduced to a sodden, steamy mass, no
longer a threat. At some point the alarm bell had either run
down or someone had turned it off, and in the ensuing silence
she heard only dripping water and the slosh of Nick's footsteps through the mud.

"Thank you," he said. But he didn't wait for a reply. A
hundred feet away, his crew was battling the fire in the haystack, and they needed all the help they could get.

Nick took the hose from Emma's leaden arms and started
forward with it. Exhausted though she was, she followed.

Apparently the men worked under a prearranged plan.
Though they were only shadowy forms through the smoke,
she could see them working as a team. They'd controlled the

open flames with water from other hoses. Now they pulled the smoldering bales off the stack to douse the fire eating away inside.

Nick dragged the hose to the extent of its length, and Emma took it back from him, knowing what needed to be done, freeing him to help dismantle the burning haystack.

The minutes dragged by, each one a torturous effort to breathe, each one a torment to her burning eyes, until she lost track of time. One by one someone pulled the bales down. And one by one she flooded them with water while someone else broke them apart, searching out hot spots.

She fell into a curious, hypnotic rhythm, breathing through a damp towel that someone thrust into her hands. Numb with fatigue, her focus narrowed to the burning bale in front of her, and she sprayed it until the fire was extinguished, then moved on to the next one.

Then, suddenly, gentle hands pried the hose loose from her fingers. Someone pulled her away from the hot, suffocating hell into clear, cool air. He unwrapped the towel from around her face, and held her upright as she took in a lungful of blessedly clean air. Confused, she looked around.

Daylight had replaced the murky darkness. The first rays of sun shone on the stack house, still enshrouded in wispy lines of vapor rising from a sea of charred bales, but through the smoke she saw a core stack, untouched by fire. Around it, men leaned against the support posts, each still gripping his tool of choice, each sagging with exhaustion.

"Is it out?" she asked, hardly recognizing the raspy sound that erupted from her throat as her voice.

"Yeah, it's out." Nick sounded worse than she did. She turned to him. His face was an unrecognizable mask of black. His eyes were reddened and watery, but she would have recognized that unbelievable blue anywhere. He remained shirtless, and across his arm, she saw a reddened, ugly stripe seared into his skin.

"You're hurt," she said, reaching for him.

"It's nothing," he replied. "I did that on the first bale I pulled away from the door."

"You should get it cleaned up. It'll get infected."

"What about you?" He reached for her.

"I'm all right." But his fingers touched angry skin on her cheek, and she jumped back.

"It's only singed, I think. Like a bad sunburn."

She put her hand to her face. Her skin felt dry and hot.

"Come on," Nick said. "Maria will have something to put on it," and he escorted her into the house.

"How many bales do you think we lost?" Nick asked over the breakfast table.

He counted himself lucky. His entire crew lined both sides of the table, still damp from a perfunctory rinse at the faucet outside the door, and none had been injured more seriously than singed eyebrows. Anger would come later, he supposed, but for now, the group as a whole celebrated winning a battle that could well have gone the other way.

Maria had served up a mountain of pancakes with bacon, eggs and gallons of hot, fresh coffee. Even Emma, who'd claimed to be too tired to eat, had polished off a plateful of food. Now she relaxed beside him with a second cup of coffee, her heat-singed cheeks shining beneath a coat of ointment.

Nick was near bursting with pride in her. If it hadn't been for her quick thinking, he didn't know how he would have coaxed the horses out of the stable. She'd worked like a trooper alongside the men, and when he'd dragged her away, she'd been close to dropping, but she was still fighting.

"Five, maybe six hundred bales," Pete answered. "We'll probably lose the top layer left on the stack, too. It's pretty wet."

"Well, it could have been worse." Nick's voice remained

raspy, but with the aid of plenty of coffee to soothe his dry throat, he sounded more like himself.

"Any idea what started it?" one of the hands asked.

Pete sputtered. "Better to ask who."

"Or why," Bob added. "What's the point in burning a man's haystack? It wasn't close enough to damage anything else, and any fool could see that a metal building wasn't going to burn."

"He didn't mean to burn the stable," Nick answered. "He was after the horses." As soon as the words were out, something clicked in his brain. Of course! That's what had been bothering him all along. The problems that had plagued him for the past weeks hadn't been directed at the ranch. The cattle and outlying areas would have made an easy target, yet all of the attacks had been aimed at the horses. Only the horses.

"What is it?" Emma whispered at his elbow.

Nick looked around the table. None of these men were responsible for setting the fire. He'd stake his life on it. They'd worked too long and hard to put the fire out. But if not them, who? He looked down at Emma. "We need to talk." If Andrew Warren was out of the picture, who else was responsible?

Talk turned to cleanup, but Nick forestalled the plans bandied around the table. "Before we get into that, we'll let the sheriff look around," he said. "I doubt if there's much to see in that mess out there, but we'll give him a go at it. When he's through, we'll see what we can do to salvage what's left."

"What about the horses?" Emma asked when the men scooted back their chairs to head for much needed showers.

"I've called Jack. Bob and I didn't see anything wrong with them, but the building was filled with smoke. I don't want to take any chances."

* * *

"So who's ticked off at you?" Jack Wyatt asked as he studied the blistered paint on the stable doors an hour later.

"Good question," Nick replied. "I'd have put my money on Andrew Warren, but he dropped out of the picture a couple of days ago. Now, it looks like we're back to square one."

"Well," Jack said, shaking his head, "two heads are better than one. Tell me what you know."

Nick told him while Jack checked the horses Nick had pulled from the stable. Jack listened thoughtfully as he worked, interrupting only once with a question.

"You say the attacks have been aimed at Ms. Reardon, too?"

Nick nodded. "That's why I brought her here. To try to keep her safe."

Jack's eyebrows lifted, but whatever his opinion, he kept it to himself. "And you say all the strikes have been directed at your horses," he thought aloud. "You need to find a common denominator between your horses and Emma Reardon."

True, but if there was one, Nick didn't know what it was.

"The horses look fine," Jack pronounced. "Grayson has some lung congestion, but with a few days' rest, he'll be okay. Just don't run him." He put his stethoscope away, then turned his attention back to Nick's problems. "Why don't we sit down and hash this out together?"

Nick called Emma to join them. She'd bathed and changed her clothes, and she looked dewy and fresh, with only rosy cheeks to show for her morning's work. His first impulse was to pull her close and keep her there, but he reminded himself that the fire had changed nothing. Maria had gone into town for a repair manual, and as soon as Emma's car was fixed, she would leave. So instead of tucking her next to him as he wanted to do, he folded his arms in front of him and settled into a chair opposite her and Jack.

Emma wanted to help, but sitting opposite Nick made her

feel cold and alone. She recalled other moments sitting in the warmth of his embrace, and a wave of emptiness washed over her. But if Nick wanted Jack Wyatt to go over it with them, she'd do her best to concentrate. Too aware of Nick's every expression, she answered Jack's questions while a knot of tension formed in her neck. She covered territory she and Nick had crossed and recrossed before, but nothing new came to light. If Andrew Warren was not the culprit, she didn't know who else it could be.

When Jack seemed satisfied, Nick started brainstorming. "The first incident happened before Emma arrived," he said, "but whoever is behind this is after her, too. So it has to be related somehow to the interview."

Emma could hardly imagine the connection. She rubbed her neck in an effort to ease the tension.

"Name everyone you talked to since you got here," Nick said, picking up a pencil and paper.

It was easier to think on her feet, so she stood up and began to pace. Page by page, she went through her notes. The president of the Cattlemen's Association. The owner of the co-op. The townspeople. Jack Wyatt. There was nobody else.

Nick doodled as he listened, following her back and forth with his eyes. The knot in her neck tightened.

"Didn't you tell me you talked with Dr. Hendricks at the university?"

She nodded. "I talked with him on the telephone."

"Who else did you call?" He went back to his drawing.

She flipped to another page. "I called Native American Show Horses to confirm that Cochise would be named Stallion of the Year."

He looked up again. "Who did you talk to?"

"A Mr. Carson. He spoke very highly of both of you."

Nick went back to his drawing. "I doubt if Carson is our man. Who else?"

Emma flipped through more pages, but everything there pertained to Andrew Warren. "All of these people were connected with Andrew Warren's arrest," she said. "The prosecutor, the arresting officer, witnesses for and against him."

"What about Lynette?" Jack asked.

Emma dismissed that notion. Lynette's only thoughts were centered on her upcoming wedding. If she meant Nick harm, she would have collected the money that could well have crippled the ranch forever. She flipped through her notes again. At the bottom of one page, an unfamiliar name caught her eye. Bill Stratton. Her notes below the telephone number said only "No comment," and her mind remained steadfastly blank. She stopped pacing. "Who's Bill Stratton?"

Both men looked up.

"Bill Stratton owns the NASH Stallion of the Year for the past five years," Nick said, watching her with new intensity.

Finally Emma remembered. She turned to Jack. "We talked about Stratton. You told me his stallion was throwing bad foals—something genetic."

Jack nodded. "Unpredictable, especially in a crowd."

"Did you talk to Stratton?" Nick asked.

"I tried. I called to get his reaction to the news about Cochise. He wasn't very cooperative, and when I asked him about the problem with the foals, he hung up on me."

Nick threw his drawing down—a remarkably accurate, remarkably flattering portrait of her deep in concentration. Was that how he saw her?

Nick steepled his hands in front of him. "I saw Stratton at the horse show before the trailer accident," he said. "Cochise took the championship, but the point spread was small. I meant to congratulate him on a good show, but by the time I broke free of the reporters, he'd already left."

"Stratton tried to buy Cochise last year," Jack said.

Nick stood and walked over to the window. "He offered me more than he was worth at the time. Cochise hadn't even won a major show." Emma sat down and rubbed her neck. "It wasn't long after that I heard the rumors about Stratton's horse."

"I just read a paper about the problem last week," Jack said. "Several of Stratton's foals were test subjects. As I recall, the chances of defect are high. As much as one in four."

"So," Emma said, rolling her head against the tension, "with a new champion on the horizon and word getting around about substandard foals, Stratton stands to lose a lot of money."

Nick turned. "Someone told me he's bought into race-horses. That costs money, and it takes years to see a return. If he's counting on his Appaloosas to tide him over, he's got to be in trouble."

Emma agreed, but it didn't explain everything. "That explains why he's trying to discredit you, but what about me?"

Nick moved behind her, nudged her hand aside. Warm hands took over the massage. "You told him who you were, didn't you? He probably thought you meant to write about him. Bad publicity, especially in a major financial magazine would spell the end to his breeding business. My guess is he panicked." He found the knot and worked it, easing the tension with knowing fingers. Everything she'd always suspected about his gentle touch proved true. She relaxed against him.

"Does he live around here?" Jack asked.

"No. He lives in Oregon." He kneaded her shoulders, and she reached up to touch him, forgetting that Jack watched. "If he's behind all of this, he's hired someone to do his dirty work for him."

Jack rocked forward, planting his elbows on his knees. "Whoever it is knows your operation inside out."

Her relaxation evaporated.

* * *

The sheriff had come and gone, and though Nick had told his men to take the rest of the day off, most of them were working on the dank heap beneath the stack yard shelter. The clean hay had been removed, and Hank and the others were loading the rest to be hauled away. Emma circumvented the noisy activity and directed her steps around the corrals toward a lane she hadn't noticed before. It led past a cottonwood grove beyond the barnyard. The cool shade beckoned, and she followed it curiously.

Weeds growing up the middle showed little traffic, and for twenty feet or so, her sandaled feet crunched on gravel washed clean where irrigation water pooled from the pipe opposite the fence. Lost in thought, she listened to the sound, unmindful of its musical quality. Then, in the back of her mind, she recalled other, heavier footsteps running across gravel. Stopping suddenly, she turned. She stood no more than fifty feet from the storeroom, though the corrals stood between her and the door. On a quiet night, the sound would carry clearly.

The driveway lay opposite the barnyard, and anyone watching it would miss someone approaching from this direction. Thinking she was onto something, she followed the lane into the trees. A man could easily hide a vehicle there. In fact, as she rounded a stand of willows growing wild on the ditch bank, she saw a vehicle there now. She stopped, and her blood ran cold as she recognized the distinctive silhouette.

Turning, she ran back toward the house. "Nick!"

Chapter Fifteen

Frank Howell stepped out in front of her so suddenly that she collided with him. "Nick isn't here, little missy."

Stumbling back, Emma fought to calm her runaway heart.

"But I wouldn't mind stepping in for him." He rubbed his hand across his unshaven chin and smiled, sending a ripple of fear down her spine.

"What are you doing here?" Her voice shook, but she stood her ground.

"Oh, just a little unfinished business."

Her eyes fell on the veterinary-type syringe he held. It was a common sight on a ranch—stainless steel with a spring-loaded plunger—but it took on evil new meaning in his hands. "What's that?"

He held the syringe up. "This? Let's just call it a little equalizer." He chuckled unpleasantly.

Emma couldn't take her eyes from the sinister-looking instrument. Was he headed toward the barnyard or returning?

Had she stumbled across him too late? He aimed the syringe toward her, and she took another step backward. A drop of clearish liquid gathered on the needle's point. If he'd already used it, it would be empty, wouldn't it? She dragged her eyes back to his face—the face of a man who held all the aces.

"Nick ordered you off the ranch," she said, trying to bluff her way past him. "He won't like this."

"No, I don't suppose he would. But then, there's no reason for him to know, is there?"

The insinuation sent another chill down her spine. "Know what? That you're here at all? Or that you've obviously hidden your truck out of sight where you can sneak into the barnyard?"

His glance shifted over her shoulder to his truck tucked in the trees. "You can't blame a man for parking in the shade, can you?" He merely smiled, making her flesh crawl.

"Give it up, Frank. We're on to you."

Frank looked around, undisturbed. "I don't think so."

She gestured toward the syringe and took a gamble. "You haven't used that thing yet. There's still time to save yourself. Go on home." She tried to brush past him, but he stopped her with a painfully tight grip on her elbow.

"Not so fast, little lady. I'm afraid you're going to have to stay with me for a while." His voice took on a hard edge. "This time, your snooping's gotten you in over your head."

Stale sweat and staler cigarette smoke permeated the air around him, and she strained against his grip, wanting only to break contact with his unwashed body. He held on with a viselike grasp, and when she felt his breath on her neck, waves of revulsion made her stomach turn over. "Nick knows where I am. He'll come looking for me if I don't come back."

Frank chuckled again and shook his head. "Nick's busy." He pulled her into the thicket of willows. "See for yourself."

Behind the cover of the foliage, a small hollow afforded

space to stand undetected. Beyond the branches, she had a clear view of the ranch yard. With a sinking feeling, she realized Frank spoke the truth. Nick was bent over her car, his head under the hood. Closer, the men worked on the burned haystack, but noise of the tractor would drown any sound she made.

Frantically, she looked around, but the area was clear of weapons. A pile of cigarette butts littered the ground at her feet, but not even a rock showed itself through the grass lining the ditch bank. Frank truly had the upper hand.

"That was a nice little fire this morning," Frank said. "I had a real good view."

From the looks of it, he'd watched more than the fire. Even a dedicated chain-smoker would be hard put to inhale that much tobacco in one sitting.

With chilling accuracy, Frank answered her unspoken question. "I enjoyed that little rodeo a couple of days ago, too. Nick rode in like a real hero. Of course, I had things to do, so I missed the first of it, but I saw your part in it. Tell me, what do you think of those damn stallions now?"

He wouldn't be willing to talk so freely if he meant to let her go. Panic threatened to snap her tightly strung nerves, but she fought it down. Losing her head would only hasten things along. She glanced through the shrubbery toward the people working nearby. If she could keep Frank talking, maybe she had a chance of drawing their attention somehow. "Why are you doing this?"

He laughed, not even trying to keep his voice low. "You said you had all the answers. You tell me."

Hoping to buy time, she strung him along. "Bill Stratton hired you. Tell me, what kind of money did it take to turn you against Nick? A thousand? Two thousand?"

Goaded, Frank sneered. "Hell, that's chicken feed. Stratton offered me—" He stopped when he realized what he'd done. Then, with an evil leer, he finished, apparently willing to take the chance. "He offered me fifty thousand—and another ten for you. I'll take the extra ten grand, but with your uppity little nose in the air, I'd almost have done you for free."

"What did I ever do to you?"

"You mean besides wave your fancy little backside in my face? I see your expression when you look at me. You wouldn't even wipe your boots on the likes of me, would you? But I'm honest enough to admit I'll shaft a man for money. How do you explain your little schemes? You must be some wildcat in bed or Nick'd see right through you."

His leering accusation held her paralyzed, and not for the first time, the possibility of rape flashed across her mind.

"What's the matter? Cat got your tongue?"

Somehow she managed a reply. "Would it do any good to deny it?"

He eyed her narrowly. "You're a smart one. I'll give you that. Was it your idea to set the trap in the storeroom?"

So he'd known all along. She played along with him, buying more time. "It worked. We caught you."

He laughed. "But you didn't have sense enough to know it." As if admitting a confidence, he added, "Stratton told me to back off after I cut your brakeline." He paused, as if to gloat. "You knew it was cut, didn't you?"

Her fleeting courage failed her, and she couldn't stop a mechanical nod. She knew by his expression that he felt the shiver that chased through her.

He grinned. "He said he didn't want any part of murder. I would have left it at that, but for the storeroom. Nobody makes a fool of Frank Howell and gets away with it."

"But you said yourself, we're the fools. We let you go."

He glanced out from his vantage point, ignoring her logic. "I think slashing the car seat was a nice touch, don't you? It scared you good."

Had he been watching then, too? She felt another measure

of control slip. There would be no reasoning with him. He'd make his move soon. They'd wasted time talking, and even Frank wasn't fool enough to let it go on forever. But she couldn't give up.

Nick had once accused her of throwing herself at him to get what she wanted. Clearly Frank considered her fair game, too. Would he believe her if she tried such a ruse on him? The idea revolted her, but she had to try.

Twisting around in his arms, she looked up at him, calling on every ounce of acting ability she'd learned in the past ten years. "You've got me figured out, Frank," she said softly. "I'll make a deal with you." Ignoring the odor that emanated from him, she rubbed her palm against his chest. "I can help you."

He didn't quite believe her, but she could see that she had his attention. His grip on her arm loosened, and, encouraged, she redoubled her efforts. "As soon as Nick gets my car fixed, I have to leave. He didn't pan out like I'd hoped, but now that I've talked to you, I know just what to do."

Intrigued, Frank raised his eyebrow. "What would that be?"

"If Stratton paid you off once, he'd pay again to keep you quiet about it."

He looked up. "Hell, I already had that figured out."

She raised her other arm to his chest, and he released her elbow. She lowered her voice to a seductive whisper. "I could help you."

Frank turned to spit, apparently in preparation to take advantage of what she offered. She saw her chance and took it. Jumping sideways, she shot away from him. Branches tore at her shoulder, and Frank caught the tail of her shirt as she fought through them. She heard the fabric tear and put all her weight against it. Suddenly she was free again, and she broke out of the foliage, screaming as long and loud as her lungs would allow.

For a big man Frank moved surprisingly fast. He caught her in five strides and clapped a dirty hand over her mouth. The next instant, she felt the pointed tip of the syringe against her throat. "Bitch!" he said as he dragged her backwards. "If you so much as twitch, I'll inject every cc of this into your neck. Got that?"

Emma relaxed her grip on the arm clamped around her neck, too frightened even to nod her head. But instead of easing his hold on her, Frank dragged her back into the undergrowth. With his elbow, he shoved the leaves aside and peered through them. Branches slapped against her face, but the syringe remained solid against her throat, and she endured the pain, barely breathing.

It seemed as if even the birds fell silent as she listened with fading hopes. Her heart sank when she heard the continued roar of the tractor's engine. No one had heard her. It might be an hour or more before anyone thought to look for her. By that time it would be too late.

Nick pulled the distributor cap free and stood up, glaring at the octopuslike contraption in his hand. New irritation with Maria boiled up as he reread the manual. It had been a hell of a morning. A hell of a night. A hell of a week. Now he was fixing a car that shouldn't have needed fixing in the first place, the last thing he wanted to do. Because when he finished, Emma would drive out of his life, taking his reasons for caring with her.

He needed all of his attention on the ranch. Instinct told him this whole mess was about to come to a head. Instead, he couldn't even form a rational thought. Couldn't even read a simple repair manual. Sorting through the wires, he found the one he was looking for and consulted the manual again.

"How's it coming?" Pete sounded as if he still found the whole job amusing.

Nick backed out from under the hood. "I've about got it."

If he could keep his mind on what he was doing. His eyes automatically scanned the horizon, looking in part for anything unusual, but more in hope of spotting a glimpse of red hair glinting in the sun. "What's up?"

"We'll have the stack cleaned up by tonight. As soon as the ground dries out, we'll put down some new pallets—what're you looking at?"

Nothing. A dust devil? But there was no wind. He squinted against the sun. "I thought I saw some dust behind that ridge over there." He tried to dismiss the uneasiness that came over him. "Where's Emma?"

"Last I saw she was headed up the ditch road," Pete said. "She disappeared behind the willows up there about twenty minutes ago." He gestured in the direction Nick was looking.

The ditch road wound behind that ridge. But no one used it unless he was running the ditch. "You haven't sent anyone up there this morning, have you?"

"No." Pete began scanning the horizon with him.

Suddenly Nick remembered the irrigation pipe that had separated last summer. Water had washed out one track of the road, even flooded the corral. It had left such a hole that he'd had Hank haul in a load of rock. "There's gravel over there behind the corral."

Pete stood stock-still. "And the ditch crosses the Uintah road above here. Anyone who knew about it could use it to get into the barnyard without being noticed."

Nick threw down the distributor in his hand. On a hunch, he said, "I'm going up there. Why don't you head out to the road and see who comes by."

In three strides he was in his pickup. Chances were Emma was just walking along the ditch. Lord knew she had enough on her mind. He was probably just overreacting.

The winding, narrow track showed recent traffic—too much for the weekly run Hank made to check the ditch. Weeds growing down the middle were bruised and broken, and the edges of last spring's ruts had been knocked down, ground into powdery dust.

The road was hardly a secret, but no one had any reason to be on it this time of year. Frank Howell had talked him into letting him use it last fall during hunting season. He'd given permission, but Frank was so volatile he hesitated to allow him on his property with a loaded gun. He didn't know what was wrong with the man. In the past few weeks his attitude had gone from surly to hateful. That scene yesterday had been the last straw. He should have fired him months ago.

A mile rolled past. Then another. Emma was nowhere in sight, and she couldn't have come this far even if she'd been running. He pulled up to think. Something didn't add up. If he could just clear his mind, he knew he'd be able to figure it out, but a nagging feeling told him time was of the essence.

He tried closing his eyes, but he saw only Emma struggling in Frank's grasp. Damn the man! Frank had been a thorn in his side for weeks, and he'd managed to turn the job of getting the horses shod for the summer into full-time employment. It was time to start training the young horses, but they still didn't have shoes. Now he had to find another farrier.

What was he doing thinking about Frank? Emma was missing, and every time he tried to concentrate, his mind turned to Frank Howell. He put the truck back into gear and started up the road again, pressing harder. *Think!*

If Emma had wandered off the road to climb one of the hills, would he have missed her? What was she wearing? A yellow T-shirt. The same one she'd had on the day he'd shown her the new foal and Frank had—

Wait a minute! Frank had been the attending farrier at the horse show just before the tire came off Nick's trailer. In fact he'd come around just as Nick was loading Cochise, and typically, set the horse off when he'd tried to help. Nick had gone off to get a bandage for a scraped knuckle, leaving Frank alone for—

God, it had been Frank all along!

Ice spread through his veins. Emma was missing, and with chilling certainty, he knew where she was. Frank had her. Nick saw again the scene he'd come upon yesterday in the stable, and with near-frantic haste, he pressed harder on the gas pedal. The cell phone lay on the seat beside him, and he reached for it, struggling to dial with one hand. The truck slid around a corner, gaining traction only inches from the edge of the ditch bank. Reining in his runaway fears, he forced himself to slow down. He'd be of no use to Emma if he put the truck in the ditch. But if Frank hurt her, he'd kill him with his bare hands.

Emma braced herself against the seat of Frank's truck. He'd shoved her onto the floorboard and told her curtly to stay there. With the memory of the syringe against her neck still fresh in her mind, she did as he said. The winding road was full of bumps and holes, but Frank drove slowly, as if not to raise attention to himself.

Fear spiraled through her, and she began talking simply to keep panic at bay.

"Let me go, Frank. You haven't done anything serious until now. You could still get off easy. But kidnapping is another matter. Don't add that to your list."

Frank ignored her, dividing his attention between the road and the rearview mirror. Was somebody following them? Had he seen something behind them? His foot pressed marginally harder on the accelerator.

"I won't press charges, Frank. Let me go now, and no one will know what you've done." She wished she could see out the window. Was there something back there, or was he just getting nervous? She pressed on. "If Nick comes after you, he won't be nearly so forgiving."

Finally, Frank looked her way. "Don't count on it. Nick's got his own problems to worry about."

What did he mean by that? Had she stumbled across Frank too late after all? Had Frank already finished with that syringe? It didn't take much imagination to guess what was in it. Cochise could already be dead.

No. Frank was bluffing. He had to be.

"Nick will hunt you down, Frank. He won't rest until you're behind bars. Have you thought about that? What it'd be like to go to prison?"

"Shut up!"

"Think about it. Years behind bars. Nothing to look forward to but—"

"I said shut up!"

He was already edgy. What would he do if she pushed him too hard? But if she stopped talking, she'd have too much time to think. Too much time to worry.

"I've met men like you before, Frank. Caught in a job they hated. They felt like they were trapped. But it doesn't have to be that way."

Frank stopped the truck at the end of a long straightaway. He left it idling, while he stared into the mirror, and she wasn't even sure if he'd been listening. To her surprise, he answered bitterly. "What do you know about it?"

"If you don't like your life, just walk away."

He took his eyes off the mirror for a moment. "That's exactly what I plan to do. Walk away with sixty thousand in my pocket."

"What will you do when the money's gone? Sixty thousand isn't so much, you know. It won't last a year. Two at the most."

Frank glanced in the mirror again, then turned on her. "You just let me worry about the future, little missy. If I were you, I'd be more concerned more with what's going to happen in the next half hour."

His words put a chilling lid on her ability to focus. Suddenly, the next half hour took on the importance of a lifetime. For her, chances were it was all of the lifetime she had left.

Had it been only yesterday she'd rejected happiness for fear of what the future would bring? She'd turned her back on Nick and everything he stood for because she couldn't take a chance that the future might not turn out right. Hysterical laughter bubbled up. She'd spent the last twenty-four hours torturing herself with what might have been so that Frank Howell could drag her into the mountains and leave her dead in a ditch.

Nick had said the only guarantee was that they'd all die someday. Too late, she realized he was right. She'd wasted her last hours pushing her dreams away so that she could move forward unfettered by the past. Well, the joke was on her. She'd had a short, bright future, and she'd squandered it on fear.

"What's the matter, little missy? Don't tell me I finally said something to shut that mouth of yours. You're right. I have to kill you now, but don't worry. That syringe will work on you as well as it worked on Cochise. You won't feel a thing."

"You're lying!"

He looked at her. "Am I?"

Anger replaced the morbid thoughts swirling through her head, and she lunged for the gearshift knob. He might very well kill her, but she wouldn't go without a fight.

Her angle was awkward, and though she managed to throw the truck out of gear, her shoulder glanced off the dashboard. Frank had her wrist in his viselike grip before she could catch her balance. A heartbeat later, he had her arm twisted behind her, the bone threatening to snap. Technicolor starbursts exploded in front of her eyes, and with a muffled scream, she quit fighting.

Frank spewed a litany of curses as he fumbled under the

seat. He pulled out a roll of duct tape and wrapped it around her wrists until she was helpless to move. When he finished, he threw her back on the floorboard with an oath and a promise of retribution if she moved again.

She braced herself against the seat the best she could, grinding her teeth against the pain still radiating up her arm, but instead of the expected lurching over the rough road, the truck remained still. Glancing up, she saw Frank's gaze riveted on the rearview mirror again. Tension had replaced his formerly complacent attitude, and with a fresh eruption of blasphemy, he threw the truck into gear and carved a new track with the rear wheels.

The force threw Emma against the seat, then back under the dashboard, but for the first time since Frank had thrown her in, she took heart. If he was suddenly in a hurry, it could only mean he'd spotted someone behind them. And from his urgency she could only assume whoever it was, was coming fast and hard.

Frank took a short, sharp curve, and the truck bounced hard on a gravely surface, slamming her face into the floor. When she regained her balance, he was speeding up the road. Rocks and dirt flew up from the wheels, filling the cab with dust. The road surface had changed—it was harder, wider, marked with the trademark washboards of a heavily traveled road. Somehow they'd come out on the Uintah road, and from the general uphill slant of the truck, she knew he'd turned toward the mountains.

What little she could see of the trees changed as they climbed. Pinyon trees graduated into pines. Pines into aspens silhouetted by an ominous dark cloud. All the while Frank drove like a madman skidding through the corners while he looked over his shoulder. With each apparent sighting of their pursuer, he edged down the accelerator until Emma wondered how he kept the truck on the road.

Then, suddenly, he turned the wheel sharply to the right.

The truck bounced sideways, sliding headlong. Emma closed her eyes tight, waiting for the impact, but miraculously, the truck bounced onto a softer, quieter surface. She caught a glimpse of rocks above her. Cliffs.

There couldn't be two roads leading to the area Nick had shown her before. This road went nowhere. She glanced up at Frank, but he'd all but forgotten her. He wasn't watching the road at all, but looking behind him. Was their pursuer so close that he—

Something slammed into her chest. Starbursts filled her vision, and somewhere, far away, she heard the crush of metal against rock. Further away, it seemed, Frank cut loose with a fresh outburst, then the lights blended together, and the only sound was the roaring in her ears.

Chapter Sixteen

Rough hands grabbed and pulled Emma out of a gray fog. She shook her head, blinking against the bright lights as she felt herself dragged up and abruptly set on her feet.

"Stand up!" Frank Howell's raspy voice broke through the roaring in her ears, and the world spun as she swayed unsteadily. He let go, leaving her to topple against something—the front fender of his truck.

Trying hard to clear her head, she focused on the fender. Something was wrong with it. The metal was crumpled. Steam hissed from beneath the hood, bringing with it the sweet smell of antifreeze escaping from the radiator. She stared stupidly at the wrinkled metal, then at the rock in front of it. A ragged white gouge marked the rock. She would have reached for it, but for some reason her arms refused to work.

Behind her, she heard the slide and click of a well-oiled gun, and she jerked her head around, sending the world into a tailspin. When it came back into focus, Frank was stuffing bullets into the chamber of a high-powered rifle.

Sight of the gun brought her upright, but her arms remained steadfastly unresponsive. Only when she began to struggle did she realize her hands were bound behind her. Gathering herself, she turned and lunged away.

"Wrong way, little missy," Frank said, grabbing her upper arm and dragging her with him.

He took an erratic course between enormous rocks, twisting and doubling back, constantly checking over his shoulder. Emma stumbled along, propelled by his grip on her arm. The uneven ground was marked with craters and dirt heaps where rocks had apparently fallen and dislodged the earth. With each turn, the way became more and more confusing until she was lost.

These were the rocks Nick had pointed out to her. He'd played here as a boy—gotten lost so many times he'd finally learned his way around. She had no idea if it was Nick who followed them, but on the slim chance that it was, she meant to give him every chance to catch up. At every opportunity, she threw herself off balance, slowing the pace, forcing Frank to literally drag her behind him.

Overhead, thunder rumbled. The wind picked up and as the clouds thickened, the light grew flat. When they stumbled through the same crater with the same cluster of columbines growing in it for the third time, Emma knew Frank was as lost as she was. She feigned tripping and threw herself on the ground, flinching as a rock dug into her ribs.

Rolling over, she taunted him. "You're lost, Frank. Admit it. You've screwed up again."

Frank was sweating, his breath came in ragged gasps. A cut on his forehead looked livid against his pale skin. He glanced nervously around, then slung the rifle onto his shoulder.

"Get up."

"Nothing you've tried has worked. What did Stratton hire

you for? To kill Cochise? The little accident you arranged didn't work, did it?''

Frank centered his gaze on her, his eyes wild.

"Did he want you to kill the mares, too? You couldn't even manage that on a busy road. Running them out like that was a big mistake on your part. After that Nick was on to you.''

Frank wiped his eye, inspected his bloodied sleeve, then wiped it again.

"You didn't even have sense enough to know Nick uses twine to tie his bales, not wire.''

She was getting to him. He looked over his shoulder again.

"What did you hope to accomplish with those three stallions? To discredit Nick? It didn't take him a minute to get them out of there. In fact, Martin Johansen was impressed by the way he took control. You did Nick a favor.'' She let that sink in for a moment. "Stratton should have hired someone else.''

"Shut up.''

"Even a kid would have spotted that bag of feed. Was that the best you could do?''

"Shut up!''

"And the fire! Metal buildings don't burn. The men had that fire out before it even ruined the hay.''

"Shut up, *now*, or I'll shut you up myself.''

"You can try. But it won't help. Nick's smarter than you are, Frank, and he's out there right now. You can't win.''

Frank glanced around uneasily and pulled the rifle back off his shoulder. Then he backed into the shelter of a massive boulder and trained the rifle on her. "I'll shoot you. I swear I'll shoot.''

Her palms went clammy, and she fisted her hands behind her. "Go ahead. With me out of the way, Nick won't even have to bide his time. He'll tear you limb from limb.''

The rifle shook, and Emma tried not to notice the size of

the hole staring at her from the blue-black barrel. Instead, she kept her eyes trained solely on Frank. She could see doubt in his face. He didn't know what to do. A fat raindrop hit her in the forehead, and she struggled to sit up.

"Stay where you are." He shook the rifle at her.

She gave up trying to move in the face of the gun. With her arms bound so tightly, there was little she could do, anyhow.

"Stratton won't pay. You know that."

Frank shook his head defensively. "He'll pay."

"Why should he? You're just a pawn to him. You're doing all the dirty work, and when you're through, he'll toss you to the wolves. It'll be your word against his, and he's a respected breeder. Who's going to believe you?"

Another drop of rain hit just above her eye.

"Face it, Frank, you're up to your ears here." She laughed, a hollow, mirthless sound that echoed her desperation. "All for nothing."

Like a cornered animal, Frank backed closer against the rock, all the more dangerous because he was no longer sure of himself. Too late, she realized she'd pushed him too far. When he cocked the rifle, she closed her eyes and prayed for the courage to see this through.

She was about to die. Nothing short of a miracle would save her now. Futile tears threatened, and she squeezed her eyes against them. She would not let Frank see her cry. *She would not cry.*

Thoughts of Nick crowded past her fears. She wished she could see him once more. She wished she could kiss him, tell him how much she loved him. Tell him how right he'd been. About everything. Oh, God! Frank was stealing it all away just when she'd figured out who she was. She wanted another chance.

She opened her eyes. When Frank pulled the trigger, she

meant for him to see her eyes. She meant for the sight of her to be burned into his brain for the rest of his life.

Frank had the rifle raised, the sights already lined up. He was trying to work up the courage to pull the trigger. She gritted her teeth and stared at him, refusing to let her fear show.

Then, above him, her miracle appeared. Out of the corner of her eye she caught the movement of someone creeping across the top of the rock above Frank. *Nick!* Dropping her eyes lest she give him away, she grappled frantically for something to say. A distraction. Anything.

Rain was falling steadily now, but Frank was sheltered by the rock, out of Nick's reach. Somehow she had to get him out into the open. Struggling against the tape that held her hands bound, she tried again to sit up.

"Don't move," Frank warned, still holding the sights shakily on her.

"You're scared to pull the trigger, aren't you? You don't have the balls to do it."

Like an angry bull, Frank roared, charged out into the rain.

Behind him, Nick gathered himself to spring.

Frank waved the rifle only inches from her face. "What kind of balls do you have? Let me see what you're made of."

Garnering the last of her flagging courage, she dragged her eyes up to meet Frank's. "Let me tell you something about fear, Frank." Her voice was surprisingly calm. "You're too late. I've been running scared for years, but I'm through. I'm taking control back." Despite her words, she couldn't keep her eyes off the blue steel so near her face. She swallowed hard. "You've got me trussed up like a pig. I can't possibly get away. But I won't lie here and grovel."

"Up here, Frank!"

Frank spun around in surprise, just as Nick leaped off the rock, landing cleanly on the big man's shoulders. The rifle exploded, then skittered across the ground. Acting more out of instinct than conscious thought, Emma rolled away, not stopping until she came up against a hard, cold surface of stone.

Behind her, she heard the sounds of a desperate struggle. Flinging her hair out of her eyes as best she could, she risked a glance at the life-and-death battle taking place. Frank had regained his feet, and he stood opposite Nick, his concentration restored to deadly focus. Like wary lions, they circled each other, watching for an opening.

Suddenly Frank lunged at Nick. Nick feinted left, but not quickly enough to avoid Frank's flying fist. He reeled from the blow, and Frank turned on him, wading in for the kill.

It wasn't a fair fight. Frank outweighed Nick by thirty or more pounds. His years of wielding a hammer had earned him a massive barrel chest and powerful, overdeveloped shoulders. Against him, Nick rained short sharp strikes, but Frank landed bruising blows. Nick broke loose.

They circled again, almost feral in their intensity. The next time Frank lunged, he landed a glancing blow to Nick's ribs, but this time Nick held his ground. Afraid to watch, afraid to look away, Emma wondered how long Nick could take such punishment. Already an angry bruise swelled across his cheekbone. In another minute the eye would swell shut, and Frank would finish him off.

Suddenly, Frank changed tactics. He dropped back, blowing like a winded buffalo, and Nick followed, staying just out of Frank's reach. Then Emma saw Frank's intent. She tried to cry out, but her voice caught in her throat. Bending quickly, Frank swept the rifle off the ground. Nick lunged at him, but the bigger man blocked his charge, using the heavy weapon as a shield. Nick fell back, and Frank took advantage of the lapse to cock the gun. The empty shell popped out of the chamber, twirling through the air and landing with a ping against a rock. Circling again, Frank grinned in triumph.

Overhead, lightning split the air, bathing the combatants in blue-white light, and for Emma, time slowed to a standstill. In seeming slow motion she watched Frank make his move, while thunder rolled across the rocks, drowning the sound of her scream. Frank swung the gun around, but the bulky weapon was his undoing. Nick kicked it aside before he could take aim, and the gun went off harmlessly in the air. Frank stumbled, dropping the rifle and losing his footing in the wet rocks. Nick drove his shoulder into the big man's stomach, and Frank fell backward, his mouth forming a perfect O as the air rushed from his lungs. Nick dove after him, driving a fist into Frank's meaty jaw, and like a downed bear, the big man went limp.

Nick reared back, still astride Frank's inert body, his chest heaving from exertion. Emma expelled the breath she'd been holding, and for a moment her vision clouded from lack of oxygen. By the time her head cleared, Nick was up. He retrieved the rifle and staggered over to her side. Dropping to his knees, he leaned the rifle against the rock where she lay.

His eye was swollen nearly shut. Blood flowed from a cut on his lip, staining the rain-soaked fabric of his shirt. His eyes asked questions he couldn't voice, and hers answered: I'm okay. He didn't hurt me. Thank God you're alive.

With gentle hands he pulled her up and supported her while he unwound the tape binding her wrists. When he'd freed her hands, he reached out to her, and she clung to him with every ounce of strength she possessed. Chanting a prayer of thanks, she buried her face against his warm, hard body and let the rain cleanse her of fear.

Nick struck a match to the kindling and waited until the flames caught. The early afternoon rain had settled into a steady drizzle, and he hoped the fire would dispel the chill—

not that it would soothe the blazing tide of emotions surging through him.

In the space of only a few hours, he'd answered hundreds of questions, told his story to the sheriff and two of his deputies, only to repeat it again for the district attorney. He'd allowed the doctor to poke and prod at him—all to no avail— he felt like he'd just gone ten rounds against the heavyweight champion. All the while, he'd been sick with worry for Emma. After the storm of tears on the mountain, she'd retreated into herself, and despite her insistence that she was unharmed, he was afraid Frank had somehow managed to inflict permanent scars. Damn the man!

Nick had refused to come home until Emma could come with him. She might not want him around, but he was the best friend she had here, and he refused to leave her alone. She wore a grisly bruise on her forehead, and her skin was marred by a hundred tiny abrasions. But the real damage didn't show. She had it tucked carefully out of sight, buried along with so much other baggage he wondered how she found the strength to walk beneath the weight of it all.

No, he hadn't left her alone, but bringing her home hadn't been such a good idea, either. She'd insisted on seeing Cochise, checking him over personally to make sure he was unharmed. After that she'd been bombarded with the full weight of Maria's hovering anxiety until she'd retreated to her room. Withdrawn as she was, he'd let her go.

Finally, he was alone. Frank was in jail. By morning Stratton would be, too. The sheriff was satisfied, the doctor had done what he could, Pete had taken his not-so-tactful hint to leave, and Maria had exhausted her efforts to smother him with concern. Now he meant to pour himself a drink and sit in the dark, letting the tightness inside him drift away with the smoke up the chimney.

The fire caught, and he added another log, then stood and replaced the screen. When he turned, Emma was sitting on the sofa in front of him. Her eyes were dark and luminous beneath the ugly bruise, but she was calm, and she met his glance before she turned her gaze to the flames.

Seeing her so pale, seeing the fresh reminder of what Frank Howell had done to her, pumped a new shot of adrenaline through Nick's veins. Weary as he was, he was consumed with wildly inappropriate urges. He wanted to make love to her, savage sweet love that would burn away the tension, prove to them both that they were *alive*. But Emma had endured enough for one day. He wouldn't make her fight him off, too.

Instead he poured them both a hefty shot of brandy. He handed her the glass, switched off the lamp, and sat down beside her—not touching, but close enough that her presence soothed his battered body and spirit. She accepted the drink, though she only held the glass, and he leaned back, propping his feet on the coffee table.

Outside, the steady drip of rain off the eaves seemed to seal out the rest of the world. The fire dispelled the gloom inside, and the brandy spread a pleasant warmth through his body. For long minutes, they sat side by side staring at the fire. Emma still said nothing, but her silence seemed restful now. The curtain she'd drawn around herself was open a crack.

"A penny for your thoughts," he said, watching her out the corner of his eye.

She took a sip of brandy and leaned back against the couch. "I was just thinking about my father."

Surprised, he turned to look at her.

"He was a good man, but he was no farmer."

"Maybe he was just caught up in circumstances," Nick suggested.

"Perhaps," she said thoughtfully. "I blamed what happened to us on the way of life, but now I'm not so sure."

Nick waited.

"You've had your share of problems," she continued. "It can't have been easy for you. Your wife married you for your money. She left you. The divorce settlement could have crippled the ranch. It'd be easy for you to be bitter." She sipped the brandy again and swallowed. "Dad would have let it get him down. *I* would have let it get me down."

"That's not true. You never gave up. You pulled yourself together, moved on. You made a life for yourself."

For the first time, she looked at him. "I've learned a lot the past few days."

"Such as?"

"Some people take what they get. Dad was like that. I—" She stopped when he threatened to argue again. "Others— like you—take what they're given and work with it. Make it better. You'll never settle."

She was talking about money, of course. Success. But the faith in the words she chose, her very nearness, turned a switch somewhere in his brain, and all the urges he'd carefully suppressed surged back to life. If he didn't touch her soon, he'd lose his mind. Taking the brandy from her, he dropped his feet to the floor and set the glass along with his on the coffee table. "I'm glad you think so," he said, turning back to her, "because I can't settle now. I want it all."

Firelight softened the scars on her skin, set her hair aglow, but he couldn't see her eyes. Reaching up, he stroked his bruised knuckles across her skin, ignoring the painful stiffness in his shoulder.

Her hair felt like cool silk to his battered hand, and he brushed it carefully away from her face. She watched him with luminous eyes, and even with the bruise on her forehead, he didn't think he'd ever seen such beauty. A single tear trailed down her cheek, and he brushed it aside. Then, because he could no more stop himself than halt the rain, he kissed her.

The moment their lips met, a dam burst inside him. He'd

come close to losing her today, forever. Consumed with the need to reassure himself that she was really there, really in his arms again, he pulled her down with him, trying to temper his urgency with gentleness.

But she wasn't fighting. She threaded her hands through his hair, wrapped her arms around him, until he felt her breasts crushed against him, until her body was stretched hard against the heat of his arousal. He ran his hands along the length of her, soaking up the knowledge that she was alive and well and responsive in his arms. He couldn't get close enough. He wouldn't be close enough until there was nothing between them, just skin on skin and he was moving deep inside her, listening to the sounds of her release. Her kiss was like a second chance at paradise.

But paradise was still an impossible dream.

Nothing had changed between them. He still lived on a ranch. Much of his future still rested on the whims of fate, and no matter how much he loved her, he still could offer her no guarantees for the future beyond his love. Frank Howell had proven only too clearly how quickly circumstances could change. If Nick had been only a minute later—

He'd heard what Emma said to Frank about fear, but he'd also seen the desperation in her eyes. Self-preservation was a powerful instinct, and years of living in fear couldn't be erased overnight. She kissed him like there was no tomorrow. Perhaps, in her mind, it was true.

She sensed his withdrawal. He knew it by the sudden stillness in her body, by the way she hid her head on his shoulder. She would have pulled away, but he didn't release her. Instead, he shifted, settling her beside him on the sofa, keeping her close with his arm tucked in the small of her back.

She was crying. Silent, unrelenting tears streamed down her cheeks, catching the firelight, reflecting it back at him. The tears tore at him until he would give anything to dry them.

Including her freedom.

"I didn't get your car fixed this morning, Emma. But I promise you I'll finish first thing—"

"I don't want to leave."

I don't want to leave. I don't want to leave. He listened as the words echoed in his head. But no matter how many times they played, his mind refused to accept them as truth. What else would cause her such misery? Why else would she cry?

"I am such a fool," she said. "I thought I was going to die today. All the way up the mountain, Frank talked about his plans and how I'd gotten in the way, and all I could think of was how stupid I've been. You offered me everything I've ever wanted, and I refused because I was afraid of what the future might bring. Then, all of a sudden, my future was up. I'd thrown everything away, and for nothing!"

"Emma, don't do this to yourself."

"Let me finish." She took a ragged breath. "I've spent half my life running from fear. It feeds on itself, grows until it takes over your life. Bit by bit I gave up everything, because without guarantees, I couldn't take a chance. I'd wait for the sure thing. And then today Frank turned that gun on you and I thought—"

"I love you, Emma." She looked up at him, surprised into silence. "I can't offer you the kind of security you want. I have no guarantees but that I love you. That's one thing you can always count on."

Her expression softened. "You're wrong, you know."

"Wrong?" Panicking, he wondered which of his statements she took exception to.

"Security is you, Nick. With your love, I have all the security I need."

Her words spread over him like a soothing balm, easing the aching bruises in mind and body. Smiling, he kissed her, pulled her close and let the healing begin.

                          *   *   *

"Let me warn you," he said sometime later, "I wasn't lying before." He stuffed a pillow under his head then let himself sink into the soft cushions, secure in the knowledge that Emma lay snuggled against him.

"What do you mean?" Emma traced the bruises on his shoulder with gentle fingers. Her languid response made him think she wasn't taking him seriously.

"I'm not taking any chances. I want it all." He lay a proprietary arm across her gold-flecked skin, bringing a telling smile to her face.

"All?"

"Everything. I won't let you leave here until I have your word."

She didn't look as if she were going anywhere soon, but, apparently deciding to play along, she let her gaze rove over their nude bodies shining in the firelight. "What more do you want from me?"

"I want you to get a new car," he said. "A good one. The sooner, the better."

Her eyes danced. "But the one I have holds such fond memories."

"No arguments."

Smiling, she nodded assent.

"And from now on, you write only about subjects of your choosing. No more corporate takeovers."

"What about successful ranchers? Can I cover them?"

He pretended to think it over. "Maybe those would be okay—as long as they're old and have loads of grandkids."

"What else?"

"First I want your promise."

She gave it, so convincingly that he lost his train of thought.

"You were saying?" she reminded him long moments later.

He tried to clear his head. What *had* he been saying? Ah, yes. "I think you should work here."

She looked dubious. "No travel? No exotic ports? No handsome, mysterious strangers?"

"*Especially* no mysterious strangers."

She smiled again. "That's easy. You have my solemn promise to—"

He stopped her with a kiss. "Be careful what you promise, Emma. There's more."

"Anything you ask," she breathed. "I love you."

"Marry me," he said. "Marry me and live with me on the Uintah forever."

She didn't meet his eyes, and he realized how nervous he'd become, how very much her answer mattered. But when she looked up at him, all his fears evaporated in the face of her love.

"I wouldn't settle for anything less."

* * * * *

Silhouette Stars

Born this month

Donald Pleasance, Alice Cooper, Mia Farrow, Burt
Reynolds, Peter Gabriel, John McEnroe, Yoko Ono,
Ivana Trump, Tom Courtenay, Elizabeth Taylor.

Star of the Month

Aquarius

The year ahead holds great promise. You may
have to make some difficult choices early on but
as the year progresses the way ahead will seem
very clear. An unexpected encounter could lead
to a new romance bringing the promise of
future stability into your life.

SILH/HR/0201a

Pisces

You could be feeling confused over your long term plans. Get your mind off your problems, try a makeover, change your diet and take some exercise to feel more positive again.

Aries

Reckless moments could lead to some embarrassment and you may need to eat some humble pie to get a relationship back on track. A lucky win lifts your spirits.

 Taurus

Romantically a brilliant month lifting your spirits and self esteem. Any difficulties will be on the work front where someone may be jealous of your new-found confidence.

Gemini

Last month's appraisal should start to pay dividends as you feel confident that the choices you made were the right ones. A night with someone special proves to be unexpectedly passionate.

 Cancer

Time to start planning for a much needed holiday. By getting your mind off your problems and refocusing you will restore your flagging energy levels and end the month feeling happier.

Leo

Career moves are uppermost in your mind and you need to think carefully about how they could affect your personal life. An invitation brings old friends back into your life.

Virgo

You need to consider a realistic financial budget to allow yourself the funds for the plans you have. Take care with how you handle a friend who is in need of your support.

Libra

You may feel frustrated by red tape or authority but keep trying as by midmonth the constraints that have held you should weaken. Late in the month there may be reason to celebrate.

 ## Scorpio

Popular is your middle name - everyone wants a piece of you and it will be difficult to accept all the invitations. Late in the month you receive news that may lead to a change of address.

Sagittarius

You are full of ambition and there is little you can't achieve this month. Career opportunities abound and while your home life may suffer a little the rewards will more than compensate for this.

 ## Capricorn

Whilst those around are doing their best to keep you focused at home your thoughts are fixed on more distant horizons. Finding out just how far you can go may lead to some turbulence in your life.

Look out for more
Silhouette Stars next month

▼™ SILHOUETTE
SPECIAL EDITION ®

AVAILABLE FROM 16TH FEBRUARY 2001

IRISH REBEL Nora Roberts

She was practically royalty and he was just a hard working horse trainer. But her wealth and position didn't deter Brian...and her innocence simply beguiled the wild Irish rebel!

DESIGNATED DADDY Jane Toombs

That's My Baby!
Steely government agent Steve Henderson needed no one, until compassionate nurse Victoria Reynaud placed a new baby girl in his arms! The orphaned little one needed his protection, and Steve found he needed his new 'family!'

MAN...MERCENARY...MONARCH Joan Elliott Pickart

Royally Wed
Laura Bishop and John Colton shared a night of anonymous passion, little knowing that John was a king's son about to meet his own baby. Could John become all that he was intended to be: father, lover, prince...husband?

DR MUM AND THE MILLIONAIRE Christine Flynn

Prescription: Marriage
Dr Alexandra Lawson wasn't the type to faint over a handsome man, but then she'd never met anyone like tycoon Chase Harrington before...

A COWBOY KIND OF DADDY Cathy Gillen Thacker

The McCabe Men
Travis McCabe was the most serious, the oldest of his brothers—the perfect role model for three lively little boys...the perfect husband for any woman. And Annie Pierce, the single mum next door was tempted...

AWAKENED BY HIS KISS Judith Lyons

Abigail Richards was twenty-eight and had never been kissed, and now loner Luke Anderson was the only man to whom Gaby wanted to risk offering everything: her innocence, and her heart...

2 Books
and a surprise gift!

We would like to take this opportunity to thank you for reading this Silhouette® book by offering you the chance to take TWO more specially selected titles from the Special Edition™ series absolutely FREE! We're also making this offer to introduce you to the benefits of the Reader Service™ —

- ★ FREE home delivery
- ★ FREE gifts and competitions
- ★ FREE monthly Newsletter
- ★ Books available before they're in the shops
- ★ Exclusive Reader Service discounts

Accepting these FREE books and gift places you under no obligation to buy; you may cancel at any time, even after receiving your free shipment. Simply complete your details below and return the entire page to the address below. **You don't even need a stamp!**

YES! Please send me 2 free Special Edition books and a surprise gift. I understand that unless you hear from me, I will receive 4 superb new titles every month for just £2.80 each, postage and packing free. I am under no obligation to purchase any books and may cancel my subscription at any time. The free books and gift will be mine to keep in any case.

E1ZEB

Ms/Mrs/Miss/Mr ....Initials...
BLOCK CAPITALS PLEASE

Surname...

Address...

....

....Postcode ....

Send this whole page to:
UK: The Reader Service, FREEPOST CN81, Croydon, CR9 3WZ
EIRE: The Reader Service, PO Box 4546, Kilcock, County Kildare (stamp required)